Frost and Flame

A tale of the Eververse

Stella and Audra Price

TEASE PUBLISHING

www.teasepublishingllc.com

Frost and Flame: A Tale of the Eververse
A Tease Publishing Book/E book

Copyright© 2007 Stella & Audra Price
ISBN: 978-1-60767-182-4
Cover Artist: Stella Price
Interior text design: Stacee Sierra

Tease Publishing LLC
www.teasepublishingllc.com
PO BOX 234
Swansboro, North Carolina 28584-0234

Prologue

Fuerety stood on the balcony and watched the gathered assembly leave with disgust. They were pathetic excuses for demons, barely worth his time and intelligence. *They all have their uses though.* He reminded himself. *Every creature has a use, a purpose.* They left with the aid of the escorts he'd sent them, back to their different houses. He watched as Amos and Camions left separately as always. The Conglacio people headed back to their frozen plain.

He watched the Ice demons leave with joy. He hated Conglacio's, hated everything ice. He had more or less singly-handedly destroyed them. Their monarchy was in ruin. *Leviathan destroyed, nothing more than a whimpering wreck. The youngest son was not even worth mentioning, no more than a worthless whelp. The bastard...* Fuerety laughed out loud, a rare occurrence for him indeed. *The bastard is mine, has been ever since I convinced him that a duel between his mother and Jolie would make her queen.* The only ice demon that had ever really posed much of a threat to Fuerety's rule was firmly in exile, his soul in Fuerety's tender care.

Next to leave were the Celo's, Aldinach and his pathetic powers of illusions, his simpering daughters and concubines following closely behind him. He'd noticed over the years that the illusion court had become gradually less tolerant to their kings wanderings and madness. There would be an uprising soon, and just in time too. Fuerety had never trusted Aldinach; the man had a tendency to live in his own illusions. He hated anyone that dealt in anything other than his scalding reality, and for that he would die. His replacement had already been chosen and put in place.

The last to leave was his friend old Addu, lord of the shadow. The King was his oldest supporter and yet, he still couldn't bring himself to believe the excuses he gave earlier on Faris' absence. They just didn't ring true. The man had a habit of losing children, his youngest son having disappeared eight years ago. Vanished completely into the shadows, but not before sharing certain words and a few hand gestures with Fuerety himself, in front of all the courts no doubt. The boy would die for such insolence. *Now, if only I could find him.* He had sent his best after the boy, yet those who had come back had found no trace, those had failed to come back, well, the old king could only guess.

He heard a scuffle behind him and turned his back on the burning plains, knowing that his face would be shadowed by the sharp burning contrast. He saw Sallos, the head of his guard kneeling before him with his head respectfully bowed.

"You find him?"

"No my lord. There is still no trace of Amaro, sir."

"And you watched the girl?"

"Yes, we haven't stopped watching her since she moved topside, but it seems that the prince has broken off all contact with her, even with Cassiel. But she has taken up with a vampire, there seems to be rebellion beginning within their ranks. The younger..."

Fuerety cut him off, holding up his hand. "Spare me. I have no interest in vampires. The fledglings always rise and they shall fall, as always."

Sallos bowed his head lower, "Yes my lord."

"Take your people off her, the annoying thing about a shadow demon is that they hide so well. But a man cannot hide forever, if he's not watched then there's no call for him to hide."

"Wisely said."

"Now, what of my daughter? Was she there, as Addu claimed?"

"No, she was not. I did find her hand maiden though." Sallos paused.

"And?" The king demanded angrily. "Out with it."

"She was not so forth coming as to the princess' location."

"I trust you got the information out of her."

Sallos grinned evilly up at his king. "Yes, she spoke. She told me everything that she knew... in the end. It seems the princess left, at some point this morning. She left no note and has not returned."

"Find her, bring her here, to me. It seems Jacob cannot control his wife, as well as I had hoped. She is becoming a problem. What more does she want? I practically hand her the shadow court, and she runs off at the first opportunity she gets." He broke off shaking his head.

"Maybe she only went to see a friend, what was that human's name..." Fuerety glared at him and Sallos, wisely held his tongue.

"Find her! Bring her to me. You have all the authority you need. Question whomever you need, torture whomever you need. If anyone challenges you, kill them or send them to me. Bring her home, and report back if you find anything that you think I should know."

"As you command my lord. I shall return her to you." He bowed low once more before standing smoothly to his full height and backing out of the door.

Fuerety smiled as he noted that the gesture was more to protect his own back than keep his king from insult. The fire plains blazed brightly in the distance as the great king returned inside his castle to inspect the damage left by the ball.

***

The mists swirled about the vast openness of Jolie's own personal hell languorously. This in truth was the closet her kind would ever come to heaven, as peaceful as a demon would ever be allowed, but it bored her to no end. Her time was taken up by watching, watching her husband self destruct, watching her second born corrupt innocent women and watching her beloved first born slowly go crazy. That's what was killing her most of all.

Levi had been getting better as of late, the girl he had taken keeping him occupied and above water. She owed the young girl so much, even if she was sleeping with the only man she ever loved, but that was neither here nor there, as Levi never disrespected her memory, because he never loved the Winters girl, and what's more, the girl knew it, but never held it against him. Theirs was an easy relationship, both gaining from each other a semblance of what they needed. For the girl, it was protection and adoration, and for her beloved husband and king, it was companionship. *Darling, if I could only get back to you.*

She sighed, thinking on Dimitri. He had indeed done right in letting Snow go, no matter how much he cared for her. Her second born was more like herself in actually having real emotions and not hiding them. Snow was a fantastic girl, but Colette was always the one she saw with her son. *She's exactly what he needs; its wonderful Cassiel has given her up to the most worthy of demons. She will be well cared for with my beautiful Dimitri.*

Ah Cassiel. She thought to herself as she smiled. He was given a second chance, and she hoped that this time he would do it right and what was left of his mind would be healed. Her first born and reason for still existing, she watched over him as he went and saw Faris, when she told him that the little boy in her tummy was his. His Sorceress was top rate, and she approved of her greatly, knowing that what he felt for her was as close to what he felt for Faris as it was ever going to be. *And she's much better than that flake Natalia; at least she's got a man of her own and a life that doesn't involve Cassiel.*

She had been watching all of the events play out with all those she held dear, including Oscar and Drake. Drake had it in him to be great, and he just needed the right incentive, and Jolie knew, he was going to get it sooner, rather than later.

She moved effortlessly through her prison, knowing that the time was coming for her to make a major choice, either move on, or do the forbidden to her kind, return. It was no contest, she would have to return to them. They needed her more than ever, and her purgatory sentence was just about over. *I believe Sookie would love to hear that I have decided* she thought as she left the cloudy dimension that surrounded her ethereal home and mounted the steps into the house she had called home for the last two hundred years.

The stairs lead to a tower and at the top of the tower, a place she had never been, stood a room that would help her return. She wouldn't enter the room unless her resolve was clear, so she veered to the lower room of the tower, the room of communication. She sat on a pristine rug and relaxed, mentally calling out to her friend and confidant. *Sookie? Sookie, I believe the time has come...*

One

Sallos watched the exchange between the general and the girl with no less enthusiasm than he would a fly and a cow. In fact the whole courtship bored him. *Drake's obviously the more interesting brother.* Once the altercation was over he followed the general home, playing a little game with the ice demon. Eventually, after a sloppily long time Oscar realized he was being followed and stopped. Sallos walked forward into the light, grinning.

"Greetings Oscar and how are you this fine evening?" He greeted with false enthusiasm. It wasn't a fine night at all, it was cold. He hated the cold. Not only was it cold but also he'd been sent to find the princess; a task that he knew would prove as difficult as the princess herself. *With any luck she'll have wandered home by now, safe in the arms of that bastard of a husband.* Sallos hid any doubts and anger at his given task and outwardly beamed at Oscar's back. *That's right just two old friends meeting accidentally in the night.*

Oscar stopped and turned smoothly, eyeing Sallos. "Same as I was at the ball Sallos, or weren't you there?"

Sallos grinned savagely, "Oh I was there, friend." *No friend of mine.* "However, I must regret that I did not have the chance to inquire after your health, or that of your lady friend. I trust you are both well?"

"As usual. So what can I do for you Sallos? Lord knows this isn't a social call." *No, Lord knows.*

"No? Yet me and your brother get on so well, we have never had the chance to get on Oscar. How about we remedy that right now?" He answered back cheerfully.

Oscar sighed heavily. "Sallos, I don't know what the hell you want so quit pussy footing around and get to it already." his eyes glittered. "And have a care, you are on Conglacio land Cento."

Sallos glared at the general, *it's all Fuerety's land Conglacio,* "Very well Conglacio, but you should tread lightly... I'm not in a good mood. It would be a shame if something happened to your pretty little girl in there." He nodded towards Milo's house, a very different grin on his face. "I'm looking for Cassiel, I assume you know where he is."

"Cassiel? How the hell would I know where the exiled prince is? I don't leave the verse, and since he's been exiled he doesn't come here. So, how the hell would I know where he is?" he scoffed. "And Sallos, watch your ass. You're just a fucking guard, and you might be all big and bad at the Cento court but I'm a general, and you can threaten me all you want but I will eat your fucking heart if you look at Lady Uriel sideways." He smiled and stood at parade rest watching the Cento.

Sallos laughed holding his hands up in mock submission, "Relax, no need to get your panties in a twist. I just thought that you might know. Would your brother?"

"Drake? You should know damn well unless it has to do with whores and the action of fucking them till they cry, and not in the good way, he doesn't know or doesn't care. Last I heard he was in Morocco, but that was months ago. You're more than welcome to ask him, but he's a bit more volatile than me."

"Well Drake always did have a better grasp on life than you, but why be so hostile friend?" *Stupid Conglacio, you think I even care about your "status"? Give me a reason, just one.*

Oscar laughed. "You come to me and threaten my date looking for info and you don't think I'm going to get hostile?"

Sallos smiled charmingly. "Threaten? I didn't threaten... mealy stated. It would be a shame, wouldn't it?" He shrugged. "Either way you must have heard some rumor as to where the exiled prince is located." *Tell me Oscar, save us all a little time. I will find him.*

"Last I heard about Cassiel, he was all buggy nuts-o laying naked on an iceberg somewhere in the Antarctic Ocean. His father doesn't even know where he is. So that's about all the info I can give you Sallos. Why are you looking for him? I thought Feurety had him watched."

Sallos frowned before he could stop himself. "No, we haven't kept track of him for a while." *We lost him, have no clue where he is or what magics he's using to hide.* "Have you seen Faris lately?"

"Faris? Not since her wedding. Isn't she with her husband? Or wedded bliss falling short?" Oscar asked smugly, a little smile on his face.

"Bliss is just fine, only her father wishes to speak with her. Where would I find Dimitri?"

"*Prince* Dimitri is where he always is, Russia. Why?"

I want nothing more than to melt that smile from your face. Sallos checked around, he couldn't afford to fight the Conglacio on his own ground, so he held his tongue. "No reason, maybe Prince Dimitri would know where his brother was, or he may have talked to Princess Faris."

"Dimitri speaks to Cassiel? You guys are really behind. Unlike some of the courts, the Conglacio heeds Fuerety's law and has no ties with the exiled, not even King Leviathan speaks with his first-born and he has clearance to. As for Princess Faris and Dimitri talking? Dimitri also heeds Fuerety's word that no royal house Conglacio may speak with the Royal crown princess of the Cento."

He smiled at Oscar through gritted teeth. "Well said, friend. But I'm afraid it sounded a little too rehearsed. The King I believe but that the Prince should forsake his brother? Never going to happen, Prince Dimitri is too much of a soft touch for that."

"You'd be surprised Sallos, Prince Dimitri even lets Drake beat his favorite whore. Prince Dimitri isn't the same Demon anymore."

The pretty little one? His mind searched for her name but he could not remember it. He had seen the prince with the girl a few times, she always had seemed so happy. "Truly? So those stories are true?" He considered for a few moments before speaking. "Well, whores are whores; the prince has thousands more, but only one true brother." The thought of Drake being allowed to beat the little whore sickened him more than he would ever admit. *Maybe we'll have to see how the Conglacio likes it himself.*

"Sallos, Prince Dimitri didn't stand by Prince Cassiel when he was exiled, what makes you think he'd do it now?"

Sallos smiled, "Most true, so you have no inkling about the whereabouts of the exile?"

"Not a damn clue, unless you count the Arctic Ocean."

No, I don't. "Well, it would be a little cold there. I'll try your brother. He does get around more than you."

"Yeah but not in circles the prince would, unless Prince Cassiel has become a drug addicted hooker."

Sallos laughed at the thought. "Well, that is always a possibility, stranger things have happened. Speaking of which, do you recognize your courted woman?"

"Uriel? Recognize? Yeah she looks like her Father."

Sallos grinned at him, "Yeah, sure... her father's double. Friend, you have no idea."

"Look Sallos I don't know what you're talking about." *No, you wouldn't and I'm not going to tell you.*

"You'll figure it out, but her eyes are most unusual, are they not?"

"Pure Conglacio Blue, most unusual."

Sallos rolled his eyes clearly frustrated at Oscar's stupidity. *Typical Conglacio, never see what's staring you in the face.* "Yes, blue is far more unusual than say a green. Speaking of which, I must go pay Prince Dimitri a visit. I shall bid you farewell."

"Enjoy trying to get past his guards, the dogs and the drug addled hookers. Even I'm not stupid enough to visit him at home..."

"I have nothing to fear, from the things you have mentioned, friend. Dimitri and his toys pose no threat to me, unlike the likes of you." He grinned again. "I shall see Drake first, though. Would you like me to pass any messages onto your little brother?" *Like how you instigated his beating?*

"No thank you Sallos, Dimitri's bodyguard, my brother, knows if I wish to get him a message, I'll do it personally. Enjoy playing with Drake." *I shall.*

"Very well, then enjoy the rest of your night, friend."

"You too Sallos."

Sallos bowed slightly then blinked off in search of the younger brother.

Two

Faris looked around the room that she would now share with Cash and nodded in approval. *His Sorceress is quite skilled in decorating.* Everything in the room, from the window treatments to the carpet was nothing but the finest cloth, furniture and electronics. *The witch certainly knows how to treat royalty, although I would have rather had burgundy or eggplant for color in here, but then again she wasn't expecting me now was she? This room is prefect for Cash, or at least I think it is.* She realized just then that in all the years she and Cassiel were courting, she had never once seen his bedroom. *I really must remedy that once we get back to the Afterverse.*

She walked over to the bed and sat, it was perfect, just soft enough and the bedclothes were of the highest quality silk. She touched the cool material and then stood walking into the large bathroom that was attached to their suite. The tub wasn't as big as the one she had at the fire palace, but it would still hold both her and Cassiel comfortably.

The closet that was between the rooms, a walk-in of the highest caliber, all lined with cedar paneling was enormous. She noticed a few suits of Cash's hanging in one corner, a pair of jeans and a few shirts. *And it looks like he hasn't been here as long as I thought. Well that's a good thing. At least I know he's a new arrival as well. I will have to be getting out shopping soon.* She turned to the other door across from the closet and opened the door to reveal a closet filled with everything you could ever need for a bathroom. There were three shelves stocked with towels in varying colors of blues and purples, of which she was grateful. *I will have to ask her about changing the bedclothes a bit.* She looked down at the rest of the shelves. They were filled with Loofah sponges, pumice stones, wash clothes, scrub brushes, exfoliating mitts, seven kinda of body wash, four male scented and three female scented, bubble bath, bath salts and bath bombs. Faris was truly in heaven. She laughed. *Well if I'm hiding out, this is the best place; it's a fantasy, a true fantasy.* She moved away from the closet pulling two towels out, purple, and a bottle of citrus bubble bath, a loofah and a bath pillow. *Since he's out talking to them, I might as well make myself comfortable. It will be nice to have him catch me in the tub.*

She thought back on one of the times he had shown up at her room at the fire palace and she was in the tub, candles the only light in the room, the oil in the water given a rosy glow.

He walked in and saw her naked and wet and oily and smirked at her standing against one of the marble pillars that surrounded her tub. She didn't open her eyes but smiled, knowing he was there, the cold touch of his power playing across her exposed flesh, sending goose bumps here and there, puckering choice bits of flesh that just rose over the waterline. She sighed and smiled. "So, are you getting in with me or what?"

He let the room get a lot colder and she giggled and sat up, her body coming up out of the very warm water, reacting to his magic. She watched him strip and sink into the bath with her pulling her to him, kissing her. "Now Princess, you did all this just for me?"

She giggled as she remembered the night they had after he grabbed her and she blushed. *I think I can recreate that night all over again, and if I can't, well then we'll just have to make a new memory for me to blush at.* She smiled and started the tub, pouring the bubble bath into the tub and got undressed, then walked around, and lit the candles with the touch of her finger on the wick. Seconds later she was sinking into the tub's hot water and sighing, waiting for her prince to come and join her.

***

Cassiel left Astrid and sauntered on up the stairs to find what type of mess Faris had left him in her urge to sleep. He smiled to himself thinking about how good it would be to hold her in his arms again. He still couldn't bring himself to believe it, she was his again, and no matter how many times he repeated those words in his head they still didn't ring true.

He didn't deserve a second chance, not after everything he'd done, was going to do. He paused shaking his head lightly. *Human standards, I'm setting myself to their standards now.* He groaned loudly, the weight of his years in exile pressing against him. *Oh god, I've got to get back home soon or I'm going to turn into one.*

"Fucking humans." He cussed gently.

Tiredly, he continued up the stairs to his room and the waiting Faris. He was going to be a father, he thought trying to lighten his mood. He still couldn't believe it. *I wonder if the world is ready for a little cross between me and Faris?* He laughed, reaching the top stair and turning into the hall, which led to his room. *Doubtful, I don't really think the world is ready for me and Faris never mind the little one.* He gently opened the door, not wanting to wake Faris up, and creeped in looking for her.

"Cash? I'm in the bathtub." She called out softly hearing the door open.

He grinned wolfishly. *In the tub eh? Well, that's much more fun than sleeping.* "Well then that's where I should be also, don't you think?" He called back as he walked to the bathroom.

She giggled and he watched as the water sloshed over the side. "That was the general idea prince."

He walked in the room and smirked down at her naked body, the heat showing plainly in his eyes. "I do love it when you get all wet for me, love."

She moved closer to the edge of the tub and rested her arms on the lip, resting her chin on them. He grinned down at her and she licked her lips. "Yeah I like it too. You going to join me prince? Or do I have to beg?"

Why is it that women these days are always begging me for things? He grinned again and started to undress. "No, you never have to beg me to do anything princess. Never."

She smiled and moved back against the far wall of the tub. "That's good to know, get your sexy self in here Cashy, I missed you. Everything go ok with your Sorceress and her demon?"

He finished undressing and slid into the space she had created for him. He stroked her smooth thigh absentmindedly as he answered her. "Well, we agreed to talk to him in the morning. He'll be alright with the situation, he doesn't really have much of a choice." He said feeling a little bit guilty for having caused Fallon any distress at all.

For all his whining and moping around the man can be handy sometimes. He quietly sighed to himself hating Astrid's emotions and decency, for the millionth time. *I can't really wait to be me again, this is getting fucking old.*

She moved over to his lap, sliding her thighs over his hips and kissed him. "Well you do what you have to baby. So, did you miss me?"

He gratefully kissed her back. "I don't think I've ever not missed you."

She giggled. "Good." She put her right hand on her little bump of a tummy and sighed. "Cash, you sure you're happy about this?"

He smiled happily and nodded. "More sure than I have been about anything. It still sounds weird as hell coming off the tongue; we're going to be a family, a real one. Not like the ones we have now, but a good one. A mummy and a daddy and baby. The three of us, and if more come later down the line then that would be great too. But for now, I'm just thankful for what I have; a second chance."

She kissed him, nibbling on his bottom lip, making her way down to his collarbone. "Ummm it's not a second chance Cashy, it's us doing things right this time. Speaking of doing things right," she giggled and pressed her body against his, wiggling on his lap.

He shivered and groaned, pulling her further onto his lap. "What is it that you would like to do right princess?" He asked teasingly.

She nibbled his neck and reached down and squeezed him, "Darling, it hasn't been that long, you forgot already?"

He laughed, "No, I think I can remember." He easily lifted her and slid her onto his hard, waiting length with a hiss of pleasure. "Oh, I think it's coming back to me now..." he trailed off growling.

She arched and groaned into him. "Ummm god Cash, no, no I don't think you ever forgot, ummm this is perfect."

He leaned forward getting deeper, before he whispered in her ear. "How gentle do we have to be? I don't want to hurt our baby or you..." he groaned again. "But, my body's screaming at me to go harder and faster."

She whimpered. "Just don't break me, and we'll be fine" She nipped his bottom lip again, and squeezed him. "Please Cash... make me yours again."

He swallowed hard and tightly gripped her thighs, moving her up and down him as her kissed down her neck to take one of her swollen nipples into his mouth. He gently rolled the rock hard pebble in his mouth with his cold tongue. "You'll always be mine Princess." He whispered into her.

"Damn straight Cash, only yours, only yours ever." She sobbed and arched as she took him deeper, whimpering. She purred and whispered. "Cash, please... don't hold back, I missed this..."

At her words he sped up, losing all thought and control to the desire to be inside of her, to hold her, to own her as he had so many year ago. He pounded deeply into her, her moans and yelps of pleasure only driving him on faster. He lived and breathed for those noises, he needed her like he had never needed anyone before. Only her, his princess.

She screamed his name and arched closer, letting her power go, scorching his chest and turning the water to steam around her. She bucked on his lap. "Cash" she panted, "Cash, you're amazing, oh god... Cash!"

"Shit!" He called out as he felt her come around him, his power instantly cooling the boiling hot water, as he arched deeper into her.

She clawed at him, "Cash, baby!" She panted as her orgasm wore down and smiled. "Sorry about the water Cash."

He smiled and began to work her again, without giving her much time to calm down. "Don't worry about it. I've always loved playing with fire."

She giggled and purred in the back of her throat. "Ummm well that's good. Cuz this fire loves playing with you." She kissed him, hard, letting loose her power once more, burning his shoulders and he instantly cooled down her body. He brought her once more over the edge. "Casha!" She looked at him with unbridled heat in her eyes and arched, clamping him hard from the inside. "Casha...Oh god..."

"Fuck!" He cried out, as he unsteadily got to his knees to gain more leverage to force himself ever deeper into her. She wrapped her slick legs tightly around him as he pounded into her as fast and hard as he could manage letting go once more. He kissed her deeply as his freezing cold hands explored her body.

The feel of her molten hot core tightening around his now ice cold shaft sent him over as he released himself violently inside of her.

"You're always so fantastic Prince, Ummm, what a wonderful welcome home present."

He groaned and sat back, pulling her down with him. "It was for both of us I think."

She giggled and kissed his chest. "Thank you prince. You sure you're ok with me being here?"

"I don't think I could live with you being anywhere other than right here." He kissed her softly on the head.

"Good, cuz the only place I feel safe is in your arms. I am sleepy, you wore me out." She cuddled closer to him, "Cash, we never have slept together. I mean in a bed, you never spent the night."

"Well, then I think we should both remedy that. Let you fall asleep and wake up in my arms." He picked her up and carried her through to the bed, settling them both down and pulling the covers over their slightly damp bodies.

She smiled at him and took his hand and put it on her belly. "We both thank you love. Please be here when I wake?" She cuddled closer to him, sighing. "I really am happy baby, and I'm glad I got you back." She closed her eyes and turned her head into his shoulder and breathed deeply. "You smell so good Prince, so good."

He smiled caressing her belly, his baby. "I smell like you Princess. I'll be here when you wake up, I promise." He kissed her head again. "Now Angel, sleep well. I'll be the first thing you see when you awake."

She smiled and closed her eyes, sighing. "Ok baby." she yawned and held him closer. "I'm safe." she murmured as she drifted off to sleep.

"Yes, princess. You are." He pulled her closer to him and drifted off after her.

Three

It had taken him all of an hour to find the younger brother. Sallos shivered pulling his coat around him. London was always so cold and wet. After scouring several bars and a few of Drake's other haunts he had found a nice little witch who had been more than happy to divulge Drake's whereabouts. Turns out he'd bagged himself a chick and was busy at her place doing whatever it was Drake did to girls before he killed them. Sallos smiled and shook his head. *Let's just hope Drake's more forthcoming than his brother was.*

He walked up the darkened driveway and immediately saw the naked Conglacio in the kitchen. *Raiding her fridge already Drake, some things never will change.* He walked up to the window and tapped the glass, scaring the demon into a little jump. Sallos smirked and motioned to the door, Drake nodded in understanding.

By the time it took Drake to find the door and open it he had also managed to find a towel and wrap it around himself, and for that Sallos was most thankful. He didn't need to end his day talking to a naked Drake. *Although,* he mused, *if he tells me where Casha is I'll let him do a fucking little jig hell, I'll even join in.*

"This better be good Sal, I'm kinda busy." Drake growled as Sallos pushed past him.

"I bet you are. I won't keep you long." He sneered.

Drake smirked at him. "I bet you won't. What are you doing topside this late anyways? Shouldn't you be home playing house?"

"Don't even go there, Drake, I'm really not in the mood." He laughed. "You know how many times I've said that today?"

"Not really, why the hell am I supposed to care if you can't get it up Sal."

Sallos ignored him, and carried on. "I'm looking for the Prince."

"D? I'm not his keeper, go see him. I'm not really in his good books right now... he doesn't want to see me for a few weeks. Why do you want him?"

"The other prince Drake, Cassiel... where is he?" He questioned the semi naked demon.

"Casha? How the hell should I know... didn't he go crazy?"

"You tell me."

Drake shook his head. "Can't mate, haven't seen him in years. You mean that you're out here looking for him, at this time?" *Unfortunately.*

"I'm looking for Faris, at this time of night."

"What makes you think she's with him?"

"Where else would she go?"

The Conglacio shrugged. "I dunno, shopping? Faris liked to do that... what about Baster? You seen her recently?"

"Not for a while." *I really am not going there with you, tonight.*

"Really? Cuz last I heard you two were real tight in the..."

"This isn't a social call, Drake." Sallos cut him off as he turned from the other demon. "If I want to brag about fucking the Succubi I'll do it on my own time, and not when I'm on the job."

Drake held his hands up a little, "Ooh, it got messy didn't it? What happened, she find out how small your dick really is?"

He never saw the hand that hit him. Sallos watched contentedly as the Conglacio flew across the room and dented the wall, his towel flying off in a different direction. *Fucking prick.* Sallos smiled down at the demon, trying not to show his discomfort at having nearly broken his hand on Drakes thick skull.

"You know Drake, that made me feel so much better. Stand back up and I'll hit you again." He said flexing his aching hand his grin turned into more of a ghastly grimace.

Drake laughed from his place on the floor. "Yeah, sure... cuz your hand's not just as sore as my face, right now. Can I stand back up and get my towel or are you gonna hit me back down?"

Sallos shrugged. "Depends, are you going to answer my question?"

"Can't, like I said; I don't know where he is and I couldn't care less. I never got on with that fucking prick. As for Far, I stay away from all the Centos, safer that way. The last one I talked to was you. Besides Faris hated me. Why would I know where she is?"

"Fine, I'll believe that you're too busy with beating and fucking whores to pick up any information not pertaining to the task at hand."

"Yeah, that's it... who said anything about whores? I'll have you know the one down there is nothing of the sort."

"Yeah, I bet she is."

"How's little Tammy?"

Sallos blinked in surprise, he couldn't remember the Conglacio ever meeting his niece, but he answered the question anyway. "Tam?" He shrugged. "She's ok, you know... it comes in waves, she does fine for a while, then it gets worse. We're getting there though."

"Yeah... So, is that all? Can I get back to my evening oh fiery one?"

"One last thing..."

"What?"

"Dimitri's whore, the blonde one..."

Drake smirked, cutting him off. "Why? You want a piece of that, cuz I gotta tell you, I put that little whore outta action for a long while..."

Sallos hit him again sending him into the wall. "Fuck!" He shook his hand loosening it up. "Have a little respect, they are still women Drake. The blonde one looked like a child, fuck!"

"Mama never taught me respect for women and children." Drake said as he slumped against the wall.

Sallos sighed. "That's because your mama was a gold digging tramp of a woman... and her sons are no better. Next time I'm just going to melt you, but there's just something about you that makes me..." He shook his head. "I would never get tired of beating you Drake."

"You're not the first person to say that."

"Absolutely useless, and I'm not the first person to say that either." He shook his head, turned his back on the Conglacio and walked out the house.

The cold rain soaked him the instant he left the house. *Why is London always so cold?* He sighed as he thought to where he was headed next; Russia was always cold, no matter the year.

Four

The key to Dimitri's apartment had been exactly where Cash had told her. Cole let herself in steadily fighting down the butterflies that had been working her way through her stomach. She hadn't seen or spoken to the prince since she was last in Russia, throwing herself at him like some lovesick teenager. Which, in all fairness, she had been. He'd been her first and the only one that had ever meant anything to her.

It was just the way things were though, he was a prince and she was barely even a witch anymore. They could never have had anything more than those two passion-filled nights in Russia. They were ships passing in the night and could never be anything else. No matter what she wanted. She'd played a key role in his brother's exile and she knew that he could never truly forgive such an act.

Today, though, things were different. She'd get to see him again and the thought of his strong arms holding her satiated and sweaty naked body against his made her heart skip a beat. His memory did things to her body that she'd never felt with any other man. Not even Arcady, Mr. Fantasy himself, could best Dimitri in her eyes.

She was skipping ahead though chances were that wasn't what this was about. Chances were that he didn't even want her; he'd always been polite to a fault. It wasn't too far fetched to believe that he'd been too nice to turn her away. If those two nights turned out to be all that she'd ever get then she'd cherish the memory like she had been doing for the past six years.

She knew that Dimitri had changed. Just because she hadn't spoken with him didn't mean that she hadn't heard the stories. Working so closely with Alcyone and seeing Arcady on a semi regular basis had made her privy to most of the stories. She knew all about his business and its fall into drug-addled degradation. Of course she didn't believe all of them but some were hard to ignore, especially when she took into consideration the bitter rivalry between Dimitri and Al.

All in all, Cole didn't know why she was meeting him other than she was doing it for Arcady. Still she could hope that D would sweep her off her feet, but giving the evidence she wasn't holding her breath. She closed the door to the apartment taking the time to look in the mirror.

Choosing an outfit had been hard. After all what did one wear to meet the love of ones life when one wasn't exactly sure of his intentions. Dresses were certainly out of the equation. She was not throwing herself at him again. She'd grown up since then and hoped to show him that. What had happened in Russia was because she'd wanted him, not because she'd been using him to get out of the city. God, she really hoped he knew that. Her belly flopped over again, the nerves and nausea returning.

If anything happened between them it would be because he wanted it to, not because she'd lost control of her hormones. Taking that into consideration she'd opted for jeans, nothing too flashy more something that you'd wear to see an old friend. Her top was figure hugging and sexy without being too slutty. She'd left her hair down falling in waves around her neck and shoulders and her make-up was natural and light.

Around her neck was the simple gold chain he'd gotten her for her birthday one year. She'd considered taking it off but it so rarely left her skin that she'd feel naked without it. She stalked over to the sofa and sat down wringing her hands and watching the clock. Cash had said twelve and it was now ten past. Her heart dropped into the pit of her stomach, she'd never even considered that he might not show.

Minutes later she heard the lock click as the knob was turned. Dimitri walked in, the light from the hallway framing him. He saw her, stopped and smiled. "Long time, no see." he said quietly, leaning against the side wall.

He took her breath away, impeccable as always. It took her a few seconds to recover from just the mere sight of him, and she managed a rueful smile back at him. "It's been a while."

"Too long I think. How have you been?" he asked and fidgeted with his tie.

"Good, well..." she looked down at the floor. "Better than most. Can't complain. You?"

"The usual. Business is business, that's about all I do." He looked up at her with a smile. "You don't look ok. Is it me?"

"No!" her eyes shot up to meet his stunning blue ones. "I..." She stuttered to a stop. Smiling at him she shrugged. "It's good to see you again."

He smiled at her again and sighed. "You probably want to know what's going on then? I mean you look like you could bolt any second."

"I'm not going anywhere... chances are Cash would kill me if I did." She winced inwardly, this wasn't how she'd planned on this going. Sure as hell wasn't close to her dreams, they were both wearing far too many clothes for that. She was curious to see what he was willing to offer. "That's not why I'm staying though, I missed you."

He looked over at her and for a second, she thought she saw what amounted to hope shining in his eyes. "I missed you too. Look. Why don't we have a drink, and talk? I could use one," he said and loosened his tie. "I think we both could."

She relaxed smiling gratefully. "I could go for that."

He pushed off the wall and walked over to the small bar just ahead of her and looked over. "What's your poison? Lord knows we don't drink the same thing."

"It's doubtful," She smiled knowing only too well of Dimitri's penchant for potently lethal cocktails. She seriously hoped that he wouldn't partake here; she wanted a conversation with him not to watch him drink his immortality away. "Wine would be great, if you've got any...?"

"I do, Merlot actually." He pulled two glasses out and poured the wine, picking up both glasses. He went to her and offered her a glass, sitting in the armchair next to the couch. He was quiet a moment, swirling the wine around the fine crystal that held it. "You look amazing Cole. Grew up better then I ever thought. Dancing has been good to you I take it?"

"It has, you should swing by one night and see a set. That is if you and Al can stay away from each other's throats long enough to actually see a whole set." She winked playfully taking a sip on the smoky wine taking her time to enjoy the rich flavor. "She's hardly at the club nowadays anyway. The chances of you running into her are pretty slim."

"I had heard she had other... interests. No matter though, I have been in to see you, twice really."

"Really?" she asked surprised and maybe a little disappointment in her voice. She'd never once seen him; he'd hidden from her.

He nodded. "About a year ago. I stopped in to see you, but you were on stage. Took my breath away actually."

She felt her cheeks burning and knew they'd just turned a deep shade of red. "Now you're just teasing." She looked away glad that the blush was her only obvious reaction to his words.

He chuckled. "No, no I'm not. You were beautiful up there Cole. Look I'm sure you have questions for me, so please...."

She took another sip of wine trying to build up some Dutch courage, which was funny considering she was from Holland originally. "I suppose the simplest one would be asking what do you want? Why am I here and what exactly does it have to do with Arcady? Your brother wasn't exactly forthcoming with the knowledge and while I hope I've pieced it together..." She paused swallowing her next words. "I just want to hear it from you."

He relaxed visibly and then sighed. "I'm sure he was quite the ass when he visited. Truth of the matter is I want you, always have. As for the Incubus, he's happy and content with Snow, my recent enforcer and companion.

Cash wanted Snow, and I let her go because it was the best way to get you. Bastard probably planned this from the off, though I really don't care. It gave me a way to get you back in my life." He looked up at her and then back down at his glass. "You're here because I can't live without you anymore."

She blinked not sure if she was hearing him correctly, he just told her that he needed her he wanted her. It was something she'd dreamed of but never dared believe. "Truly?" Her voice asked quietly.

"I don't play games Cole. I'm not Casha. It's been too long without you. I won't live with half a heart anymore. You with me is the *only* thing that can change that."

She smiled at him, "You have no idea how long I've wanted to hear you say that."

His gaze went from tentative to smoldering in about two seconds. "Now you're teasing."

She flicked her tongue out wetting her lips. "No teasing D... not between us."

He sat up and grinned. "Cole you don't have to do this, I may need you but if your heart isn't in it, I won't force you. I'm giving you an out right now."

"Because you're a good guy, but it's not what I want. Dimitri I want you, I always have. Only you and in any capacity I can get you in."

"Any capacity?" He grinned and patted his lap. "Come here Cole, I need to touch you."

"Any and every capacity D." She returned his grin setting her wine down and slipping perfectly into his lap. "You always were comfy," she breathed quietly resting her head on his shoulder.

He sighed and wrapped his arms around her, holding her tight. "And you fit perfectly around me. Always have," he said quietly, stroking her side. "There's a few conditions though Cole..."

She relaxed into him, "Isn't there always?"

"I think you'll be ok with most of these though."

"I don't think anything would be too much as long as I get you."

"You're being entirely too accommodating pet."

"I am?" She smiled up at him.

He chuckled. "Yes you are. I could be asking you to jump off a bridge here... Where is that wary girl I knew years ago? The one that learned the world wasn't a nice place? Dare I think she isn't so jaded anymore?"

She chuckled, "Not really... I just don't believe that you'd ask me to jump off a bridge. I'm plenty jaded, you just don't bring that out in me... not yet anyway."

"Well thank Christ for that." He kissed her forehead and then sighed. "Cash isn't going to hunt you anymore, so you don't have to be wary of him. And you don't have to give up your job."

"Good I couldn't give up the club, not with Al absent."

"I liked seeing you dance, so that's not even a worry."

She smiled again glad that he liked her dancing. If he played his cards right he'd be getting a private viewing "So where's the bad?"

"Well I'm not sure it's really bad..."

"D you're beating around the bush." she chastised.

"Well the apartment for one. It's yours."

"All of it?" She asked looking around.

He laughed. "Yes all of it."

"Mmmm..." She purred happily against him. "So far there's nothing I hate."

"Well that's a relief. But there's just one more thing."

She nodded pulling away from him and met his eyes. Whatever it was she wasn't going to like, she knew it would be this one. "Okay shoot."

"I have to bind you to me as my sorceress. It's the one thing he insisted on." he sighed and stroked her side again, only lower.

"Oh..." She swallowed looking away. "Dimitri I'm not a witch anymore. I don't have a goddess remember? I wouldn't be much use to you... If you want my soul then it's always been yours but I'm no sorceress."

He chuckled. "Cole, love, you are more powerful then you'll ever know, that's why he wanted you. Why else did you think he was so good to you? So what, you don't have a goddess, you have the power as part of you. You can be a sorceress without a goddess."

"D, Casha only wanted me because of that damn book. It had nothing to do with my powers."

"Sure it didn't Pet. You keep believing that."

"Plan on it..." She sighed. "So a sorceress? Is that what you want?"

"What I want is you, Cole, with me for as long as I live, as my lover, my companion, the woman that holds my heart. Making you my sorceress ensures that, so yes that's what I want. What do you want though?"

"I don't know... but I do know what I don't want. I don't want to live without you anymore. Never again. Having powers again might take some getting used to but I think I'll adjust. I want you D... always have."

He groaned and kissed her then, moving them to a sitting up position, his hands possessive around her body. "Then that's one thing we agree on my love. We shall have each other..."

She slid her legs to either side of his, straddling him. Jeans were definitely not the best choice she decided as she wriggled down on his lap. She looked deeply into his eyes. "Promise me."

"Anything..."

"Promise me we'll always be together," She shook her head. "No more being alone."

"I can promise you that Cole... You're mine... have been since that weekend in Russia"

She nodded knowing that she'd been his well before that day. "Nothing will ever come between us D... it can't."

"And I won't let it.. You're mine now, fully, nothing can change that."

"Thank you." She leaned in kissing him deeply her arms wrapping around him and pulling him against her.

"And just so you know, I'm staying the night..."

"Mmmm then you should know that I'm not wearing any panties." She purred in his ear.

He growled and grabbed her hips situating her over his groin and the hard length imprisoned therein. "Neither am I" he winked and slid his hands up under her shirt. "You sure you wanna do this? Once you're naked you can't say no..."

He drew a groan from her as his fingertips brushed her nipples. "Like I could say no to you... even clothed."

He grinned. "Still such a naughty girl Cole. So shall we take the tour?"

She trailed her tongue down his neck, breathing in his spicy scent, "As long as the first stop's the bedroom."

"The only stop is the bedroom Cole... You think I'm going to wait any longer to have you?" he said as he stood, wrapping her legs around his waist.

"We've both waited long enough." She agreed.

Seconds later they were stumbling into the bedroom, her small fingers unbuttoning his shirt, as his supported her back. They tumbled onto the bed, still kissing and Dimitri laughed. "Eager aren't we?"

"Shouldn't we be?" She lightly bit his lower lip tugging him gently closer to her.

"There's no rush love... we have all night..." he kissed her, "And tomorrow..." he kissed her again, "And the day after that..."

She giggled, luxuriating in his attention. It felt so good to finally be together as they were meant to be. "I know but it doesn't make me need you any less..." She slipped her hand down to cup him, squeezing gently yet firmly.

He groaned and closed his eyes. "Fucking hell Cole."

She smirked pulling on his pants. "Off!" She kissed him again. "Off or I'm going to start ripping... and I know how much you'd hate that."

"It's just a suit... And I like seeing you lost in yourself like this... " He kissed her and helped her get his clothes off as he was liberating her of her own. Jeans open, shirt off and displaying her to his gaze he growled and took a pert nipple into his mouth as she helped him out of his pants.

Gasping she ran her hands through his hair tugging it tightly as his tongue and teeth played havoc on her body. "And I love being lost in you."

He sucked hard at her nipple then let go panting. They rolled on the bed, his pants rolling down his legs in a very comical way. He grinned with Cole under him, her nipples stiff and at attention, the fly and button of her jeans open, soft tanned flesh peaking out. He looked up and then back down, grinning." As stunning as you look in jeans, I'm afraid they need to come off."

"They do." She agreed wiggling her way out of the denim and making quite a show for him. Kicking them across the room she grinned lustfully up at him, her hair now messily spread across them both.

"God damn are you fucking perfect. And I see someone tans in the nude... So sexy."

She flashed him a wicked grin. "Can't have tan lines in my job."

"Very true." he ran his fingers down her belly slowly, a thoughtful look on his face.

She shivered to his touch looking questionably at him. "What?"

"I just can't believe you're really here. I mean that I have you..." he looked up at her with a sheepish grin. "Fantasies coming true," he offered by way of explanation.

"You do have me... all of me." She let her hands drift up his chest stroking him gently. "This is a fantasy alright."

He kissed her again, and smiled, lifting her hip and thigh. He was settled between her legs quickly, his length nestled in her warmth. "This isn't going to last long I'm afraid."

She chuckled as her back arched to further accommodate him. "You know that's not what you say in my fantasy." She grinned squeezing him teasingly. "God but you do feel so damn good."

"Well I don't say it in my fantasy either, but it's the truth." He kissed her and shifted, slipping into her waiting heat. "Gods I barely touched you and you're soaked."

"Been this wet since you first walked in the room." She wrapped her legs around his waist pulling him further into her. He filled her better than she remembered touching everything that he should. "I love you Dimitri."

"You better pet, cuz you're stuck with me." He kissed her and moved slowly, groaning. "Fuck you're so tight," he said and moved to her ear, his hands lifting her hips up off the bed partially to get deeper. "And I love you too Cole, only and always you."

"Good." She slipped her hands around his back holding herself to him as she thrust her hips up to meet him. "Please... please don't stop."

"I don't plan on it pet, you're too fantastic..." he worked her deftly, seemingly remembering her body and all the things his taught her in seconds. "Gods baby...So sweet."

She panted hard, both their bodies glistening in the pale light. She needed him, this. His body drove harder into her sending her higher. His touch and kisses were all that mattered to her spurring and coaxing her on. "Ummm that's it! Make me yours D..." She cried out her body crashing into his as orgasm built rapidly within her.

"Not yet love... Soon you'll wear my brand.... but now, I want you to come for me... I miss feeling you fall apart around me... fucking shit you're amazing."

"Oh Dimitri!" She screamed his name as she came hard, wave after wave of pleasure burst through her rippling over her skin. She bucked hard against him pulling him even deeper still.

"Sweet Hell that's good!" he groaned and followed her over, panting and kissing her shoulder. "Told you that wasn't going to last...."

She purred rolling them over and sprawling over the top of him. "Mmmm true but that was much better than the fantasy."

"Well then I'm glad I don't disappoint. Give me about twenty minutes and we will change that."

She giggled, "What, you plan on disappointing me?"

"No, god I hope not... I mean I'm going to fuck you senseless so this last one seems like a bad dream."

Chuckling she kissed up his neck pausing to nibble gently on his collarbone. "Now that I like the sound of," she sighed contentedly.

"Of that I have no doubt... You are so beautiful...."

She beamed up at him her face inches from his. His intense green eyes practically glowed sending shivers though her body. "I'm glad you think so."

"How could I not? So my lover, my companion and my sorceress soon... I can't wait to have you wear my brand... where shall we put it?"

"Anywhere you want, but I want to show it off when I dance." She kissed him nuzzling closer. "Everyone has to know that I'm yours."

He grinned. "And everybody will know. Perhaps high on your hip? Or maybe the small of your back? Something sexy I think..." he nibbled on her fingers slowly.

"Sexy we can do, love. Maybe on my hip... I'd like that."

"Ummm... I could see that... pretty and sexy...." he grinned. "So what do you say to a ride love?"

She chuckled up at him kissing his cheek. "It's a bit late to be running around in cars don't you think?"

He shook his head. "I'm not talking about a car pet."

"Oh?" She raised a questioning eyebrow shifting her weight slightly so that she straddled him.

He smirked and gripped her hips. "I think you know exactly what I mean love...though we should take care if this bargain don't you think?"

"Mmmm I think so..."

"So then... what is it you want my love?"

"Other than you? Not much..."

"All bargains have to involve something... what is it you want. Astrid wanted power and the ability to help her family... While Cash just wanted to shag her..." he chuckled. "Well there's more than that but you get the idea..."

"Ok..." She nodded thinking carefully. If this was her one shot then she sure as hell wasn't going to waste it on superpowers. She took her time considering. "Ok I think I know. You might not want to go for this D and that's ok. I want you... body and soul. You get mine right? I don't need any power to protect my family but I do want one...eventually. Lord knows this body isn't ready for stretch marks, but if I have kids I want them to be yours." She swallowed hard.

"I want you to be mine, which means no one else." She smirked at him, "A little playtime now and again is different, I mean relationships... and whores. I'm not sharing you with whores, I don't plan on sharing you at all very often." When she was finished she took a deep breath and waited for his answer.

He smiled. "They all pale in comparison to you pet. In exchange for this, I ask that you wear my brand, be my sorceress and use your powers to serve me, and the family. I accept, and hope that someday that children thing will be possible."

"I think it's a definite possibility." She beamed kissing him. "Someday."

He bucked under her, and winked. "It will. Now, about that riding? I think we have a mark to make."

"So we do." She kissed him slipping her tongue into his mouth as she slid herself down onto him.

***

Dimitri opened his eyes to see the angel of his dreams still sleeping on his chest. Her hair was like a honey curtain covering where her skin wasn't on his. She was a rare jewel, and now she was all his. She stirred and he touched her hair and down her shoulder and back loving the silky texture of her skin. *How did I get so lucky? Brother I do have to thank you.*

She moved and he slid down a bit wrapping his arms around her and sighing. The night before had been nothing if not magnificent. Having her back in his arms, for good, the place he knew she was meant to be the morning he put her on a train for London was a dream come true. She was so responsive to his touch he nearly wept with the joy he felt when he touched her.

"Colette, pet, you awake?"

She groaned burrowing herself deeper into their warm nest of covers, she smiled sleepily up at him, "I think so. I had the most amazing dream... then I woke up and here you are."

"Oh? Well I'm sorry to disappoint..." he said and wiggled his eyebrows.

"Oh I'm not disappointed." She chuckled moving up to kiss him. "Good morning."

"How do you feel? Sore?" he asked, hoping their evening's activities didn't hurt her too much, and the brand which ran high on her hip wasn't in any way painful.

She took a moment really thinking about the question. "Not really, maybe a little tender if anything. The brand feels good though. I can feel you through it."

Her answer pleased him. He knew the brand, an intricate snowflake that glistened blue and pearlized purple, felt cold to her. He pushed a little power out, making the symbol pulse.

She gasped, her nipples tightening instantly. "That's cheating." Her voice was low and throaty, her eyes darkened with heat.

He chuckled and shrugged. "Get used to it Pet, I plan on cheating a lot." He pulled her to him and settled in under the covers. "I think it looks spectacular on you. Thisbe is going to be quite jealous isn't she?"

"Why? Because you get me all to yourself and she doesn't get to play anymore?" she asked teasingly.

"I never said you couldn't play pet, lest of all with the fetching Thisbe. Dad chose well with that one. No, I meant because your brand is prettier then hers..."

"Ah..." She smiled. "Of course she will be, but mostly because my brand means something. Hers is mostly for show.

"True, but she seems ok with that, doesn't she? So what's on your agenda for today? Not going to fuck and run are you love?"

"No running here, today's my day off." She sighed, "And yes Thissy is ok with it... I just think she deserves better. So..." She walked her fingers up his chest. "What will we do today?"

"Anything you wish pet. I suggest we move your stuff from Pinky's to here. But that's for later I think. You might wanna think about decorating this place, giving it your special touch."

"Some shopping then. Some personal touches from you wouldn't hurt. No offense but I know for a fact this place looked like this when you bought it. Since you'll be spending more time here, hopefully a lot more, it couldn't hurt to have your touch in the place. Something to remind me of you in those long cold nights when you're gone."

"I don't plan on spending any nights away from you pet, but yes, it will be good."

She beamed at him. "Excellent."

"So a nice lie-in and then some shopping? Maybe dinner out? I don't know about you but I can't really cook for shit."

She laughed, "My cooking's edible but its pretty basic. I guess I could learn and have a hot home-cooked meal ready for you coming home after a hard day's work doing whatever it is that you do all day."

He laughed. "Let's not get that domestic... I don't think you need to learn to cook. This town has more then enough restaurants, and if not, then I can always blink us somewhere. And you really don't know what I do all day?"

"Do you know what I do all day?"

"Sleep most likely, and you work the evenings, am I correct?

She frowned at him managing to mock looking offended, "Only on some days. Tuesdays and Thursdays and Sundays I work out with Thissy. Then recently I've been running the club punching numbers and sorting out the set."

"My little career girl. You still didn't answer my question."

"I have no clue what you do all day and I may even like to keep it that way."

"It's not as bad as you think."

"Oh no?"

He grinned. "I'm a businessman. I meet clients, set up meetings, and visit with my management..."

"Ah well if you put it like that it's not bad at all." She rolled her eyes.

"Seriously I don't deal with the girls at all. That's all Drake, Sandor and up until two days ago, Snow's job."

She smiled and shook her head. "What will you do now? Without her that is. I take it she is here with Arcady... that was the swap deal... right?"

"Sorta...it's a bit more complicated then that."

She shrugged. "So what will you do?"

"About Snow? Nothing. She's where she should be, with someone who can love her, warts, or should I say homicidal tendencies, and all. I have what I want, and business goes on like normal."

"I was talking about business, that thing that you do all day."

"Oh, well I can work from here. Unless I have to meet clients, I usually work online."

"Sounds like you'll be spending more time here than me. Maybe you should be the one learning to cook."

"I set fire to water when I try to make tea," he grinned and kissed her. He looked over at the clock. "I was going to suggest breakfast, but it seems lunch is more in order."

"Let's order in," she chuckled kissing him. "For fear of burning water although I'm guessing that may be more alcohol related than bad cooking. Who shall we call? Sully's or Treacles?"

"Sully's I think... better coffee." Somebody knocked hard on the door. She looked questioningly at him and he shrugged as he stood, causing her to roll over and pull up the blankets around her to keep warm. She jumped slightly as the door was knocked louder, somebody sure was in a hurry. Dimitri finished putting on his clothes and turned to her.

"Stay here pet, I'll go see to our guest... but hold that thought." He leaned down and kissed her gently on the cheek, before turning and leaving the room.

Five

Sallos was losing patience. The bodyguard had been just as hopeless as the general. *Next time I'll start at the top instead of working my way up.* His hand still ached from hitting Drake's face and he knew it would take a painfully slow time to heal. *Stupid ice demon.* Sallos had quickly found out that Drake had neglected to mention, the prince was not currently at his home. *I went to Russia for nothing, I should go back and beat the bastard some more.*

He made his way to Shadow Heights, a loathsome town teaming with demons and vampires and all the different types of supernatural. He blinked strait to the prince's apartment door and knocked with his good hand. He was no longer in the mood for games, he would find Cassiel and he would do it tonight. He had Fuerety's authority to do anything he deemed necessary and he had run out of patience. He stood, blazing in the corridor and waited for the Prince to open the door.

Dimitri opened the door and frowned at the fire demon standing there. "What the fuck are you doing here Cento?"

Sallos suppressed a sigh; a glare and the urge to just hit him all in the space of a few moments. "Prince Dimitri, how good it is to see you again," he answered in a monotone voice that even he couldn't force himself to believe. "May I come inside for a moment, so that we may talk?"

"Why not, you came all this way the least I can do is be hospitable. What can I do for you, and do you want a drink?" He moved aside and Sallos entered the spacious apartment as Dimitri walked into the kitchen.

"Thank you." He followed Dimitri to the kitchen. "I'll drink anything strong you have."

"I have scotch?"

"That would be very good, thanks."

Dimitri fixed two double scotches, neat, and handed one to Sallos, then walked into the living room and sat on the couch motioning for Sallos to sit as well. "So? Do what to do I owe this honor?"

Sallos took a seat next to the prince. "I'm looking for your brother, or more accurately Princess Faris." He took a drink.

"And what makes you think I would know where either of them are? Last I saw Princess Faris was a year and a half ago at the Incubus ball. And I heard she married Jacob, I was meaning to send my wedding gift as soon as I was back in the Afterverse. As for my brother, I haven't seen hide nor hair of him in more time than it's been since I saw the princess." Dimitri answered as he sipped his drink and relaxed further into the couch.

Sallos suppressed the urge to roll his eyes. *Because I haven't heard that already, tonight.* "So, you really haven't had any contact with him? So, you truly heed Fuerety's law?" He asked, faking surprise.

"He is the overlord isn't he? The only one that might not heed that decree is my Father, but as we all know, my brother and my Father don't get along. So your guess is as good as mine where he is."

Sallos took another drink, choosing his words carefully. "Well I do need to find him. Feurety wants him found, and more importantly Princess Faris."

"Faris is missing? I thought you guys kept her under lock and key since the recent unpleasantness twelve years back. And hasn't she been married like for a few days? Jacob can't control her? Does she still have the apartment in Paris?"

The word unpleasantness caused Sallos to shudder, *Unpleasant? It was a fucking disaster.* The memory of the night the child was terminated would haunt Sallos till the day he died. He could still hear the princesses screams and pleas, all of which he'd been ordered to ignore. In the end he'd gone in to talk to her, try and calm her down. She'd lashed out at him, kicking, scorching, even biting. He had taken it all, let her take it all out on him, let her do anything but escape. Eventually she'd tired herself out and fallen asleep in his arms. *We all suffered, but to the Conglacio it was nothing but unpleasant.*

He hated admitting the loss of the princess to the Conglacio, "No, it seems that Addu cannot control the youngest of his court. They will be dealt with. Apparently not all the courts are as good as the Conglacio at following Fuerety's laws." He answered a little too sarcastically. "But that is another matter, it is the problem of locating your brother that I have brought to you, in hope of your help."

"Sallos, he may be my brother, but we hold no love for each other. Christ if he ever finds out I have his old ward, I'm sure he'll kill me."

Perfect, such lies are hard to get out of Dimitri. "Good, I'm glad you said that, Prince. I need your assistance with a locating spell. Being the closest he has to a blood relative." *Both mother and father.*

Dimitri laughed. "Would that I could Sallos, but if you remember his old Sorceress charmed him, he can't be found. Believe me I would help if I could." He smiled at Sallos and turned seeing Colette walk in. "Sal? Have you met Colette? Cole? Love, come meet Fuerety's Second. He's here looking Casha, can you believe that? Here?"

Colette walked in and smiled. She kissed D and perched next to him, her hand playing with the hair at the nape of Dimitri's neck. "Looking for Casha? Why would you know where he is D? Hello Sal." She smiled warmly at him.

Sallos smiled at her, deep in thought. *Natalia, of course. That's why we can't find him... but that would mean that the spell can be easily reversed. She would be able to locate him at least, she hates him, and she'd love the chance to get Faris into trouble. Petty little witch, but she'd love to rain on Cassiel parade from the grave. I'll try the brother first, milk this uncomfortable situation for all its worth. Loyalty to Feurety, not likely.*

Sallos smiled at the prince. "Oh, Nat's spell wouldn't matter for this spell Prince. The spell isn't really to find him per say. So, you see you can help me. Hello Colette."

"Colette is his old ward, aren't you pet?" Dimitri said absent-mindedly.

Cole nodded. "Yep."

Sallos smiled, he had a plan for the first time in hours. *No more chasing my tail.* "Then congrats on getting the bastard exiled in the first place." He turned to Dimitri. "Will you help me?"

"What exactly will I have to do Sallos? I don't spill my blood for anything."

Sallos smiled, deciding to toy with the prince that he no longer needed. "Not even to save your girl here from almost certain death at the hands of your brother?"

"She's bound, he could not hurt her if he tried Sallos." He pulled her down into his lap and kissed her, his hands going up and under her shirt, stopping just under her breasts. She giggled and nipped at his mouth and he looked from around her at Sallos. "So what's the dish Sal? Gimme your idea and well see how it goes."

"All I need is some hair, prince." *No blood, what will you say to that, I wonder.*

"Hair? Blood? Locating spells... honestly Sallos you're grasping at straws here. You think I'm insane? I know exactly what another demon can do with fluids or parts of another demon... so let's just leave it as, the last place I saw Casha was at my father's place in the Andes, check there, bet he's got hair lying around there..."

"You're right Dimitri, I'm clasping at straws. I want nothing more than to go home, I wanted nothing more than to go home at the end of the ball last night. But no, I'm stuck here looking for the princess. If you honestly think I want to go to the Andes looking for fallen hair in the snow then you're sadly mistaken. The hair will not leave your sight, it's a simple spell I can have it done and be out of here in ten minutes. So I'm asking you now, please do this willingly." *I could have made you do it ten times over Conglacio.*

Dimitri ignored him and slipped a hand down from under Cole's shirt and up under the skirt she was wearing, eliciting a groan from her. "Why does Feurety want my brother? He already ruined the guy's life. So let him go insane by himself, you can't take that from him as well."

"He doesn't want your brother, he wants the princess."

Dimitri moved his hands while Cole reached down and unbuckled his pants completely oblivious to Sallos. "If Casha was with Faris at all, I would have heard from him, and he would be gloating that he got his princess back, but as far as I know he hates her with more fire than her father. Last I heard Bethany had been visiting him at his place in Monaco."

Keep your lies strait Prince. "I thought that the last you heard he was at your father's in the Andes?" Sallos smirked at him.

"Same fucking difference... I do know one thing, the night Faris went and had the little problem taken care of, he was boning Bethany, at my father's place in the Andes. Sorry If I can't think straight but," he motioned to his girlfriend who was unzipping his pants. "You understand."

He was where? Sallos' face lost all color as he fought to control his temper. He fought to control the memories of Faris screaming for her Casha as she beat at him. *And he was with Bethany? I'll kill him* "Of course, but you must tell me why the change? I thought the little blonde one complemented you perfectly, or did your negligence finally allow Drake to beat her to death?" He asked nastily.

"Snow?" Dimitri chuckled carelessly. "Does it matter? Cole is much more suited to be a royal concubine, if you wanna see why you can stay... I think she's about to show you."

"No, I don't think it does matter." He stood and shook his head in disgust. *Wasn't good enough so you had her beaten to death by your pet bully.* "You Conglacio are all the same."

"Meaning?"

Meaning that you're all self obsessed, arrogant pricks that wouldn't know a good thing if it bit you. Meaning that you don't look after or even care for your own. You have no morals and no regard what so ever for... well, anything.

His face hardened. "Meaning nothing. I know you're still in contact with him, if you weren't you would have taken the throne by now, Gabbe's an ass. You're more powerful than him and you know you could do a better job than he. So something is holding you back and that something is Casha. You tell you brother and Faris this; that the longer she hides the worse it's going to get. You tell her that daddy wants her home and fuck knows what he'll send after me."

Dimitri laughed. "Sallos honestly, I don't want the throne. I don't even like being home. And I'll tell you one thing; I haven't seen my brother or the princess and if I do I'll be sure to tell her exactly what you told me. Now unless you wanna hear this pretty little pet scream my name in five different languages, I suggest you bounce." He turned back to kiss Cole. "You know exactly where the door is."

Sallos nodded, "Just pass on the message Dimitri."

He turned his back on the ice demon and walked out the door, his next move was already playing in his mind. He had to go home briefly. He needed to make sure Tammy was safe, let her know where he was and find someone to look after her while he found the princess. He also needed to pay a little visit to the halls and have himself a little chat with Casha's dead sorceress. Dimitri had been very helpful indeed.

Six

The ringing pulled him out of his sleep, he grabbed the stupid phone with its stupid noise and pressed the button that answered it.

"What type of fucking idiot calls in the middle of the fucking night." he whispered threateningly, careful not to wake Faris up. *Mal if that is you I'll gut you and stake you out in the sun.*

"Well you sound like I woke you out of a sound sleep, so I'm not feeling too guilty at calling. I had thought I might be interrupting something. She okay?"

He smiled at his brother's amused voice in spite of himself. "No, that was a few hours ago, she's fine and sleeping in my arms, or at least she was sleeping in my arms." He smiled down at her.

"Well I'm sorry to hear I have interrupted something after all. I thought you would give the princess her own room there, you never took me as one to share through the night."

He frowned. "Yeah, me neither. You know I think that this might be the first time I've ever shared a bed with a woman on purpose. It's not all that bad really," he said a little surprised at the realization.

"And the Sorceress' emotions rearing its ugly head. Hey don't knock it Cash. But sadly I didn't call to speak of your lavicious activities with the princess. We have a major problem I thought you would want to know about."

He groaned. "Oh, just don't tell me, I really don't want to know. Let me live in ignorance till morning..." He pleaded.

"Sure why not... then he could have found her by then."

Cash sighed lying further back into the pillow. "Who?"

"Sallos. Seems Feurety knows the princess is topside. And he thinks she's with you."

"What makes him think that?" He looked down at her sleeping form. "Shit!" He swore loudly. "I thought we would have had more time before he sent that bastard after her."

"Hold up, Sallos isn't as bad as you are thinking, hell he knocked Drake out for dealing with Snow the way he was," Dimitri defended. "He's pissed as shit. I played the affected Heir and denied your existence, but he cares deeply for Faris. He told me to remind her when I spoke to her that the longer she hides the worse it's going to get, that after him, lord knows what Old fire pants would send to find her. He's the least of your troubles. I think he just wants to see her happy, and I think he's going to try to buy her some time. Also, I think he went to shake down Nat."

Casha sighed. *Poor Nat, doesn't have much of a chance against him.* "Which means he probably already knows where we are. Don't think for one second that just because he's got morals that he's one of the good guys D. He wouldn't think twice about dragging her kicking and screaming back to Feurety. Don't forget that he believes she's far better off without me."

"Well yeah duh Cash, but he's not in possession of all the facts. He's always hated you. I mean, tell you the truth seeing how you were at court with her I would have hated you too if I didn't know for a fact she thrived on how you guys were." He swallowed hard. "But I think he's got a new reason to hate you, I think I kinda slipped."

Cash's face fell and he closed his eyes silently praying. "Oh god, what have you said?"

"Bethany. I mentioned Bethany."

He sat up strait. "You would have, wouldn't you? Fuck!" He shook his head. "Sometimes I doubt your parentage... Well, your mother anyway. What did you say about her?"

"Look Cash, I had Cole on my lap and I couldn't think. No excuse I know but still... it's better than me blurting out other stuff." *Don't count on it.*

"Why was Cole on your... no I don't want to know." He eased himself out of the bed and walked to the other room shutting the door securely. "Now what did you say?"

"That the last time I saw you, you were at dad's in the Andes boning Bethany."

Fuck, fuck, fuck! "Do you have any idea how much Faris would kill me... you know I hardly even remember that. If he tells her, it would kill her, then it would kill me. Then I'll find some way to make it kill you, you hear me?" He said angrily.

"Look Bro, I told you then it was coming back to bite you in the ass... Christ Cash that's the only one Faris forbade you from... She was willing to share you with the entire court if need be... I might have fucked up by telling Sallos, but you fucked the wrong woman there. And Sallos cares for Faris more than Feurety does, he won't tell her, cuz he knows what it will do to her."

"I was out of my mind at the time, I wouldn't have known up from down let alone right from wrong. I can't undo it, no matter how much I want to, and I do want to. Now the witch's emotions have set in again, so thanks for that little trip down memory lane. Why don't you really kick me while I'm down and mention mum's anniversary?" He felt instantly guilty as the words left his mouth.

He heard Dimitri take a shot of something. "No need, you and I both remember it well enough." He sighed. "Faris will be able to handle it one day, or she'll kill the bitch. What she did to ensure she was still your only princess when you left was wonderful, but maybe those are stories she should tell you."

Casha shook his head, knowing he couldn't see it. "Yeah, sure... because I'm sure I appreciated the gestures so much while I lay in a pool of my own... No you're right, don't listen to me. It'll take me a long while to get back to myself again, but I'll get there." He searched the room for a bottle of some kind and eventually finding a bottle of sherry. He drank some from the bottle, wincing at the taste. "Eventually. How's Cole settling in at the apartment?"

"She's a dream. She loves it, and she's redecorating and everything. She also told me to send her congratulations about the princess."

"Good, I'm glad she's set about feminizing the place." He swallowed another gulp of the vile alcohol, bracing himself for the next question. "So... have you heard from Levi recently?"

"I saw him. Seems he's going to be paying you a visit at the mansion."

Casha raised his eyebrow. "Yeah?" He asked surprised. "Why?"

"Why would I ruin that surprise?" *Dick.*

"Because you're my brother and you love me, plus you've already caused me a massively big surprise in the future, when Sallos beats the hell out of me for the whole Bethany thing." *Which he's bound to do, instead of hurting Faris.*

"A surprise I think you wholly deserve. I told you then I didn't approve, but you just had to drown your sorrows in a warm body."

"Maybe I do, and that's a surprise I'll willingly take. But when it comes to Levi, forewarned is forearmed. I need to know, please?" He asked, his tone pleading.

"Shine up your crown Cash, I'm going to go. I think I have said too much already. Night."

"What?! Don't you dare hang up." *Surely not.*

Dimitri chuckled and sighed. "What? Come on Cash. You're not stupid. I think I hear Cole waking up, something I fully intend to take advantage of even before she opens those gorgeous eyes. So say what you gotta say so I can go fuck my girlfriend."

"When's he planning to come over?" He asked stunned.

"Soon I think. Tomorrow? Day after. He wants to see Faris and the Heir."

"Huh, well that certainly is food for thought. Go and enjoy yourself with Cole, I better get back to Faris."

"Cash, a parting thought, treat her like the princess she is, not the princess you created, then maybe she won't be so pissed when she finds out. Enjoy your love brother." He hung up and went back to bed with Faris. He had a lot to think about.

Seven

Fallon brought up his coffee and sat it next to the bed, then he threw himself on the bed and propped himself up with some pillows. He could hear Astrid in the shower and knew it wouldn't be long before she came back out again. He'd picked up a magazine from the kitchen table and opened it for some light reading while he thought about what had been going on.

Something was wrong, and it wasn't this stupid Forbes thing he had picked up. Astrid had been so jumpy of late and it was always around the demon. The bargain had gone wrong, at some point, something just wasn't right. Astrid came out of the shower all wrapped up in a blue fluffy towel. He kept his eyes firmly on the magazine, pretending to read, while he watched Astrid drop her towel and wander around the room naked. She turned her back and stopped dead, hitting her head silently against the doorframe.

He sat the vile magazine away from him and watched her intently. "Are you going to tell me what's wrong, or are you just going to continue to brain yourself against things when you think I'm not looking?"

She turned and sighed. "I'm having an issue, and it's going to hurt you if I tell you what it is."

He sat up in the bed. "Let me guess, you can't stop touching Cassiel?" He sighed and took a drink of coffee. "No offense Ast, but I didn't exactly see you running up and hugging Morrison yesterday when he came back from Russia. Yet, Cash goes to the coffee shop..." He trailed off.

She shook her head. "You think I'm enjoying this? Do you?"

"No, I hope to god you're not, vixen. Just...just answer me this, it's still temporary, right?" He asked her quietly pleading with her.

"God I hope so. This is not something I wanted...and I don't think he meant for it to happen either. Christ Faris is here! And pregnant!"

"I know, but 'God I hope so' isn't the definitive answer that I'm looking for love. Am I going to have to share you with him for the rest of my life?" *Because I will, if I have to. I'll just be very upset about it.*

She shook her head. "I don't want that, and I don't think he wants that either. Fallon, it was a lot of power that he poured into me. A lot, Christ the last two weeks my skin has been crawling with the amount of power. I... I think it wants to go back to him."

"And me?" He swallowed hard, trying not to sound pathetic. "Do, you still want me?" He failed.

She smiled. "Fallon, I always want you, nothing ever changes that. You're mine cookie." She giggled. "You are way too sexy cookie you know that?" She moved to the bed and crawled up his body, laying kisses on his tummy and chest.

He shook his head and held her to him, laying a kiss on her forehead. "Well, in that case. I think we should find that demon of yours and find out exactly how long it will take to fix and then set about fixing it. Don't you think?"

"Umm I do. You are so warm Cookie." She said as she kissed his collarbone. "Let me get dressed and we'll go from there, ok?" She kissed him sweetly on the lips and climbed off the large bed and walked back into the closet, grabbing a pair of jeans and a pink t-shirt. "Ready. You getting dressed? Or does Feyd have to bitch about seeing your 'naked ass' again?" she asked giggling.

He laughed and sighed, "I'll have you know that Feyd loves my 'naked ass'. But no, clothes are good." He slid on a pair of jeans and a pale blue shirt, which he buttoned half way.

"God damn Cookie, you are so hot." She giggled as she walked closer to him and kissed him soundly.

***

He still hadn't told Faris about Sallos. She should know. He knew that she should, but he just couldn't bring himself to do it. Sallos would never hurt Faris; he wasn't that type of demon. But he would hurt Cash, a lot. A much deserved pain in Cash's eyes, he'd done wrong, horribly wrong. So wrong that there was no denying it and Casha never admitted to being in the wrong, ever. He could talk his way out of any problem, till people thought white was black. But there was just no good spin to be had from this, sure there were excuses. But that didn't stop the guilt, he should have known better.

60

Then there was Levi to consider. If what Dimitri said was true, and he always believed his brother, then he would soon be king, Crown and all. Which meant that he would have to start thinking about killing Feurety a little sooner than he had originally planned. He was going to have to talk to Snow, and then talk to Arcady about her soul. But even with the Incubus support and the Succubi, he was going to need more. He needed the Effusio and the Caligo, which meant that he would need to speak to Donavan and Amaro, both of who were in exile and none of whom were talking with him.

He rubbed his temples to the headache that he knew would soon be coming. *Why did I only plan on getting back home and not what I would do when I got there? I'll have to talk with Oscar.* He fed the dog on his lap some cold toast.

"Cash, why is it you're down here with the dog when you have a princess lurking around the house?" Astrid said from the doorway as she came in with Fallon.

Great, just what I need. "You just answered you own question there. I think she's in some sort of mood. I'm staying out of her way. Besides I like the dog, he doesn't talk back." *Or expect you to juggle too many balls.*

"Trouble in paradise?" Fallon smirked irritatingly.

Casha glared at him then smirked at Ast, "You tell me..." He looked smugly back to a glaring Fallon.

"Both of you stop ok? My morning started good, I'd like for it to continue that way. What's wrong with the princess Cash?" She shook her head, trying to stop the attraction that he knew she felt. "Look, we need to deal with the little problem Cash, it's getting worse."

"Yeah, I know. Sorry, I'm in a strange mood today. Antsy, I think is the term. I'm expecting a few visits." He sighed, as the headache arrived.

"Well, then we should address this situation quickly don't you think Cash?" He watched her squeeze Fallon's hand then move forward, Linus bounding towards her, leaping up and licking her face.

"Yeah, quickly. Fallon, I need to..." *Fuck your wife to be, senseless.*

Fallon sighed "How many times?"

Casha fought to keep his face straight. "Two maybe three, five at the most. I reckon if we spread it out over three days, everything should be back to normal. Then she'll be all yours again and we can all move along."

Astrid frowned at him. "I'm not a piece of meat to be bartered over demon!" She said appalled as she looked at Fallon.

Fallon blanched and stood behind Astrid apologetically while Cash nodded. *Wimp.* "Oh, I agree completely. However, I'm already having a fucker of a day, and I still have to talk to Snow, Spinner, my father, and to top it all off, Sallos. Fuerety's captain of guard and right hand demon, who's hunting for Faris, to take her home to kill my unborn child. So, you'll forgive me for being a little less sensitive to your feelings Astrid. I've got bigger things to worry about. So, do all parties agree?"

"Go to hell Cash!" She got up from where she was squatting and seethed. "The quicker I can get this gnawing need out of my system the better you oafish pratt!" She turned and kissed Fallon in the cheek. "Cookie I'm going to go upstairs and scream a bit, then I'm going to help Feyd with breakfast ok?"

Fallon kissed her back, "Sure thing Vixen. Sorry for my part in making you mad." He smirked at Cash who sighed deeply.

Fal you really need to grow a pair, but you're right, no need to upset her. "I'm sorry too, Astrid. I didn't mean to make you feel, well, cheap. I just want to speed things along a little. Now I realize that this wasn't one of those conversations that could get sped along. So, I'm sorry for hurting you and for being an oafish pratt," he said. *Damn women and their fucking feelings.*

She didn't turn around. "Uh huh. Whatever demon. Cookie, do me a favor after you have finished talking with the brat prince, make sure Linus goes out?"

"Will do, Vixen."

Casha saw red. *Look who's talking you selfish little bitch, it was exactly that kind of attitude that made you a fucking orphan in the first place. I never should have bothered with you, or yours. Fuck you, I'm outta here, you think you give me protection? Just see how long you last with Fallwell over your head.* He gritted his teeth, stopping the words from leaving his mouth. He liked Astrid; he didn't want to shout at her in anger. His day really didn't need a crying Sorceress.

He took a deep breath, and then answered a little more calmly. "Hey, I could have meant that! It's not my fault that I don't understand your damn emotions. Fine, you go in a huff, that's real big and clever, Astrid." Casha shouted to her retreating form, before sighing and shaking his head. "Yeah, real big and clever. Go in a huff; don't help protect your family... I was sorry, you know," he muttered under his breath.

She ran back in the room and looked at Fallon. "Cookie, could you excuse us a minute? I think I need to educate Cash in something called tact ok?" The glint in her eye was nothing if not predatory.

"Yeah, ok." Fallon kissed her on the cheek. "I need to let the dog out anyway." He left the room.

She shut the door to the sunroom and glared at him. "Look, it's not my fault everything is coming to a head for you," she said as she sauntered closer to his sitting form. She stood in front of him, hands on her hips, legs parted. "Sometimes I really hate you Cash."

Well, sometimes you're not my favorite person either. "Astrid, I'm a demon. I've spent hundreds of years being hurtful and causing pain to people, just for fun. I'm not being hurtful to you, I don't want to see you cry, and I could have you in tears if I wished. I've never been particularly sorry for anything in my life." *Except for the whole Bethany thing.* "However I was less than gentle with your feelings and I apologized for it, I was genuinely sorry. Do you have any idea how many people have called me the brat prince to my face?" He took a deep breath. He hated that name. "They don't. I find it hurtful. I also find its hurts when my sorceress tells me that she hate me. So, I'm holding back, because I like you, and you're not holding much back at all. Tell me, why is that fair?"

She sighed. "Cash, I am sorry ok. I'm just not used to being treated like a whore, that's Spin's thing, not mine. And I hate hurting Fallon. And the way you just dealt with this situation hurt him too, and I know you don't care about that either. Let's just drop it ok? You have things to do and people to see, so I'll talk to you later."

"Actually, I think it would have hurt him more, if we had treated the whole situation like some sort of romantic liaison. I think he much prefers to think that it's an awful chore that we have to do, rather than what it really is. So, what's really your problem?"

She smiled and leaned down and kissed him on the lips, sliding onto his lap. "What do you think my problem is Cash?" She asked with a slight purr to her voice.

He smiled slightly, sliding his hands along her bare arms. *Ah tension.* "Well, I hope it's something that I can help you with?" He kissed her lightly.

She shivered. "Only you can demon," She shifted on his lap and then sighed. "I think maybe I should take a cold shower."

He raised his eyebrow, "Didn't we get the all clear?" *I could give you all the cold you want right here.*

"We did, but you have a full day, and an upset princess moping around." She sighed.

"She's not upset at me, just in general. I'll tell you what. Go for your shower, I'll see to Faris and Fallon, and I'll meet you there." He grinned up at her.

She kissed him hard, and then nibbled his bottom lip. "Second one of the day. See you in the shower, okay?"

He nodded, "Deal." She got up off his lap and sauntered from the room leaving Casha once again with his thoughts.

Eight

The shower was hot and steamy, all seven showerheads turned on. Astrid reveled in the moist heat, relaxing. She had the music on loud, her version of telling everyone she didn't want to be disturbed, her eyes closed. She never saw nor heard the shower door open. The next thing she knew she was up against the corner of the shower stall, being lifted up by her waist. She opened her eyes, expecting to see Fallon but none too surprised to see Cash. She wrapped her legs around his rock hard stomach as he nibbled on her neck.

"Cash? Something I can help you with?" She smirked and looked down to him.

He growled into her neck as he positioned her just above his waiting, throbbing cock. "Yeah Ast, there is. Scream for me." He quickly slid her body down impaling her on him. She moaned deep in her throat as he fought her tightness and it was seconds till he was sheathed inside her to the hilt.

He fucked her hard and fast keeping time with her sobs and pants. She clawed at his back as he worked her, whispering lewd and suggestive ideas into her ear the whole time. *Yes* she thought *He knows what gets me hot.*

She came minutes later in screams and sobs, Casha still working her heated body. He blew a cold breath onto her nipples and she tensed again. She knew he wasn't finished with her. He backed up and sat on the shower ledge, her still riding his cock. He was giving her the chance to play dominant and she wasn't going to pass it up. She began riding him slowly.

"Come on Ast, come on, I know you want me Astrid, harder." He dug his fingers into her thighs and moved her how he wanted, the illusion of her being in control shattering. "Harder Luv." She leaned back as she rode him, exposing her tight nipples to his gaze. He bent his head and took one into his mouth and bit it, hard. She screamed and came instantly. "That's it Astrid, That's it. Let go" she curled herself around him as he stood once more and pressed her against the other wall.

He wasn't gentle, he just needed, and he talked a lot of shit to her while he railed her. She was close and he knew it and urged her on, daring her to come with him. "Take it Astrid, fuck, take it!" They came together moments later, Cash growling his release in her ear as she sobbed.

Both of them sated, Cash put her down. He patted her ass and kissed her sweetly on the cheek. "Finish your shower Pumpkin. You were great."

He walked out of the shower stall and she heard him open the door, it was then she realized the music had finished.

"You're welcome Cash." She screamed at him as he closed the door. *Damn, that demon is going to be the death of me...*

***

He walked up behind Snow smiling, whether he was smiling because of last night's events or because he was glad to see her he wasn't sure he wanted to think about it. *Then again it could have been my time with Astrid.* He stood silently behind her, smiling.

"Hey there Snowflake." He said suddenly hoping to surprise her.

Never one to disappoint, she yelped and jumped back a little. "Snowflake? That's a new one."

"It is?"

She shrugged, "This morning it is anyway. How many kitchens does this place have, I'm sure I was in a different one yesterday. I've been lost like three times already this morning. The cat showed me to the kitchen."

We have a cat? He raised an eyebrow. "Cat?"

"Yeah, you know, black and white," She shook her head. "Doesn't matter. So, I'm going to need my own expense account. Ooh and card... I need new clothes, I'm sure I didn't bring enough." She giggled.

His eyes widened, and he laughed, "Hey, you'll be getting no such thing. I've got a baby to save up for. I can't go giving the likes of you my credit card."

She rolled her eyes. "The likes of me? Cash, you're like a bazillionaire."

"So's your boyfriend." He watched her intently for a reaction.

She blushed a little and ducked her head down, scuffing her bare foot on the floor. "He's not my boyfriend, I barely know him."

"Like that's ever stopped you." He muttered under his breath, silently pleased that the mention of Arcady could make her blush.

She sighed and poured a coffee from the pot. "You should stop being so tight with your damn money. So, care to tell me why I'm here?"

"Your cousin wanted to see you." He answered simply.

"Bullshit. Why would you do anything Fal wanted you to do? You only ever do what you want, for your own nefarious plans and schemes. So, I must be here for some other reason, not for Fal." She frowned, pausing for a few seconds before continuing on her tangent. "Something that, I wouldn't mind..."

"Enough!" He cut her off lightly, worried at where her logic was taking her. "Are you even allowed to drink coffee?"

"What D did or didn't allow me to do doesn't matter anymore, as I'm clearly yours now." Her voice broke and she looked up into his eyes, tears filling hers. "What did you give him? Was I worth it? Did he want rid of me, is that why I'm here?"

He placed his hands on her bare shoulders, giving her as much comfort as he could offer. "Snowy, no. I gave D..." He trailed off with a deep sigh. "You know, I don't think I've ever seen you so weepy."

She shrugged, wiping her eyes. "It's been a rough couple of days, sorry." She took a shaky breath.

"How rough?" He asked, knowing she would never tell him.

She shrugged, "I don't really want to talk about it. Let's just say I've had better weeks."

"Yeah, I hear that. I don't think today's going to get much better."

She nodded. "Yeah, I heard Astrid shouting about being bartered over like meat. You weren't very nice to her. She's not used to being owned yet."

Like you? "I hope she never gets used to it Snowy, I don't own her. I just had other things on my mind at the time, I didn't consider her feelings."

Snow smiled at him. "I wouldn't fuss about it. Besides there's no real reason to worry, I liked your father."

He laughed loudly. "Yeah, well, you were under him at the time, so your opinion doesn't count," he said in a tone that clearly told her to drop it.

She shrugged. "So look, what's the deal here? What is my purpose? Faris is here, so it's not that kind of gig. To be honest, I'm pretty confused in my whole part in this."

He shrugged. "You won't just believe that I want you here because it's safer for you than at Dimitri's?"

She rolled her eyes and took another drink of coffee. "Nope, I'm not that kind of gullible."

Well, maybe I can shock you into believing Snowy. "Fine, in that case I have someone in town that I want you to keep service." He watched her lower lip tremble, and then looked out the window. "The sun's up so he'll still be out for the count, but he'll wake up soon and I'll send you right over. He should be hungry."

"You, I... A vampire?" She hugged herself and looked to the doorway.

"Sure, you want to be my whore, so you can go be dinner," he said cruelly. "You met Mal right?"

"Well if it's Mal... I suppose, I could," she nodded weekly, looking crushed.

He sighed. "No. Snow, the word you are looking for, is no. Say it, it's not hard. I'm not Dimitri, I don't deal with whores, I don't own any to date and I don't intend to start. Understood?" he said as plainly as he could.

"No." *Great now she uses the bloody word.*

"Well, you will. It's dead easy. All you have to do, if someone offers you money for sex, say no and hit them with something large or sharp. Now I don't really have time to sit down and discuss life choices with you, but you could do anything you want."

"I'm doing what I'm here for already aren't I?" She asked.

For someone who spends way to much time in your head you're amazingly astute. "Through choice love, and choice alone. I'd never force you to do anything."

She frowned. "Yes you would."

"True, but not in the way you mean it. What you're doing with Morrison is your own choice, never an order."

She smiled up at him. "Ok, I kind of get it now."

Why do I doubt that? "Great. Now, I've got a few more things to do today, but I think tomorrow we'll sit down and I'll go through things a little more clearly with you. Just to 'Snow proof' a few things that I don't want you talking about, ok?"

"Yeah, ok. Is Mal really in town?"

Casha laughed loudly. "Yes, I'm afraid he is." She giggled. "And what's worse is that, he's been very quiet. Not like him at all."

She shook her head amazed. "No, it's really not. Why was it you keep him around again?"

Casha shrugged. *Because I'm the reason he's dead, and he does a damn fine job of running the heavy end of my businesses.* "I like him. He' amuses me."

She laughed again. "So, tomorrow. You gonna stop lying to me then?"

"Never Snowflake. There would be no fun in a world of truths."

She giggled brightly and bit her bottom lip. "Sure there would. We would just have to lie more truthfully.

"Well, there you are then. Now stop drinking coffee, and go and try not to cause too much trouble." He winked at her and left the room to find Faris.

Nine

When he returned, Sallos found his home in the Afterverse empty. In a panic, he looked around the house before finding a note for him that was taped the mirror in the front hall. He sighed with relief and ripped it off. *She always finds the most awkward places to hide the damn things.* The handwriting didn't belong to his eight-year-old niece, but to an old friend of his. He smiled picturing the little girl, dictating to the giant Cento, as he read.

Fending for myself again Sal.

God, your guardianship is a bunch of crap you know. All this sitting up and worrying if you're even going to come home, I sometimes have to wonder which one is the parent figure in this relationship. The worrying thing is I know for a fact that you're not out getting your rocks off with some demon that you met at the ball.

And don't act so shocked that I just said that because you know that I spend more time with the rest of the guards than with you. So it's your own fault for putting such a young impressionable lady with such people.

Anyway, Kris figured out that I was all alone and is taking me to Mexico. You can pick me up there, once you finish doing whatever it is he has you doing now. This loyalty thing is getting old, y'know, I thought you said you were going to try and spend more time with me? I deserve it. You're the only real family that I have and I never get to see you.

So hurry up and come and get me. Kris promised to teach me a new swear word for every hour that you're gone and he's being quite colorful about it too. Please be safe, I miss you Uncle, maybe next year we could live topside for a while... Just be ok, and I hope to see you soon.

Love you loads, Tammy.

P.S: Sallos I wrote the damn note for her, you can't leave an eight year old by herself even if she is a half-breed. Look, I love the kid like my own, but some of us resent her being here, it breaks the rules. It's great that the king granted her "special" permission, but it's not safe for her here, especially if you keep leaving her.

Your reputation will only keep her safe for so long. I'm taking her topside to your place in Mexico, meet us there. Don't go blowing up in my face but maybe she should go and live with the human's parents, her grandparents. I know it's not what your sister would have wanted, but it would be safer for her.

No matter how great she is, she just isn't one of us. Just think on it, before you decide on no. You need to have her best interests at heart, not just your own selfish need to be with her.

Kris.

Kris, you're an angel. Granted a 6 foot 8, ugly as hell angel, but an angel none the less. I'm never giving her up, though. The discussion between them was an old one, one they'd had for eight years. Thing was, he knew that she'd be better off with the humans, but he made a promise and would stick to it. He sighed and took the note, which he slipped into his pocket. Then he grabbed a bag and threw a few things into it, before setting off to the halls to see Casha's old sorceress.

In life, Natalia had been a princess. Her father had been the self-claimed king of the fey or some shit like that, and her mother had been some sort of witch. None of that really mattered, what did matter was that she was a pain in the ass. Death had certainly not mellowed the former sorceress and Sallos knew that what he was going tell her would only serve to rile her up more.

He walked down the halls, easily finding her room, which was the only one without screams of agony coming from it. Feurety had, for some reason or another, allowed her to stay in the peace that Cassiel had originally created for her. Nobody really knew why, but Sallos had his suspicions. Natalia had once been a force to recon with, it was much safer and in the long run, much less trouble to keep her happy than to give her a reason to cause trouble.

He opened her door and walked into her world and home for eternity. The place was a vast forest, teaming with life from deer to birds. It always amazed him how the rooms within the halls could be changed so easily.

Of course not by the inhabitants themselves, but Sallos knew, he could easily change the room/forest into anything that he desired. *Let's hope it doesn't come to that.* Natalia sat on a fallen tree staring into a fire. She was beautiful by anyone's standards. Sallos found himself wondering, not for the first time, on how Cassiel had managed to bind such an obviously powerful young woman.

"Never really had you pegged as a back to nature sort," he said as he approached her, hoping to startle her.

"What?!" She asked sharply, turning her attention to him.

He suppressed a shudder and shook his head, "Never mind. How are you today?"

She shrugged. "Still dead. I would ask you the same but I couldn't even pretend to care. What do you want Sallos?"

"I'm looking for Faris."

Natalia laughed bitterly. "And you think she's here with me?" She looked around her. "You're more than welcome to look around, Captain." She licked her lips and stood walking towards him, swaying her hips, seductively. "You can look at anything you want here, Captain. Absolutely anything."

He slowly backed away from her, her movements more predatory than sexy. "Still whoring yourself out to the nearest man, wasn't that how you ended up with Cassiel in the first place?" He grinned and stopped moving.

She stopped with him, reaching out to touch his chest. "Not the nearest man, just it gets lonely down here, and you are a very attractive demon. Powerful too, we could have such fun." She said absentmindedly as she stroked him.

He batted her hand away. "True, but I'm looking for Cassiel, Faris is with him."

She spat next to him and swore loudly; in what Sallos could be sure was every language she knew. "Bitch!"

He smirked at her reaction and raised an eyebrow. "Well, I'm sure we both agree that she should be found and taken away from him, so... if you would be so kind as to tell me where he is, then I'll set about doing just that."

This time it was her turn to back away. She shook her head. "You'll hurt him"

Sallos smiled innocently. "Now, would I do a thing like that?"

"Yes, you hate him." She hugged herself.

He shrugged. "As should you, look at you. You're a ghost, a shadow of your former self, sitting alone in a world that doesn't exist, next to a fire that doesn't exist. While he's out there, very much alive fucking the woman that had you killed. Not very fair is it?"

She shook her head sadly. "I know. But I won't tell you where he is. I can't."

He sighed and sat cross-legged on the soft green grass next to the smoldering fire. "Oh, I think you can. Well, at least you've admitted to knowing where he is. How about I promise not to hurt him, how about I just take Faris and leave?"

She shook her head. "You might have gotten a better response from Dimitri with that one. Its about betrayal, I just can't."

He sighed, hating himself. For all her hatred and bitterness, Talia, didn't deserve this. "Talia, you have no power here. You can't refuse me anything, I'm afraid. Just tell me, save yourself the pain. You'll have told me in an hour anyway, I promise"

She shook her head, defiantly holding it up high. "No."

He sighed and clasped his hands in front of him and cradled his head. "It's funny, how easily this place can change." As he spoke the lush green scenery disappeared into a rough barren land, full of fire and molten rock. It severely resembled the fire plains, red rock stuck up from the wasted ground. Natalia backed away quickly, but there was nowhere to go. She backed into a piece of the rock, and jumped away, hissing and she was burned. Sallos looked sadly up into her eyes and sighed. "All you need is a little imagination and there you are. Last chance; where is he?"

"I can't tell you..." She answered panicky, helplessly looking around her.

He stood, his face a blank mask. "I understand, I really do. But, that's just not good enough." He held her shoulders firmly in his large hands and looked down into her eyes. "I remember Talia, I remember, what truly terrified you." She looked behind his shoulder, her eyes widening with fear. She shook her head uselessly and tried to break free of him. "No, please. Sallos, you can't. Oh please, god no..." She trailed off mewling. He shook her forcefully, snapping her attention back to his eyes. "You tell me at any time, they'll go away. It'll all go away, even me. I just want to know where he is, he's not worth it."

She glared up at him, hatefully. "I'll never tell you."

He nodded to her. "Oh yes, you will."

She turned and ran into the vast, flame filled expanse. The pony-sized beasts, all teeth and claws, followed her, hunting down their prey. Sallos watched her duck and weave, and fall and burn. Each time she fell, she jumped back up again trying to avoid her pursuers. Her fear was of being chased, and Sallos presumed of being eaten alive.

Although let's hope it doesn't get that bad. The beasts themselves were a figment of her imagination, although real enough to touch in the halls, where your worst nightmare could and would come alive and eat you. Sallos sighed and sat down, not wanting to watch any longer, as she grew tired. *She'll break before the creatures do.* He glanced down at his watch, wondering just how long it would be until she finally told him the ice demon's location.

Ten

He'd put it off for long enough, he had to tell Faris about Sallos. She was the only one in his eyes that had the power to call him off. *I could always kidnap his niece, threaten to kill her unless he...* He sighed. *That's never going to work. Damn!* He was just going to have to tell Faris and have them come to a responsible decision together. He climbed the stairs and opened his room door.

"How are you feeling love?" He asked her.

She sat on the center of the bed in the lotus position, and assessed him. "Better, well, better now that I'm here. You look better. Getting things straightened out with the witch?" She asked with no hint of malice or jealousy in her voice, cocking her head.

"Yeah, I did. I feel better for it too. I've been going around, talking to people, sorting things out. I'm not half way through my list, but I'm getting there."

"Umm? And I rank so high that you have to see me in the middle of your list? What's wrong prince?"

He smiled and sat on the bed next to her. He gently brushed a stray piece of hair from her face then rubbed her cheek with his thumb. "With me you always rank high, Princess. But in all honesty you're on that list. I talked to Dimitri last night after you had fallen asleep."

"After I had passed out you mean. Well, talk to me prince, what's up?" She giggled and slid into his lap, nuzzling his neck. "Tell me love, I won't freak."

"Oh, you might." He placed his arms around her and held her tightly to him. "It seems that Sallos has been looking for us, that he is, in all probability on his way here now."

She chuckled. "Old Sally? Daddy sent old Sally after me? Well, he must really be desperate." She slipped off his lap and lay out, stretching on the large bed. "Don't worry on Sally. If he shows up I'll deal with him prince, he's more my father that Fuerety is."

He nodded and grinned as he watched her stretch out. *If ever there was a female version of me, she lays before me. Absolutely perfect.* "Ok, I trust you know what you're doing. I'm sure if there's anyone who can handle him it's you, although Dimitri swears he's a good guy."

"He is a good guy Cash, he's the only one who gave a shit about what I did after mum was exiled." She shook her head. "True he's daddy's watch dog, but it's only because honor dictates that he serves his lord and master, Sallos has chivalry inscribed into his DNA. He might serve my father, but he loves me."

Casha laughed. "Chivalry in a demon? What is the world coming to? He should shack up with Am..." His smile dropped and he sighed deeply. "Anyway, I just thought you should know that he's on his way."

She sat up and nuzzled his nose, and kissed him sweetly on the lips. "And if and when he does, I will take care of him. I just got you back prince, I'm not giving you up, never."

He smirked down at her. "Better not. Because you are stuck with me, for a very long time."

She giggled and grabbed him around the waist and pushed him to a prone position settling herself on him. "Damn straight prince. Don't worry, we are a team baby. So? Everything else ok?"

He laughed and sighed "Well, Snow seems to think we have a cat, Malcolm is being unusually quiet, Astrid thinks I'm treating her like a piece of meat, my father's coming to visit and I still have to find a way to contact Don and Amaro. Plus I need to find a use for Spinner before she comes over and someone kills her." He laughed. "Apart from that, everything's peachy."

She giggled. "Well you just answered your own question about how to get a hold of the princes. Send Spinner to find them. That way she's not around and doing something constructive." She kissed his neck and smiled at him. "As for Astrid thinking you're treating her like a piece of meat, well... and Mal, well you know Mal, when things get tight he gets loud. So think it a blessing he's not hemming and hawing at you nightly." She kissed his jaw and ran her hand under his polo shirt, tracing the tight lines of his stomach. "And I would mention the cat to Astrid, no doubt that dog you love so much would have a fit if he saw it."

He laughed. "I'm not touching the cat issue with a barge pole. Same with Mal, when he needs me, I'll hear about it. Good idea with Spinner though, Don's too nice to shoot the messenger. Am has issues and you can only get to his place through Shadows or Effusio, that could work, with Don's help." he kissed her.

"See? I'm helping already prince. So? Asty wear you out? I was thinking about taking a shower in that heavenly shower. I do love your sorceress' taste. Five shower heads? It's almost heaven, so you going to join me?"

He grinned down at her. "Oh, I think I've got time for a round or two." His eyes darkened with lust and he picked her up, throwing her carefully over his shoulder. "You coming?" he asked teasingly.

"No choice prince." She laughed.

"Well, then, let's go." He laughed with her as he carried her off to the bathroom.

Eleven

He was lounged across the leather couch in the study, his earlier conversations with Snow and Faris running through his head. It was quiet in the study, which he supposed was the whole point of the thing. Faris' idea of sending Spinner to see Donovan and Amaro was an excellent idea, but he planned on going one better, well, two better. He would send her to Donovan, then he would send the two of them after the other exiles, with the option of going home.

He needed to see Amaro. The door to the study suddenly opened and Astrid escorted his father in. She sent him a significant glance then left the room, closing the door firmly behind her.

"Got a minute?" His father and king asked him.

Casha looked over his father for a few moments, paying special attention to the briefcase in his hand, before sitting up and pointing to the chair that sat in front of the desk. "Sure, why not. Have a seat."

Levi nodded and placed the briefcase on top of the desk and sat on the chair Casha had pointed out.

"I know you hate me, and you've got the right. I fell into my own pit trap of misery over everything that led to your mother's death. I should have been more available for you boys while you were growing--but I was concerned with being a good king then. The list of things I should have done is a long one so I'm not going to try and atone for each one individually. All I can say is I'm sorry, Cassiel. Please forgive me."

Cash's jaw dropped and he took a few moments to recover. Eventually he cleared his throat. "I don't think I can. I'm glad you finally admitted it, though I've been trying to tell you for years. Although thirteen years ago, you could have said that... hell I would have jumped at five, have you ever been in exile?"

"Does the fact that I haven't been back to the Afterverse since then count?"

You'll never get it... "No, it really doesn't. You let me get exiled, and then you leave the place to Gabbe. If anything you should have paid more attention to our people instead of less. I shudder to think what that bastard would have done to my home and people if it weren't for Oscar."

"I know. I have him to thank as well."

Damn right you do, he's been doing your job for thirteen years.

Levi stood and moved to the briefcase, Casha couldn't see what he was doing; however he knew he was opening the case.

What now? Money? A bomb? Surely the crown didn't fit in there. Before he turned, Levi spoke.

"I can't give you back those exiled years, but I can put an end to them." Finally he turned and Casha could see what he held in his hands, his Cipere.

All coherent thoughts left Casha as he trailed his eyes from his father to the book and back. Eventually he remembered how to breathe and took a deep rasping breath. "You're kidding." He said his voice a little too high. He cleared his throat and spoke again. "Truly? I can go home?"

His father nodded. "You think you can give an old man a chance to make things up and be a part of this family again?"

Never that simple Levi. He sat back on the couch, slouching himself deeper into the leather and tried not to roll his eyes. "Is that the catch?"

Levi moved back to the chair and sat down, "No."

Cash nodded. "If you're a better grandfather than you were father, I have no real problem with your... presence. Let's just hope that you don't ever have to ask the baby for a chance. So, what is the catch?"

Levi sighed deeply. "There is no catch. Aside from my sincerity and support, this is all I have to give to you. My kingdom, my power, and three-quarters of the souls it took me nearly four thousand years to collect. I had hoped that might be enough to prove how sorry I am."

He nodded unable to keep a small smile from his face. *I'm going home, I'm really going home.* "I suppose it'll have to do." He joked slightly. "But I just have one question."

He nodded, "Go ahead."

"Why now? Don't get me wrong, I know why. But why make me live through thirteen years of hell, when you could have ended it like that," He snapped his fingers. "And don't say it was character building because I didn't learn a damn thing..." *Unless you count that people like to kick you when you're down, and if you start killing them, your friends don't stick around for long.* "Well nothing useful."

"I wasn't thinking about you, or Dimitri, or even Gabbe for that matter." He paused and Casha instantly knew that he was going to mention his mother. "I had never stopped grieving your mother and then one day, I just sort of...woke up." He looked up and over at Casha. "I realized how much of the lives of those I claimed to love I had let fall to ruin. That made me realize that if your mother were still alive, she'd have kicked my ass ten times already. So, here I am, trying as best I can to build a better future for my family and my people."

He smiled and nodded, finding that he couldn't hate the man anymore. He was giving up his kingship and after that he'd just be a sad old man grieving for his dead wife, Casha's mother. "You know, you never have to pay Gabbe any attention. Y'know the verse would be a better place without him." He said, changing the conversation away from his mother.

Levi finally smiled as well. "Well you can do with him what you see fit when we're through here. So what do you think, are you ready to be king?"

He took a deep breath his smile widening to a grin. "Yeah, I think I am." *Have been for over a century.*

Levi nodded. "Excellent. Is there anyone you want to witness this?"

"I'm not sure... should anyone witness this?"

"That's entirely up to you. I had the entire Conglacio court witness the exchange between your grandfather and I."

"Well, there's kind of a getting home issue on that one, but Faris should see this. She'd kill me if I did this without her here. Dimitri too, if just so he believes me."

His father chuckled, "Alright. Why don't we get them in here? Perhaps your sorceress as well? We'll have to arrange a ball when all the dust has settled."

"Yeah, Ast should be here too. How about I get Faris and Asty and you call my little brother?" He stood and walked to the door, smiling and shaking his head. "Balls can wait, let's just get me home first."

He walked to the bottom of the stairs knowing that Faris and Astrid would not be very far away.

"Ladies, your attendance is required in the study. So get both of your asses down here right now as I know you've been trying to listen in anyway." He shouted up at them, partially because he couldn't be bothered walking up to get them and partially because he knew it would make his father cringe.

They both came down the stairs looking bewildered and he ushered them into the room, where his very confused brother was standing already.

"Hey D, how's Cole?" He asked as their father stood back from the group, watching them interact.

"She's... Fine... Ok this is the first time I have been in the same room with the two of you and ice shards aren't being thrown. So what the hell?" He nodded at Astrid and Faris, then looked at Levi and Cash. "So?"

Cash grinned at him, practically bouncing with excitement. *I'm going to be king, little brother.* He nodded to his father, letting the man take the lead for once. They waited till everyone was in the room before shutting the door.

"Patience, my boys, patience. There is a lady present that must be attended to." He stepped up to Faris and held his hand out to her. "It's a pleasure to see you again, Faris. Come, get off of your feet." He motioned to the chair in front of Cash's desk with his free hand and smiled at her.

She returned his smile and bowed. "It is always a pleasure Highness." She gave Cash a kiss on the cheek and took Levi's extended hand and let him sit her on the chair. "Well Highness, now that the formalities are over, why have you asked for us to be here?"

He heard his father chuckle then the old man turned to face all of them. "Well now, I kind of like having everyone on the edge of their seats like this. It's kind of a rush, isn't it Cash?" The king looked over at him, and they shared a smile. "Maybe we should keep it a secret after all and leave them in suspense for a while. What do you think?"

"Well, we could... it seems we both like to keep people waiting." He looked over at Faris who glared at him. "However, death by impatient fire demon is not how I plan on leaving this plain of existence. Would you like to tell them, or shall I?" He grinned at his father, enjoying the moment immensely.

"You go ahead, son."

Casha turned to them, letting his father son comment slide. "Well, it seems I'll be going home a little sooner than planned." He turned to Faris and winked, still grinning like the Cheshire cat. "As king."

He watched as Faris' eyes grew wide. "Truly? Well congratulations my darling." She stood from her chair and walked to him and kissing him soundly, then she turned to Levi. "Thank you Highness."

Levi smiled at Faris as he removed his suit jacket and laid it over the desk. Cassiel watched a little nervously as he then unbuttoned the left sleeve of his shirt, rolling it up until Casha's eyes fell hungrily upon the snowflake brand that marked him as king.

Mine all mine.

He brushed his hand against Faris', continuing to watch as his father opened his briefcase and took his Cipere into his hands. He stood a moment looking at the book, then stepped up to Cash so that everyone could see them. He nodded to his son. "Ready?"

Faris moved away from him and smiled at Cash, truly beaming. *I was born ready.* He grinned again, then nodded as he composed himself as he tried very hard to remember why he hated the man in front of him. "Yes, I think I am."

Levi closed his eyes and turned his face to the ceiling for a moment, making Casha wonder just what he was doing. When he re-opened them Cash could see that he had assumed part of his demon form, now gazing at him was two deep blue faceted ice-crystals that replaced his father's eyes, the mark of a true demon. Casha suppressed a shudder, he hated that gaze, always had. Not that they weren't eyes, he supposed that Levi could see perfectly well out of them, if not exceedingly better.

Every demon had a demon form, whether it was a tail made of fire or horns made of ice they all had them and not one was the same. Either way, when it was shown it meant that said demon was calling on an extraordinary amount of power. Cash wasn't given very long to ponder the point or purpose to each face as his father began to speak.

"Be it known that from this day forward, the lands of the Conglacio shall be ruled by its natural successor, Cassiel, son of Leviathan, descendent of all that the Conglacio stand for, and embodiment of its spirit. I commend to thee my Cipere and all of the souls within it...let them carry our great King back to his homelands where he belongs."

Oh god, I really hope that I don't have to repeat that.

Levi reached out and took Cash's hand and pushed his sleeve back, then held his hand firmly so that both their wrists were clearly visible. "Put your right hand on top of the Cipere, Cassiel."

Cash took a deep breath, praying that this wasn't some ploy to kill him off. He could have done it in a hell of a less cruel way. He nodded and placed his hand on the soul filled Cipere, doing just as his father asked him to, for what might have been the first time in his long life. As soon as his flesh touched the cold book, the brand on Levi's wrist began to glow a bright, ice blue, as though the light were coming from inside Levi himself. The same glow erupted around Cash's hand on the book, and in seconds both father and son were enveloped with a near-blinding white-blue light as the souls transferred from one owner to the next. Casha had to fight to keep his knees from buckling with the sheer force of the power. His whole body throbbed, the power filling him and healing him, making him whole.

It seemed like only seconds had passed, although according to the wall clock it had been nearly four minutes. The lights surrounding them began to fade, and the snowflake had been fully transferred onto Casha's wrist. He stared at it for a few seconds in disbelief.

Casha was silent for many moments, his head slightly bowed. "Well, that was different." He smiled and looked around the room at everyone, his eyesight better than it had been in years. Eventually he looked back down at his wrist, resisting the urge to poke his finger at the brand that made him king.

Levi offered the forgotten Cipere out to him. "Congratulations, Highness."

Faris smiled. "It's different from your prince's brand, but only slightly." She said as she looked over his shoulder and kissed his cheek. "Congratulations my Lord."

Astrid smiled and walked over and hugged him from the front, so that he was sandwiched between the both of them. "Congrats Darling. This is a very good thing. I'm going to tell Fal and Arcady and the rest of them. Spend some time with your family." She touched Faris' hand and smiled at her, then came around Cash and smiled. "And welcome Lady Faris. I hope you are comfortable." She walked to Levi and bowed. "I do thank you." She turned to Dimitri, hugged him and left the family to themselves.

Dimitri, still recovering from the hug looked at his brother and Father. "Well, now we have a lot to do don't we?"

"Yeah, I need to see Oscar, I have to go home," Casha said still in a daze at how different he felt.

Leviathan chuckled and thrust the Cipere into Cash's hands. "Don't lose that." He winked.

Cash started, taking the book. "Thanks, it's just... I don't know, weird. I have souls again, I can feel them all." He smiled and reached out with his newly acquired power to feel them all. "I had forgotten how it felt."

Dimitri carried on. "I'll take care of Oscar, have him keep Gabbe in the dark, I know you'll want to do that little insurrection later am I right?" He smiled. "Well, welcome back Highness."

Levi nodded, "There's some good ones in there. I put stars beside the ones that are fun for visits."

Casha smiled, still far away. "Yeah, I bet. I'm sure I'll have my favorites picked out soon enough."

The old king smiled then patted Cash on the shoulder before he stepped away to give him some air. He returned to the desk next to his jacket and stood there staring wistfully at his bare wrist for a few moments. Casha felt a stab of something, as he saw the slightly lost look on the once proud and powerful king's face. Eventually Levi lowered his sleeve and did it up again, then put on his jacket and leaned against the desk quietly.

Faris spoke up, also noticing Levi's well covered discomfort. "Levi? I have to ask, Sookie will be here with Rudolph to check on the baby," Faris said as she rubbed her tummy. "Will you be present at the birth?"

Levi blinked a couple of times, gaping like a fish, before he answered, "Well...I'd like to be. If there were no objections." He looked over at his son.

Cash turned to his father and shook his head, "None from my direction." He paused. "If I haven't said it already, which I know I haven't, thanks. I do appreciate it, I know what you just gave up." He smiled weakly. "So, any words of wisdom? Aftercare advice?" *Aftercare advice? Surely I could have done better than that, it's true that too much daytime TV must really rot the brain.* He grinned, waiting for his father's response.

Levi smiled back. "Don't just listen to your subjects and underlings, pay attention to them. They speak much louder without words. Rule them, but don't cow them and most of all." He looked between Cash and Faris, "Don't neglect your family. Trust me. I know."

Casha moved closer to Faris, snaking his arm around her waist. "I think I can do that."

Faris giggled and walked over to Levi and smiled, hugging him and kissing him on the cheek. "You stay close, I find out tonight what we are having, but I do know it's Cento." She kissed him on his other cheek as well. "Don't be a stranger."

Levi smiled as he received Faris' affection and whispered something into her ear that Casha couldn't quite make out. When he leaned back, his eyes had returned to their human form and he took a deep breath. He let it out looking happier than Casha had ever seen him, well, since his mother had died. He turned to Casha. "I'm going to assume you're headed home for a visit very shortly. I'd like to meet with Oscar. If you would please get him to contact me I'd be mightily obliged."

Casha grinned at the prospect of seeing his general and good friend again. "Yeah, I'll be going home real soon, survey my kingdom and all that. I'll let Oscar know you wish to see him."

Levi stood, "Thank you, Cash. It'll be good getting to know you again." He turned and closed his briefcase then took it up in one hand and looked back to all three of them. "It feels good to know things are moving toward the better for this fucked up family, doesn't it?" He grinned.

Dimitri grinned back at him, clearly overjoyed at the turn of events and Casha couldn't blame him. "It does. Pop, Faris, Highness, I am going to leave, let you celebrate, Cole and I will be over soon to see you. Faris, good luck with Rudolph." He blinked out, leaving the three of them alone.

Casha laughed, "How long do you think it'll take before he stops calling me that?"

Faris smiled. "A very long time, as long as he knows you don't like it."

Casha winced, "I could get used to it. Did you?" He asked his father.

"To the "highness" thing?" He nodded, "Try to think of it like, "sir" if you're more comfortable with that. And Dimitri will likely stop once the novelty wears off. He gets to be the King's brother, you see.

"But I think I will follow Dimitri's lead and make my exit. Call on me for anything, anytime. I mean that. But if I don't go strait to Thisbe to tell her all of this, she'll shoot me in the street." He continued to grin, "So I best go do it."

Cash nodded to his father, highly doubting that Thisbe would do anything of the sort. "Yeah, ok. I'll see you soon then?"

Faris giggled. "Have her call me. I need to do baby shopping."

Levi nodded, "Anytime you need me." With that and another pat on Cash's shoulder as he passed him, Levi made his exit. "Will do!" He called back to Faris on the way out.

Casha smiled, as he watched the man who didn't raise him leave, feeling for once not hatred, but something else that he couldn't quite put his finger on. He turned to Faris and smiled at her taking her hand in his and giving it a small squeeze and smiled at her. Things were looking up, he would be going home very soon and he was finally King.

Twelve

Faris stepped from the shower stall in a cloud of mist to see Cash leaning against the doorframe watching her. He looked so much better now that he was freshly infused with souls. After the transference, he was in better spirits, and even dealt with Feyd without getting frustrated, which was a feat in itself.

Then when they went to bed, he was like his former self, making love to her into the night, soft, gentle and commanding, like it was when they had first started seeing each other. It was as if he didn't feel he needed to compensate for anything that his full confidence was back. Her demon was back to full power now, and it wouldn't be long till he went home, and took his rightful place on the throne in the Conglacio palace for all his race to see.

They would be happy; most of them hated Gabbe with a passion. Most of the races did. She was glad he had never tried to court her, though. Gabbe wasn't close to anything she would deem worthy, and would have married Drake and dealt with his sick issues before she even considered Gabbe.

But that didn't matter, Cassiel was back and he wasn't going to fuck about this time, she could see it in his eyes since his father left, the grim determination and cold calculation that only Cassiel could have.

She grinned at her lover, taking the towel to blot the moisture out of her hair. She stretched as she did so, loving the deliciously sore feeling she had from then night before. Her bump, the little life inside her, was growing and she was pleased. A demon gestation was about half of the time a human was, and the children grew quicker due to the dimensional time difference of the Afterverse and earth. Once the child was born, he would grow quickly, and in the space of a year would appear as if eight years had gone by. In essence that's exactly what would happen, as one earth rotation was equivalent to eight years in the Afterverse.

Their child would grow up here though, because as much as she would love to give birth in the Afterverse, and as much as Cash was back to his former self, he wasn't a hundred percent. They still needed the exiled princes, and some more support. True, now he had the support of the pleasure courts, and the Arcuo court was always in his corner, he still needed Donovan and Amaro to come home with him so that he would have the support of the Effusio and the Caligo. Once he had that, the Strigo would fall in as well as the Acers.

The only wild card was the Celo's and with Cash's constant rebuffing of their crown princess and the fact that Faris was once again pregnant with his child, she didn't think it was going to be easy to get them to their side. Unless of course, King Aldinach decided that he would overlook everything and side with the winning party. The Conglacio's all were ready for a change of guard in the rule of the Afterverse, and the Cento's... well they would be fine once she was queen and they had the heir.

"I'm rather upset you didn't join me. Astrid ok?" they had the theory that because Cash was more powerful now with the new souls, that it would be much less of a problem weaning them off each other. Fallon had been happy with that assessment, and Faris was fine with it, as long as it didn't last too much longer. Sharing him wasn't the problem; she just didn't want another issue like with his old sorceress.

Natalia was a horrible slut and she was extremely ambitious. Usually Faris could respect that, but Nat had designs on Casha. It was a good thing that Fey and Demon's couldn't mate because she kept at him enough that if they could have, Cash might have an heir already walking around that wasn't in any way legitimate. Cash had taken Natalia because of her mixed heritage of fey and witch, because she was powerful and ruthless enough but he didn't see the extent of what she would go through to get everything she wanted.

Faris saw it though, and dispatched Natalia, slicing her throat at court one night when she had said something very off color about her and Cash's sex life. Faris knew they were involved bit she drew the line of having it rubbed I her face. That was why Astrid was a godsend. She had her own love, but the ambition to be what Cash needed, an ally.

"Things are leveling out." He smiled flashing his teeth. "What are you thinking about that causes you to frown so?"

She chuckled. "Just remembering that cunt Natalia, and thanking the fates Asty isn't like her."

"Ah..." a frown flashed briefly over his face, "It's never good to speak ill of the dead, love and I'm pretty sure Asty should be thanking the fates that she's not Talia."

"That too." she winked and padded over to the sink, grabbing another towel from the sidewall to wrap around her still wet body. "You didn't snap at Fallon did you? This can't be easy for him."

"I seem to have a new found patience for the world, Fallon included."

"That's my prince..." she smiled. She walked across the large expanse toward him and wrapped herself around him. He smelled like Astrid a little, fresh and sweet, and where when he would smell of Nat she would be pissed, with Asty she really just didn't care. Astrid loved Cash, and that was something they bonded on. "So? What's on the list for today? Anything special?"

He lifted her kissing her soundly. "There's a few people that I have to see, mostly taking advantage of lay line use. I might even steal D away from Cole and sneak onto the ice plains for a little peak." He grinned cheerfully.

She giggled, his happiness infectious. "That sounds like a good idea, I can't remember seeing you this giddy and not attributing it to insanity," she teased. "I missed my prince."

"And I missed you love."

"So I need to do some shopping I think. I didn't bring anything with me really, and Astrid said she would take me, Feyd even offered to play bodyguard though I have no idea why."

"Why he offered or why you'd need an Aspectus to guard you?" He asked carrying her back through to the room and setting her on the bed.

"Both?" She let the towel drop and rolled her shoulders.

"I could ask him if you want," he offered sitting next to her kissing her bare shoulder.

"Though it's probably for two reasons, one he'll be able to keep an eye out for danger without sticking out too much. Feyd tends to blend in, unlike the others. And two because he's a pervert and going shopping with both of you would land him in his element. Also going with you prevents him from being nominated for the really hard tasks."

"Really hard tasks? Shit I thought that was delegated to Snow and Arcady when Astrid sent them to the market," she laughed. "The list she gave Arcady, I haven't ever seen the guy pale but..."

"She really goes to town with her lists. Things'll be fine. Snow likes butchers anyway, it'll an experience for him."

"That I have no doubt. So what else is there going on?" she laid back and closed her eyes.

"Not much, I assume it's Fallon's turn to lead George around town."

"Probably," she sighed and stoked her small bump.

He smiled down at her hand. "How are you both feeling?"

"Good I think. It's very agreeable." He took his hand and placed it on her tummy, letting the newfound warmth soak into his skin. "When it's content I get warmer like now... I think it's happy you're happy."

"That's my baby." He grinned gently caressing her belly. "Knows that its daddy is finally king and that its grandfather isn't a complete waste of space... well one of them anyway. Any word from Sallos?"

"Not yet..." At her words a knock came at the suite door and Astrid peeked her head in. "Sorry if I'm interrupting, but I thought you should know, a Cento just passed the wards on the west side of the mansion."

Cash whistled shaking his head, "I can say what I like about the old fucker but he does have impeccable timing."

Astrid giggled. "I take it it's Sallos?"

"We're not expecting any other, so let's hope so."

"Speak of the devil and he appears," Faris said and sighed looking at Asty. "Do you have something else I can wear?"

Astrid grinned and left the doorway, coming back minutes later with a cream colored wrap dress. "This should fit you Princess. I figured you would need something so this would be it, at least until we shop a bit."

Faris smiled and went to Astrid and hugged her, taking the dress. "It's perfect, well it's not red but it will do." She bent her head and kissed Astrid on the lips, tasting what she figured was both Fallon's and Cash's kiss as she did. It was kind of erotic, knowing that this woman allowed her to kiss her so shamelessly especially when she had recently been with Faris' Prince.

Cash groaned watching them both. "Now girls, as much as I'd love to keep you both on this track, Sallos is going to be knocking on the door soon and I have to be gone by then." He cleared his throat. "Not that I'm running away."

Astrid giggled and blushed. "You're most welcome Princess. I'll be in the kitchen after I let the Cento in. I'll direct him to the main sitting room. When you're done we can go." She winked at Cash and walked out.

Faris turned with the dress in her hand and grinned at Cash. "She's fantastic, totally thinks of everything. Don't forget you have to get a hold of her cousin my love."

"I have a lot of people to get a hold of but Spinner is at the top of my list." He kissed her cheek.

"Then do what you must love, I'll be here when you get back. Anything special you want me to pick up?"

He smirked, "I'll leave it to your own impeccable taste princess."

"Be safe love, okay? And enjoy yourself. Don't worry, I can handle old Sally."

"I know you can, if anyone can it's you Princess." He kissed her again. "Take care of yourself and the little one."

"Always." she giggled and pulled the dress off the hanger, shrugging into it. "Think of me."

"Always Princess." He beamed gleefully before stepping back into a ley-line and blinking out of the room.

She smiled. Seeing him use the lines again brought back memories of him popping in and out, the times when they were really happy. It would happen again, and they were well on their way, but things were going to have to change, and people were going to have to die for her to get her happily ever after. She didn't care in the slightest though; now and forever she wasn't the naive child she used to be. She tied the dress and squared her shoulders, ready to prove to herself and the demon hunting her that she deserved everything her way.

Thirteen

Spinner's phone rang shrilly on the side table and she rolled over the couch scrambling to get it.

"Spinner."

"Yes, you certainly are. How are you love?"

Casha she thought as she smirked. *Why the hell is the prince calling me?* She relaxed into the couch.

"I'm as well as can be expected, wasting away in this damn hotel room. If this was why I was brought here then I could have very well stayed at the flat in Paris."

"True, you could have. But then you would have missed all the fun. I have a little job for you, something to keep you amused if, you're up for it?

"Anything is better that eating bon-bons and watching daytime TV. American television sucks royally. So what's the job?"

"There are a few demons that I need you to find and bring back to me. Exiled demons. I have a list somewhere."

She listened as he rummaged around on the other end, curious as to why he would ask her. "So why ask me to do this? Or are you just getting rid of me like everyone else?"

"Spinner love, that is a hard question for me to answer, but I shall try. You said it yourself, you're wasting away. I personally would much rather kill someone than watch them get bitter with age." He sighed. "When I look at you I see potential, I want to see you reach that. I think you just need a chance, something to smile about now and again."

"You ain't the only one demon," she muttered. "Not like I have a lot options Prince. So what's the job?"

"We'll maybe you'll find some of those options when you're out playing. Like I said the job's finding exiled demons. Tell them that... fuck it, tell them there's a war against Fuerety and they're all invited. And tell them that I'm going to be king, I like saying that. If all of that sparks their interest, tell them where to find me."

"That sounds all peachy Cash, it does, but what do I get out of it aside from getting out of this god forsaken burgh?"

"Hmmm... What would you like?"

She thought about it and laughed. "Well an expense account would be nice, maybe some new clothes, carte blanche on what I think needs to be done to bring them in?"

He sighed loudly, "What is it with you women and your expense accounts? I have a baby to save up for..."

"Not like you aren't richer than Midas demon, so spare me. You don't have to worry about digs topside cuz you live with Asty, and you have your place in Europe too, don't forget I have spent some time there." *In that luscious and large bed bent over backwards.* She thought to herself with a smile.

He laughed, "Fine, all expenses paid. As for carte blanche, define your meaning of carte blanche."

That was the question wasn't it? "You know exactly what I mean Cash, let's be honest here, I'm only good at one thing, and that might be of use to you."

"No, I don't want you fucking them. If you go as my emissary then you will not just jump into bed with them, I know I wouldn't. If they're not interested then leave. I'm offering them a chance to go home. If they don't want that then they're beyond saving." He sighed. "I just told you that you deserved a chance, now I'll treat you like a person if you act like one. I don't deal in whores; I'm not my brother. Understood?"

"I do understand Cash, and thank you. You were the last person I would expect to not treat me like I'm used to being treated."

"I think you're worthwhile Spinner. I always have. You just have a lot of mess in your head that you need to get sorted out. I'll help you if you let me, because to me you're worth saving." He laughed. "If you weren't, then you'd be dead already."

She thought about his words and smiled. "I guess you're right. So who am I going after first?"

"Well, I can't really find my list. But you definitely have to get Donovan, he was top of the list."

"Donovan? Who the hell is that? Where was he last and how important is he?" She asked grabbing a piece of paper and pen from the side table.

"Donovan," he laughed. "Don is a lawyer in, Chicago. I think he goes by David Harrison, you can't miss him. He's like a huge criminal defense guy. He is the crown prince of the Effusio, or was until he stuck up to his mother, who is also known as Ammit, the bitch queen, to you cousin."

Hmm, very interesting. "So? Chicago? I could do that. The windy city it is. When do you want me to leave? And what would you like me to tell them?"

"Well, leave whenever you're ready, but this is important. You can tell Don that I request his presence..." He broke off laughing. "No, don't say that. Tell old Don, that I'm going to kill his whore of a mother and, if he doesn't want his useless waste of a sister to get his throne then he better just come and see me for a little chat."

"Right. Well I'm sure just calling him to tell him that won't work. I'll send him a letter with the royal seal on it. Cool? And tell him to meet me at the hotel? I'd just storm into his office or maybe you should make an appointment. I'd avoid letters and phones."

"Appointment, doable. Ok Prince, I'll leave in the morning. And thanks Cash, really. Thanks for trusting me."

"No problem Spinner, I'm happy to be able to and you'll love Don. Really, you will. Try and have fun, and bring back presents."

"Presents? I can do that. I'll call you when I have conformation okay?"

"Excellent, I'll hear from you then."

"Thanks again Cash, really, and give my love to your princess okay?"

"I will, Spin."

The call disconnected and Spinner smiled to herself. There was a reason after all why she had been summoned to the States, one that she felt rather privileged to be a part of. Truth of the matter was that he could have sent Astrid on this job but he didn't. Astrid was his sorceress, and in effect spoke for him, but there must be a reason why he was keeping her so close, and she didn't want to think about it. Her cousin has all the luck, becoming engaged to Fallon and being Casha's sorceress. This mission was a chance to prove that she was just as good as Astrid though, and prove that she had her own talents.

She sighed and grabbed the desk phone, ringing down to the front desk.

"Front desk, Harvey speaking."

"Harvey? Hi this is Ms. Buchamps in the Victorian suite. I need you to make arrangements for me to fly out of Newark tomorrow to Chicago, and have a car ready for me to take me to the airport."

"Very good Ms. Buchamps. I am sorry you're cutting your stay with us short."

"As am I, but some urgent business came up. Please make the flight the earliest you can make it."

"Of course. And is there anything else I can do for you today?"

She thought about it. If her memory served her correctly, Harvey was a young and sexy thing, built like Fallon with a set of lips on him that could make a saint cry. Several possibilities blossomed in her head but she shook them back. Cash was right; she shouldn't play the whore anymore. It was just an act anyway, one that she fell into because it was comfortable to be numb and without the thoughts of what the men in her life thought of her. No, she would refrain from taking young Harvey up on his cleverly veiled offer, and be the better for it.

"No, thank you, Harvey. You're a gem." She hung up and sighed. So, come this time tomorrow, she would be either conversing with the mysterious Donovan, or trying to figure out how to do so. Either way, she would be out of here, and off on an adventure that could prove life altering. Standing, she went to the bedroom and started to pack.

Fourteen

So, she knew where Cassiel was, like anyone ever doubted I'd get there. They could have just told me. It would have saved so much time. He sighed and jogged up the stairs ringing the bell, and praying that it would be Faris that answered.

A pretty woman, seemingly in her twenties with bright blue eyes answered the door with a bright smile. "Yes?"

He smiled warmly at her. "Hi, I was wondering if you could point me to the general location of Faris, or perhaps Cassiel?"

She nodded. "You must be Sallos; Princess Faris has been waiting on you. Please come in. I'm Astrid, Cash's Sorceress." She led him through the side hall and into the house proper. "She's in the living room, you're not afraid of dogs are you?"

"No, I rather like them myself. I take it you have one?"

"Yes, a large smelly bulldog named Linus. He's here somewhere. Just be warned, he's a licker." She paused in the doorway and smiled. "Please don't upset her Captain Sallos, she's in a very delicate way."

He raised an eyebrow, and turned to her "Delicate? Is she ok? He hasn't... hurt her, has he?"

"Cash? Hurt Faris? Are you insane? She's pregnant Sallos. Cash is trying to keep his child safe, he'd never hurt Faris."

Sallos stood in shock and horror. Eventually he rubbed his temples and pointed to the door. "And she's in there?"

"Yes, would you like tea? Or something stronger?" She giggled and shook her head. "There's brandy in the crystal decanter on the sideboard near the TV, enjoy your convo with the princess. You know, she has great affection for you Captain," with that she left.

He walked into the room, and picked up the decanter. He took the stopper off and sat it on the table then walked around and threw himself onto the couch next to her. "You know, I've been looking for you for days."

"And you found me Sal, so what's up?"

He sighed, "I'm here to take you home to your father and husband." He said weakly, taking a long drink from the bottle.

"I am home Sallos, with my rightful husband and prince."

"No you're not Faris, you shouldn't be here at all. Do you have any idea what I've had to do to get here?" he asked quietly subdued

She chuckled. "I do. I'm not that easily found Sal. Look, the bottom line is that I am with Cash again, and the child in my womb is not Jacob's. The oaf never touched me. So history is *not* repeating itself. I will have this child and my prince and nothing old fire pants does or says is going to change that."

He set his head back and closed his eyes, taking another drink. "Its not just you Faris, I can't hide from him. I have dependants, responsibilities..." He opened his eyes his tone rising. "Damn it Faris, How could you get pregnant again! I'm almost certain, that you know how it happens! You couldn't just leave it alone, could you?" he shouted.

She looked at him and laughed. "Calm the fuck down Sallos! I'm not an errant child anymore! You might be my friend but I am still the crown princess of your liege lord so give me the respect I deserve!" The temperature rose in the room just a tad and she relaxed a bit. "And I do know how people get pregnant. And for your information Sallos, I want this baby. It will be the Heir to the Cento throne, it is cento." She touched her stomach lovingly. "I have always wanted my prince Sal, all daddy did was delay the inevitable, and make a very, very powerful enemy. Please don't make me yours. As for "leaving it alone" as you so eloquently put it, let me ask you, have you seen Baster recently?"

He winced, but his eyes burned with anger. "Don't you dare pull rank on me! You're getting exactly the amount of respect you deserve. How dare you run away, like the 'errant child' you so vehemently declare yourself not to be." He sighed. "I don't care what the child is, it could be half human for all I care. I would never condemn it to death." He hung his head, running his fingers through his hair. "Only you could put me in such a position, split my loyalties."

She smiled sadly. "And he will. He will kill it all over again. I will not let that happen again Sal, I won't. And I didn't run. It's called self-preservation. I needed to keep this one safe, I'm not as stupid as I used to be Sal, I know what kinda monster my father is. This baby is the only way I'm going to atone for the shit that happened thirteen years ago."

"You could have come to me. We could have arranged something for you. A decent excuse, a good reason... not this running away. Now he knows you're gone Faris and he won't stop looking. You should have trusted me."

She sighed. "I didn't have a choice or time Sal, and I am sorry. As soon as Cash found out the only thing he could think about was making sure me and the child were safe. I went to him, because." she let a tear fall, "Cuz he's my prince, has always been... regardless..."

"Where is the prince?" He spat out the title.

"I asked him to let me see you alone, I know how you don't like him, and he's seeing about some business and tying up loose ends."

He nodded "Wise decision. The last thing we need is me kicking the shit out of him."

She chuckled and shook her head. "No we wouldn't want that. Look Sal, I have to know I can trust you, to tell you something, and for you to keep it to yourself."

"Other than the pregnancy?" He nodded. "Yeah, I think I'm already in deep enough to keep your secrets."

"Casha is now king."

"Oh!" He took a beep breath then drank the brandy again

"Levi did it last night. Cash is now the rightful ruler of the Conglacio, as it should be."

"So... he's no longer in exile?"

"No he's not, he's got his souls, and then some, and a very powerful sorceress, I believe she let you in."

"Truly?" He looked back to the door. "He sure knows how to pick them. I spent the day with Natalia."

"Nat? Lord knows I hate her; at least Asty isn't trying to steal Cash or get pregnant. Nat should rot. I hope you left her very pissed off. And you're right, he does know how to pick them, Astrid is very suitable for him."

"Oh, Nat was... very loyal to him. I left her in somewhat of a state, yes."

"She always wanted him for herself... bitch was too power hungry. Thank you Sallos, you know just how to lift my sprits." She smiled. "What will you do now?"

"I don't know. I'll have to hide Tammy, maybe myself. But if I go completely he'll just send something else..." He trailed off. "I'm just not sure."

"Send Tam to the place in Mexico, Daddy doesn't know about it. You'll be fine, he trusts you Sal, if you say you couldn't find me he'll believe you.... And you won't have to worry about him long once the baby is born, I'm taking the throne."

"Tam's already there, with Kris. Fari he trusts me because I'm loyal to him, he's a good king, and he has my full support."

She smirked. "No he's really not a good king. A good king wouldn't be worried about his power base or killing innocent children. A good king wouldn't have married his daughter off to a retard that she hated just to get rid of her. No Sallos, he's good to the Centos when it pleases him... he has no respect for any other race of demon, that's not a good king, that's a pretentious bastard."

"I never said he was a good father. He's just lost sight of what..." He sighed. "Ok, you're right. But when we do it, it has to be done right. I can't and won't sacrifice my life for your cause."

"Never Sal, never... I'd never expect that, he would though. No don't worry... It will be fine I swear it..."

"If he catches me being all double agent, I'm a dead demon."

"Sallos, it won't happen, he won't know. What are you going to tell him about me?"

"The truth... that I couldn't find you. That you were last seen ranting about your forced marriage, swearing revenge on him. That wherever you are you are most definitely not with Cassiel, as he hasn't been seen for five years by anyone and that I'm pretty sure he's dead. As most exiles have a tendency to die. He'll like that you're swearing revenge in a fury, think you're a real chip off the block."

She smiled. "Thank you Sallos. Myself and the prince thank you, along with this little bundle," she stroked her little bump.

"So, is it a boy or a girl? Tell me something happy Princess."

She smiled and beamed. "I don't know, but I do know it is Cento. I'm going to have a very healthy and powerful baby Sallos... That in itself is cause for celebration."

He smiled. "A Cento? Well that is good news, indeed."

"It is. So, you met Astrid, did you meet the boys or Ash? They are all around here somewhere, and the smelly Linus, he loves Cash."

"No, I only met Astrid. Who else is here?"

"Fallon, Astrid's fiancé, Feyd and Ash, their best friends and Arcady and Snow. Feyd's Mum will be here soon, and Levi visits."

He laughs, relaxing into the couch. "Snow? Dimitri's Snow? The blonde one?"

"Yep, That's the one. She's with Arcady."

"The lying bastards. I think I owe Oscar a few bad ones, actually I owe them all a few."

Faris looked at him confused. "Sal, what are you talking about?"

"Nothing, Oscar said that Dimitri had let Drake kill her." He smiled "I had to hit him a few times."

"You think that would honestly happen? They take care of their own. Granted Drake is a bit of a sick fuck, they would never let it get too far. And I'm glad you knocked Drake around, but then again the lunatic prolly enjoyed it. Where did you find him?" she asked as she smiled. "They all play like they are Neanderthals, but it's the face they show the other races... they are all very romantic and very dedicated to the women in their lives... Dimitri didn't wanna give Snow up, but he got Cole, and Snow is much happier."

"Yeah, Colette looked really happy," he said unmoved by her speech.

"Cole has always wanted Dimitri. So where did you find Drake?"

"London, he was entertaining."

Faris laughed her head off, then smiled at him. "And Tam? How's she?"

"Good, and pissed off. I think once this is over I'll take a little vacation, spend some time with her before she grows up."

"Thankfully you have more time cuz she's only half demon. Send her my best when you see her?"

"Yeah, I will. She always liked you."

"As well she should, I am very likeable."

He chuckled and stood. "Of course you are love. I better go make sure she's ok. Send Cassiel my regards."

"I will Sal, and please come see me soon? I'll send for you once he's born ok?"

He smiled fondly at her. "Yes, please do. But do it safely." He kissed her on the cheek. "It'll be good to know my future king."

"I shall have Oscar get a hold of you then Sal, it will be safe. Take care of you, and if you need anything.... And Sal?"

"Yes, princess?"

"Go see Baster huh? You look like you need it."

He smiled and looked down at himself. "We'll see, it got complicated with Baster."

"Why?"

He stretched and yawned. "Because... it just did."

"Bullshit. I know how you feel about her Sal, and she does too... Go see her, Ok?"

He sighed. "Yeah, I might."

Fifteen

Cash grinned as he blinked into the small apartment in Philadelphia. Oh how he'd missed using the lines. It felt so good to be free again, free from everything, from the limitations of mortal travel. Never again would he have to take a plane to travel, or beg another demon to carry him through. His brother's days as a taxi were long done. Not that he'd ever bothered much to use Dimitri.

Soon he'd be able to go and see Dimitri, take his little brother home. He couldn't resist its call for much longer but there were a few things he had to do first, the most important of which was the beautiful demon who owned this tiny apartment. Blythe, while she didn't know it quite yet, was instrumental in his return to the Afterverse. Without her he wouldn't be able to hold the throne for very long.

He needed her. He'd always known that, which was why when she came to his home one fateful night nine years ago in desperate need of his help he'd been more than happy to help.

Blythe, or Chastity as she was known back then, was one of the few bargained demons that Cash had known as a human. In fact it had been Faris who'd introduced them both. It had been during one Faris's frequent dalliances to the human realm, demanding that she go to a human high school, that she met Chastity and became good, if not best, friends with the girl. Like a pet, Faris took her everywhere to all the balls and parties. Feurety indulged her, as he often did, allowing Faris her human friend and Cash himself didn't really care as the human wasn't a complete idiot and could hold a decent conversation now and again.

Chastity was nothing like her namesake however, courting and flirting with every demon that looked her way. Having many of them and enjoying the casual attitude that the courts had towards sex. Cash had even set her up with Dimitri a few times. Unfortunately D had always backed out at the last moment, instead opting to look after Cole or help her with her studying. Even back then Cash had always known where the two of them were headed. If he had been anyone else Cash would have been seriously worried for the twelve-year-old Cole's virtue. Dimitri, however, just wasn't made like a normal demon.

It was one New Year that Chastity sealed her fate as the key to Cash's reentry. After yet another standing up from Dimitri, Cash introduced her to Amaro. Amaro was Cash's best friend. The two of them had grown up together as demon children of the same age often tended to do especially since they were both from royal houses. Amaro was and is the third born to the Caligo, the shadow court, and the same court his princess was married into.

Amaro was the only Royal demon that Cash knew who was embarrassed about his powers. He was also, Cash hated to admit, the most powerful demon Cash had ever known. Amaro had power that far succeeded his father's and older brothers'. The shadows loved Amaro granting him power that no Caligo had ever known at once. Am was the true king and Heir to his father's throne yet instead of claiming it he hid himself away, rarely going home to the court he loved so much and the family he pretended to love.

Amaro had morals that Cash was grateful to never have to pretend to understand. It took Cash a while to realize that Amaro hated what he was. Maybe not hate but he had a strong dislike. Am wanted to be normal, a normal demon or a normal human, it didn't really matter as long as he was normal. He didn't want to be the most powerful Caligo in history, fated to destroy his family in order to take his proper place in life. Because let's face it, Jacob and his father were hardly about to hand the throne over to him.

Which brings us back to Chastity, from that night on Amaro was hooked. With Chastity he could be anyone he liked, he could be normal. He even lied to her about his power set, claiming to be a bargained lower level Opacus. The two were good together and Cash was free to have Faris all to himself. The lies were fun too and for a while everyone was happy.

Then, one day, it all stopped. Cash had to assume that Chastity knew nothing about his exile or Faris's exile or indeed Amaro's disappearance into wherever it was that he buried himself to hide from himself. In Cash's pain and misery he'd all but forgotten she even existed. That was until she tracked him down to his English manor and nearly beat the door down.

Normally under the circumstances of his insanity he didn't open the door to old friends or allow them admittance at all. He'd even had a tendency to turn Dimitri away in those days, only the vampire did he allow by his side. Chastity had changed a lot since he'd last seen her and his curiosity got the better of him.

She was a lot thinner and not as well kept, her hair was messy something she would never have allowed back when they had all been friends. That hadn't been what sparked his curiosity though. Little Chastity had made herself a bargain and judging by the fresh black eye she'd been sporting Cash came to the short conclusion that it hadn't been a very good one.

He'd silently let her in taking her to the kitchen and making some hot chocolate for them both. In those days he'd been feeling more lucid and as she'd already bargained her soul away she'd been fairly safe around him. It took a while, and several cups of steaming chocolate, for him to get the full story from her.

She'd bargained her life away to an illusion demon named Armand. Unbeknownst to her that not only was Armand the second born prince to the Celo court but he was one mean fucker of a demon. The bastard himself was rogue, preying on women bargaining them then using them up. The Celo court didn't condone his actions but they didn't condemn them either.

The Celo's had a habit of sitting on the fence on life issues. They were sneaky opportunists more than anything else, believing the illusions that they created more than the harsh reality of the world. They also were bitter enemies of the Caligo, Amaro's own race, she'd unwittingly made herself the enemy. Not that that had ever stopped Cash and Faris but Cash had the feeling Amaro would take a different view especially if he'd seen the mess young Armand had made of his love.

Of course Amaro, hiding from himself in a cave, was in no position to help her. Cash on the other hand, had nothing to lose by killing the upstart of a Celo and stealing his souls. Unfortunately upon his death Armand's souls, Chastity's included reverted back to the Celo king. He'd lost the souls but he'd gained Chastity, who'd spent a few months recovering from her ordeal at the manor before leaving to start a new life with a new name, Blythe. It suited the red head more than her last one and it seemed to give her a little peace.

Blythe in all her stupidity had given Cash exactly what he needed, something that he'd saved up all throughout his exile and now planned to use over the coming weeks to his full advantage. Leverage over Amaro. If the demon was too thick to accept his proper place in life then Cash was going to have to thrust him into it. Cash needed Caligo support, which meant disposing of Amaro's father and older brothers. To do that he needed Amaro's support and if his old friend wasn't going to give it freely then by god Cash was prepared to take it.

Lost deep in his thoughts of determination Cash jumped when he heard the door unlock, it looked like little Blythe was home and ready for an interesting conversation. He turned his back to the door instead making for the kitchen to put the kettle on.

"You know, you're the last person I expected to see puttering around my kitchen midday," she said as she walked into the room, her arms laden with packages that she promptly dropped.

"Why? You don't expect me to check up on my favorite Illusion demon now and then?" He turned leaning against the counter.

She grinned and ran to him, jumping into his arms and hugged him. "It's been a while is all. I missed you."

He caught her with ease hugging her back, genuinely glad to see her. "I'm sure you did...so how are things?"

"Same as always." she buried her face in his neck and inhaled, then gasped. "Cash..." she said moving back. "Either you have some really weird issues I don't know about, or you have been with Faris. That perfume is unmistakable," she smiled, hope glimmering in her eyes.

He raised an eyebrow smirking. "Have you ever doubted that I have weird issues?"

"Well no, but wearing ladies' perfume, especially the perfume of your missing princess is totally beyond you, even when you were at your lowest."

"Very true..." he conceded with a smile.

"So? Are you just fucking with me, or are you and Faris back together?" she grinned.

"It would seem so... a lot has changed since we last met darling. Faris and I are one of them."

"Meaning? Old fire pants okay with you guys now?" she asked and smiled.

"Not entirely." He set her down detangling himself from her. "She's somewhat on the lamb."

"Something tells me this isn't a truly social call. What's wrong Cash?"

"I'm just checking up on you... I'm going to need you soon." Turning from her he poured out two cups of tea.

"Need me? Whatever for? Apparently not for the usual if the princess is back in your bed..."

"No it's not the usual, I have a feeling Faris would be far less tolerant of my dalliances these days. We'll discuss your actual role closer to the time but I needed to make you aware that you owe me darling, and I fully intend to collect." He passed her her cup. "It's not anything you won't like... I'm not that cruel."

"I know I owe you Cash, you don't have to even think of reminding me. You're my friend Cash, always have been. So what's up? Tell me..."

"Why spoil the surprise?"

"Fair enough. So then tell me something happy."

"Faris is pregnant." He told her strait faced taking a drink of the tea.

Blythe, who had also been sipping her tea, coughed and sputtered her eyes going wide. "Oh my goddess. Truly? It is yours right?"

"Yep and I'm king... finally."

Her jaw hung slack. "Oh... Oh Cash that's wonderful!" she jumped up and went to him hugging him tightly. "This is cause for celebration! Oh when can I see Faris? And the baby? How far is she along?"

He barely avoided spilling tea everywhere just managing to set the cup down. "Not long. She should have gone to see Rudolph yesterday but we held off so that I can be with her. You can see her soon, not now though. I just want you to go about your normal routine for a few weeks. I'll call you when I need you okay?"

"Of course Cash... but I wanna see her soon... she's my best friend... I miss her."

"And I know she misses you pet... it won't be long I promise. She'll need you closer to the birth."

"And I'll be there, just tell me when. So what else? Lord knows you didn't come over to just be all cryptic and mysterious. I know how you get off on it, but this is even a lot for you. Gimmee a hint?"

"I'd love to but not yet..." He winked stepping away from her. In truth he hadn't decided the full capacity of her involvement yet.

He knew she'd be integral for gaining Amaro's support but how to go about it depended on the shadow demon himself and Cash had no idea just how the years had changed him.

There was the slim chance that Amaro just wouldn't care about her anymore; it was a slim chance yet it was there all the same.

"Okay," she shrugged. "Well if you're done being all mysterious, I have to get ready for a date."

"A date? You getting back on the horse?" he grinned at her.

"I gotta do something, right? No Victor is nice. We have been seeing each other for a while now, I think he's going to pop the question soon," she said as she left the kitchen.

Cash laughed shaking his head. Boy did Amaro have a lot of work to do and a lot to make up for. It was his own fault for leaving the chit all by herself and going deep underground. Not that her entanglement and possible engagement meant anything to him or changed any of his plans. If Amaro were still bleeding hearted enough to care he'd take his proper place in life to save her soul whether she was still interested in him or not. Cash grinned, bleeding hearts, they were always so easy to manipulate. "You're going to marry a man called Victor... I just don't see you with a Victor. Is he human?"

She nodded. "Its not like I have so many other interesting prospects. A girl gets lonely. I don't wanna be alone anymore."

He scrunched up his face. "But a Victor? Your a stunning looking demon, you shouldn't have to settle... you know there are rules to dating humans."

"I'm a Capito Cash. I don't have to use my powers ever   if I don't want to. He's a decent guy, he's kind to me, he treats me good and he's stable. I didn't see myself with a Victor either, but sometimes whom we see in our heart isn't whom we end up with. You of all people should know that. I'm getting too old to wait forever."

"Why should I know that? I have Faris... what I do know, is that things have a way of working themselves out. Against all the odds. You just have to want it enough. Promise me something okay?"

"Of course Cash... what?"

"Let me check this guy out before you end up making any life changing decisions ok? I don't want to see you hurt, it would upset Faris."

"I can do that. But I can tell you, he's an art teacher, never married and doesn't cheat on his taxes. I don't think you'll find him in your circles love."

"I can find dirt on anyone, I have people you know." He winked.

"Yeah I do know." She turned from the doorway to her room and bit her lip. "I know I said I wouldn't... but... how is he? Do you know?"

"I have no idea." He smiled sadly needing no prompting.

She sighed. "Well now you know why I'm considering Victor. I can't wait for Am forever. He probably doesn't even remember me."

"That I doubt... Am loved you but it's not my job to convince you of that."

"I never thought he didn't. He has a funny way of showing it Cash when he goes missing out of the blue and I haven't heard a word in thirteen years. Hell I don't even know if he's still alive."

"I doubt that anyone got lucky enough to kill him. I'll have a look for him if you wish?" Cash offered knowing that was exactly what he was going to do anyway, though in truth Amaro would find Cash when it was time.

"No... no if he wanted me he would have found me... Best to let it lie." She sighed and then sniffed.

"He won't stay gone forever." Cash shrugged.

"True. I'm just wasting my youth." She went to him and hugged him again. "Unless you wanna get in the shower with me Cashy, I'm going to have to say goodbye. You'll call me won't you?"

"Count on it and both Faris and myself will be seeing you very soon." He winked kissing her cheek.

She grinned. "Send her my love won't you? You know the way," she winked.

"I sure do." He grinned blinking out of her house. He was so close to going back home with Dimitri now that that conversation was over. All he had to do now was have a short conversation with the incubus then he could go back to see the glistening ice plains.

$\mathscr{S}$ixteen

"Faris, what's the difference? Buy the damn thing!" Astrid said and giggled at the frilly and almost non-existent piece of lingerie in her hand.

"You think? I'm not going to be able to wear it any time soon though."

"He will love it, you'll look stunning."

"Okay, but only if you pick up that leather get-up you were eyeing."

Astrid blushed and giggled again. "Yeah, Fallon would appreciate it that's for damn sure. Ok deal. What color though?"

"The blue, it will look great on you with your eyes."

They had been in Belts and Baubles Boutique for the better part of an hour hunting through all the sexy goodies they could get their hands on. It was their last stop on their shopping excursion, because Astrid told her they had to save the best for last.

The Sorceress' GTI was already filled with bags and a lot of boxes from the mall, and the contents ranged from lounge pants to bath products to maternity clothes. They even picked up some goodies for Cash as well, and some baby things too.

They ordered a crib and some baby things, but not much as Faris wasn't sure how long the child was even going to be a toddler. Astrid was enjoying the baby section, but Faris saw the sadness in her eyes. She knew her own mother had cursed Astrid with infertility and it was yet another reason why she hated Lillith. She might look like her, but she wasn't her mother's child.

Faris considered the ruby colored set in her hands. Cassiel would like it, the g-string exactly the kind of uncomplicated apparel he enjoyed when in the heat of the moment. "What the hell," she said mostly to herself as Astrid has moved off towards the boots section. She turned back to the lingerie and spied a sapphire blue camisole and boy shorts set with ice blue piping and knew Cash would adore it. She picked it up as well and went to join Astrid who was trying on a pair of buttery looking blue thigh high boots with a wicked heel.

"Those are gorgeous," she said as Astrid stalked in them in front of the wall length mirror.

"I know. Ash is going to shit herself. Much more her style then mine but gods they match the leather set to a T. Fallon will drool."

"Hell Cash will drool." Faris said offhandedly.

Astrid stopped walking and looked at Faris. "Faris, you sure you're ok with everything? I know it's not the most optimal situation, especially with the baby and all..."

Faris shook her head. "Astrid, I don't mind. You know back in the day a Demon kept his Sorceress as a beloved concubine along with his wife. It's the way of it. You have Fallon so it's not all about Cassiel and you. It's a business situation, and I know that. I also know what comes with that and I don't mind sharing. It's not like you're Bethany."

"Bethany?" Astrid asked and sat to unzip the boot.

"Celo Princess. She's a lunatic and wants Cash way too much. I never liked her but when she decided that Cash had to be *her* prince, well the gloves were off so to speak. She was the only one I forbade him to see. Luckily he listened." She sighed. "I know that the power is greater if you guys fuck. I'm ok with that, it's obvious why he's attracted to you," she winked "So it's cool. It keeps us all safe, and that's what matters."

"Well you're approaching this pretty well for a woman that just got her lover back. Once this power transference thing is over, Cash told me it won't have to be often, but it's a necessary evil." She shrugged and then nodded to the sales girl, who grabbed the boots and the box and took them to the counter. "And he's divine in bed."

Faris giggled. "That's from all the damn practice. Fallon doesn't look like a slouch either."

Astrid sat back and whistled. "Lord I'm surprised I can walk half the time." She grinned. "Fallon is amazing. He's more then enough, though if you wanna have a go..."

Hearing this, Faris laughed. She and Fallon would be a wild ride, but she wasn't sure she was that interested, not that she would throw him outta bed. He was very sexy. "I might take you guys up on that one day. I think I'm set with these, though I did see some boy shorts towards the front of the store I have to have."

"Then let's get them. I'm looking forward to getting back to Fallon, and hopefully a stocked kitchen. I might have messed up sending Arcady and Snow shopping, but I guess it can't be helped now. We will have to see won't we?"

"What's for dinner?" Faris asked, her stomach growling. They had been shopping since lunch and while they had eaten before setting out, it was light. She was craving something rare and bleeding.

"Steaks I think. I sent Arcady with the specific instructions to get eight New York strip steaks; Feyd was talking about some new marinade. So we will go from there."

Faris sent a silent prayer of thanks to whoever just answered her desires and then laughed. "You know, I'm really surprised you don't have servants."

"What and have some asshole learning everyone's secrets? Not a chance in hell. No we work things out pretty well without, and I like the arrangement we have. It's like a real family."

"I can attest to that." She grabbed eight pairs of boy shorts as they walked by, to add to the bras, thongs and nighties she already had on the counter. Cash was going to enjoy this haul most of all and she looked forward to trying it all on for him later that evening. She looked at the sales girl who was smiling from behind the counter and sighed. "Okay Betty, what's the damage?"

***

"So have you decided on what to name the pup?" Arcady asked as he grabbed the last of the grocery bags from the back of SUV. They had made it to the grocery store and done all the shopping Astrid had asked for, even getting some other goodies Feyd had slipped onto the list last minute. Never in his life had he done the amount of grocery shopping he did this time. He was fairly certain that every trip to the market up until this point hadn't equaled this trip as well. It was weird, shopping for 10 adults.

On the way out Snow had gravitated towards a small box and an old lady just outside and as Arcady went over to see what it was she was looking at she had turned and showed him the small fuzzy puppy in her arms. Her face was alight with happiness and her eyes pleaded with him. He couldn't say no, and now she had the pup still in her arms cooing to him. He was fairly sure it was a husky pup, and that meant that when he got older he was going to be twice the size of the reigning king of the mansion, Linus.

"Badger." Snow answered grinning. "He looks like a Badger don't you think?"

Arcady looked at the ball of fur in Snow's arms and shrugged. He didn't really know what one looked like, and as he was all about indulging his soon to be fiancée he nodded. "If you say so love."

She frowned up at him looking away from the pup, "He's black and white, its close enough," she giggled back down at the newly dubbed Badger. "And she going to be a big boy," She said in a baby voice directed at the ball of fluff. "Just look at those big paws." She lifted the paws in question up for him to inspect.

He grinned at his girlfriend. She was adorable, and happy and that's all the mattered. "Well we will have to go out and get him some puppy stuff then. Astrid would shit kittens if he cuts his teeth on the four thousand dollar suede couch. No one is even allowed to fuck on that thing."

"Really?" She grinned up her eyes getting that sparkle that Arcady now recognized as a very wicked thought.

"Snowy you're just bad," he grinned.

She chuckled. "Maybe but I doubt the pup will be the couch's downfall and if he does wander we'll blame it on Linus or the cat."

There was that cat again. He had asked Astrid about it, and she had assured him they didn't have a cat, Fallon was allergic. Where she was seeing a cat was beyond him, but if it were the worst of her delusions, then he would have to count his blessings. "Yeah. Maybe on the cat, Linus knows better," he grinned.

He turned as they were walking in to see the GTI pull up in the side drive. Astrid and Faris got out and they waved at them and Snow went over to show them the pup, no doubt to get Astrid's seal of approval. He chuckled, knowing Astrid wouldn't ever say no, especially when she saw how excited Snow was. He walked into the kitchen to see Cash rooting through the bags they had already put on the table. He smirked. "Looking for something special?"

"Not really. Looking for some ice cream ingredients to take over to D," he said brightly. "I see you took my advice and got her a dog."

"Oddly, no she found the thing as we were walking out of the grocer. She's happy, and that's all the matters. So I suppose I should say congratulations, highness, I'm sorry we weren't at your coronation dinner last night but..." he grinned. "We had plans and you sprung it on us. How's the princess? I got the ingredients that Asty didn't have for the incubus tea for her."

"Faris is good although I'm sure the tea will make her feel much better. Have you been back to the Incubus courts then?"

"Since last I saw you? No, Astrid keeps a lot of the ingredients on hand; I just picked up the Yarrow and the Rue fresh. She doesn't grow them in the garden as they aren't a witch's herb."

"Of course," he nodded, "My witch does keep herself well stocked. Tell me something," The demon placed his hand on his arm taking him to the side. "How was Camions when you last visited?"

"Cam? I didn't see her. I saw Fi, Apparently she's the one running the Succubus courts, why?"

"Oh..." He frowned, "And how did Fi take the news?"

"What about Snow? She was ok, if not a bit sad."

"That's right, you and her were... well Amos had his hopes. I'm sure she knew that, we all did and I was in exile." He grinned. "Painful."

"She knew, and it's cool between us. She deserves to be swept off her feet, you know? So what's up?"

He shook his head. "Nothing much. Did she know where Camions went? How long she'd be gone?"

"Not sure, but you know how Cam is. What's going on Cash?"

"I'd just hate for the queen to miss my reentry," he smiled shrugging. "You two sure you're ready for a kid?" He nodded over to Snow and the pup. "It's a big commitment bringing a life up in this crazy world."

"I see it as practice for the real thing," he winked. "What about you? You ready for the trials and tribulations of fatherhood?"

"I've been ready for thirteen years."

"And do you know what it's going to be?"

"Not yet, other than Cento. I want to be with Faris when we find out... so we'll have to delay the moment." He smiled. "So do you think Snow will ever be ready for motherhood? I wouldn't suggest it just yet... Well I might just to panic her but you shouldn't."

"Honestly? Yes. Not now, but yes. She will make a great mother, like Asty would if she could. They are the kinda women that raise strong and independent children. Like Mandy. She might be a porno star, but my mother raised us right."

"That's good to hear, at least it will cheer Dimitri up somewhat. I'm a little impartial to the whole thing. Tell me, for curiosity sake, what did Amos want for my support?"

"Not sure really. Asked for a favor from me at a later date, so I took it."

Cash snorted a laugh shaking his head, "Sneaky old fuck. I hate spoiling other people's surprises but kid you're so screwed."

"Probably, but whatever it is it's worth it. And that reminds me, I'm going to need her soul."

"Of course, she's all yours." He nodded. "Enjoy her."

"I already do, we'll do the exchange later. Where's Fallon? You seen him today? I know Feyd was watching the girls but hightailed it home when they went to Belts and Baubles to see Ash. Bastard needs to get down here to cook," he grinned.

"He's in the pool room drinking. Spending time with George without killing him seems to be taking its toll."

"Beauty. I'm sure he'll wanna hit the mats then. Work out some frustrations." He nodded to Cash and grabbed an apple off the center island and skirted off just as the girls were walking in. He heard Snow exclaim to Cash about Badger and grinned, then took a bite of his apple. He was up the stairs towards the second floor poolroom before Snow could catch up with him.

Seventeen

Cash blinked himself to the hallway in the Cisco towers. He had considered just blinking into Dimitri's apartment but decided that he really didn't want to walk in on whatever he and Colette could be up to. He checked the contents of the bag he was carrying keeping it cold enough so that it didn't melt. The ice cream was a consolation to Cole for him stealing his brother away from her. He knocked loudly hoping that he wasn't interrupting anything.

Dimitri opened then door with a grin. "Shit. I thought you were the Lorenzo's delivery guy. Looks like you brought food though. Come in."

"Do I look like a delivery boy to you? At least you dropped the highness... And here I thought you would have kept that up for at least another week or two." He stepped into the apartment pleased to see that they'd been redecorating. "Now don't tell me she's had you doing manual labor?" He grinned looking around.

"I didn't drop the *Highness*, I didn't address you at all actually, and no, we hired movers for that. She's been here not even a day and has already designed several rooms. So what do I owe the pleasure, Highness?" he smirked and winked as Cole walked in.

Cash sighed markedly rolling his eyes. "I need to borrow you for a few hours." He nodded to Cole throwing her the box of ice cream. "Compensation."

"Ooh..." She grinned opening it quickly and dipping a finger in, licking it clean. "Fudge and caramel... you remembered." She perched herself on a stool next to Dimitri.

"Think you can get along without me for a little while Pet?" Dimitri asked, running his hand on her naked knee.

"I have ice cream and the food is due soon." She nodded dipping another finger in the ice cream and suggestively sucking it clean. "Just don't be too long, a girl can get pretty lonely by herself. Wouldn't want me eating the whole tub without you."

"No matter if you do..." he kissed her. "We still have to fuck lunch off you, what're a few extra calories?" he grinned.

"Nothing but I'd rather lick it off of you than a spoon." She said innocently her eyes dark with heat.

"Later pet," he winked "Have fun ok? And save me some of that tempura."

"I might." She winked back.

Cash groaned. "Oh come on. Quickly before I lose my royal lunch."

Dimitri kissed Cole and turned to Cash. "Oh Highness, where to?"

He grinned, feeling the excitement building up within him. "Home."

"Ah, was wondering when you would wanna hit that. Any place in particular?"

"Nowhere public. The meeting spot I guess, I'm going to have to have a talk with Oscar too."

Dimitri grinned. "Ah the war room... Well then to the cottage we go." Dimitri winked at Cole and blinked out.

Cash blinked after him using the lines to pierce the veils between the two worlds and slip into the Afterverse for the first time in thirteen years. It was the cold that hit him first; it penetrated every fiber of his being welcoming him back. It wasn't a cold that you could find in the Eververse, nothing in the human realm could even come close to it. The light hit him next the hazy surreal-ness of it all, the pure white light from the suns reflecting off the perfect glaciers. It drove him to his knees, the pure ecstasy of his homeland. He'd waited so long for this moment. He laid himself down getting as close to the ice as he could, pressing his face down into the cold memorizing it.

"If you start humping the ice I'm outta here" Dimitri said from behind him leaning against a glacial birch.

"Bite me," he growled into the ice. "You have no idea what this feels like to me."

"True, but still if anyone were to happen onto you like this, questions would get raised."

"If anyone happens upon me at all questions are going to be raised." He rolled over onto his back grinning up at his little brother.

"True... You feel better?"

"Unbelievably so." He stretched.

A soft growl penetrated the quiet that surrounded them and Dimitri smiled as a large cat, the Afterverse equivalent to a snow leopard, sauntered around the corner.

Cash chuckled watching the beast. "Well aren't you a surprise. I was sure you'd have taken off a long time ago." He beckoned his old pet who walked happily over to him letting him scratch his soft ears. "And at least you're well fed. Someone's been taking good care of you."

Oscar came around the corner of the ice flow they were on and nodded. "Took a while to get him to trust me..." he smiled at Cash. "Welcome home Prince, Just how the hell did you manage this?"

"He's a grumpy old thing but his vice is fish... something oily like mackerel and he's purring like a kitten." He grinned batting the large cat away from him. "And its Highness, I'm king. Which changes... practically nothing as of yet, but it's a start in the right direction." He stood up grinning at his old friend and general. "Heard you've been keeping the place ticking over for me."

Oscar grinned and bowed to Cash. "Well then Highness, It is good to see your father came to his senses... I assume he did, I mean Dimitri isn't hemming and hawing about you dispatching him."

Dimitri glowered at Oscar. "Hey, I wouldn't piss too much of a bitch about it," he said sullenly.

Cash snorted, "Yeah, sure you wouldn't. If that was truly the case I would have done it years ago and saved myself the bother."

Dimitri just shook his head and Oscar looked at Cash. "So what's the plan?" he asked and pet the large cat.

"The plan?" He shrugged. "Lay low and gather support under Fuerety's nose until the baby's born. I'm not ready yet, I still need Am and Don but they're on their way. Ammit's avoiding me; Shabiri says she'll watch from the sideline. I don't think Sookie will be much of a problem and I have Amos and Cam's support. Things are falling into place."

"Sookie will stand by you simply because Alexander supports you. He might not have gone with you when you left, but he did leave too."

"Alex is a good man... he likes me but he's a little iffy with the Conglacio thanks to something your brother did."

"Well I don't presume to know thing one about Drake, including where he is at the moment. I felt it the second you came back in... He should have too."

"Well then with any luck he should keep the hell away from here. We didn't part on very good terms," He turned to Dimitri. "I had to warn him off Snow, something you should have done a very long time ago." He faced Oscar again. "I'd keep an eye on him if I were you or the incubus is likely to gut him and I'll let him. I need that Incubus more than I need Drake."

"Understood." Oscar shook his head. "He might be my brother but he really needs to be knocked on his ass."

Dimitri looked at both of them. "Don't blame me. There's only so much I can do. But you're right I didn't warn him off Snow. But I had my reasons. And if she would have just cooperated then we wouldn't be having this conversation. See what happens when I try to be calculating and sneaky like you? Its gets fucked up. I'll stay the honest one in the bunch thank you."

"You do that, you really can't do calculating and sneaky until you learn people. Snow's an abused soul, you couldn't ask her to stand up to someone like Drake, not for herself. She doesn't have it in her... not yet." He turned to Oscar. "So we have to lay low."

"Can do. It's business as usual here, thwarting Gabbe left and right." He sighed. "How is it topside. What have you been up to? Dimitri told me about Astrid.... not a bad haul if you ask me."

"Not at all, you should meet her, she's a gem and Faris agrees," he grinned. "Other than that not much, I'm trying to round up Don and Am. Has the bastard been giving you much trouble?"

"No, his usual playing lord and master to any chit that will listen. He's been going through the courts like water. I seriously don't think there's one chick out there he hasn't nailed. Seen a lot of Bethany though. She's been an odd duck recently too."

Cash sneered. "Oh? In what way? More than usual?"

"Well it started when Faris got betrothed. She was asking me about you, if I knew if you were still about, saying all her competition was now taken care of... then the past three nights she's been holed up with Gabbe in the Palace. Cash I don't know what's going on but..."

Dimitri shook his head. "I told you this was going to bite you in the ass."

"I'll deal with it Dimitri. Besides it really wasn't my fault..." He growled out. "Okay keep an eye on Gabbe. I'll have Bethany dealt with..." He looked at his General. "If you get the chance, kill her."

"Don't have to tell me twice, that girl is a hazard. So do we know what the Heir is yet?"

"Cento. Other than that not really. I'll find out soon and you'll be one of the first to know"

He nodded. "And Faris? How is she doing? I take it Astrid and her get along better then her and Nate did?"

"Astrid isn't dead, so no, they seem to be agreeable. Faris is doing well. At least she's yet to burn anything down in a temper or kill any of our roommates; pregnancy hormones seem to be agreeing with her. Maybe I should always keep her pregnant. Although I could have done without Sallos' presence but she handled that better than any of us could have."

"Yeah well, that's what Faris does best, handle Sallos."

Cash chuckled shaking his head, "Not quite what she does best but it's a close third or fourth."

Oscar shook his head. "You'd know. So? Aside from the brat, what else do you need me to do?"

"Feed my cat," he grinned as the beast batted his head against his leg. "And if you see Ammit around get her to call me, tell her I want to make a deal."

"Can do," he bowed. "I'm due at the palace for a dinner party tonight. So I don't want my absence to be noted. Welcome back Cassiel. I'll be in touch."

With that he was gone. Dimitri looked at Cash. "So? You going to wander for a while or are you going back to Faris? Personally as much as seeing you all hot for home makes me all squishy inside I have a sorceress I need to attend to."

"True but I have to talk to you."

"Okay." Dimitri looked at him waiting.

"I'm king now." He stated looking down unsure how to broach the next topic. "And as such it's my job to set up alliances... betrothals." He looked up at Dimitri. "And you have the position of being my unmarried little brother."

Dimitri looked at Cash. "What the hell are you saying?" he asked carefully, a frown on his face.

He sighed, this wasn't going to be easy, "There's no need to curse. It's not like I'd marry you off to someone you hated. I need to strengthen my alliance with the succubus court... princess Fiona always had a thing for you and Amos would very much approve of the match. It's how things are done..."

"Cash, you can't expect me to agree to this! I just got Cole back in my life, the woman is my sorceress and chosen companion, Cash I love her."

"I know," He said softly, "I gave you what you wanted Dimitri... I always have but sometimes we have to give a little. If you think this is bad you just wait to hear what I have to say to Drake... I need bombproof alliances D. Colette is your sorceress, you'll have her for all time, but you need a wife."

"She's going to be my wife Cash... I'm the third fucking son; I don't have to deal with shit like this! I like Fiona... But I'd never love her Cash..." he looked at him pleadingly.

His heart broke at the desperation of his brothers' voice. "Don't look at me like that I've made up my mind."

"You're condemning a perfectly wonderful girl to a loveless marriage Cash. She deserves better. And I can't give it to her." He sighed.

"Could you try?" He swallowed, his resolve slipping.

Dimitri sighed. "It's not fair to any of us Cash. Not to Fi, not to me and not to Cole. But hey, I'll give it my best ok? Have two women hate me. One child Cash. One." he looked up at the king.

Cash rolled his eyes sighing deeply. "Would you name it after me?"

"Not a chance in hell."

"Fine! Marry your sorceress, do what you want, as always... I'll move on to plan B, which, for the record, I don't have. Fuck knows my bratty little brother can't take one for the team. Not that the security and well being of our people is worth you putting on a happy face now and again. It's fine, I'll suffer for your happiness as always."

"Can the martyr act Cash. You want me to marry Fi, I will."

"No, its fine, I'll find somebody that wants the job... not like I'm doing anything else at the moment."

"Quit your shit Cash. Okay? You put me in a very precarious position, especially after I just bound my sorceress. And now you're trying to make me feel bad about it. And what would have happened if Dad told you to marry Bethany? Instead of Faris because it was what was good for the kingdom? Could you do that to Faris?" he sighed. "If she accepts the suit she has to know that I have Cole and she's a priority to me, I won't stand for anything less."

"Levi was never king and if I truly believed that marrying Bethany was for the better of out kingdom I would be with her now." He sighed. "Look I know you, you're going to grit your teeth and drag your heels and that's not what I want. If she suspects she's being traded like meat she's going to be very upset. So how about we make a deal? You don't have to marry her, but I don't have the time to find someone who will. That can be your new job. Set her up with somebody and make sure it works and has to be owed to the Conglacio. I don't care who it is but if she's not betrothed by the time it takes for me to actually need her support then you're the man for the job. Does that sound fair?"

Dimitri chuckled. "Fine. Reduced to fucking matchmaker. Fine... I think I can handle it. I mean I peddle flesh for a living. Fi's hot. I think it shouldn't be too hard."

"Good, and once that's done then you can marry Cole. Then I promise this situation will never come up again."

"Better not. Cash, you're my brother and I love you, but you nearly made me stroke with this one."

He shook his head. "You're so spoiled D."

"Not at all. I have to have the woman I want Cash, anything else is just not appealing."

"I was referring to the fact that you always get what you want."

"Cash... I really don't. It took me thirteen years of hoping you wouldn't kill her and waiting for her to be mine to have what I wanted, I did my penance. I deserve to be happy with her. So what are you going to make Drake do?"

"Marry Sandor..." He winced. "But maybe that's not such a good idea either. For starters I'd have to talk to him then it would be war if he seriously hurt her. I'll think I'll leave that on a back burner for a while. We have the support of the Strigo court as it is... best not to push it."

"I think I can kill two birds with one stone there..."

"That's why you deal with flesh and I deal in death. How?"

"Who is the one person no one ever hears from?"

"Is this question multiple choice?"

Dimitri snickered. "No. One prince that's usually MIA."

"I've been in exile for thirteen years, how the hell should I know?"

He sighed. "Murphy."

"Ah... could you set that up?"

"Is Astrid a nympho?" he asked

"Of course she is but that wasn't my question. Didn't Murphy have a thing for Fiona's sister Iris? She's not going to want her sister's seconds."

"No... Truth of that is dear daddy Strigo hoped for an alliance with the Succubus. Iris was the right age. Murphy always had a thing for Fi... but when Iris refused his suit and married the human... he gave up for the same reason you just said."

"Ok, but still you know how bitchy the sisters can get. I'll leave it in your capable hands then?"

"Yeah it's going to take finesse but it's doable. You know you should have just asked me... instead of trying to get me to be cool with it myself."

"I honestly didn't think you'd take it so badly, there's a fate worse than Cole and Fi in your bed."

"I agree. But I only want Cole. Like you only want Faris. Astrid is a bonus you enjoy."

"True." He sighed looking around. "Well it's back to the mansion I think. I'm only pushing my luck if I stay here any longer."

"Wise decision. Give my love to Faris will you? I'll see you guys in a few days."

"You will. Good luck." He patted the cat's head one last time before blinking away back to the mansion.

Eighteen

Faris smiled as she roamed around the suite she shared with Casha, putting her shopping away. She had purchased a lot, and left the choice items on the bed for her prince to find while she went to the hallway closet and put the extra new towels her and Astrid had bought at the linens store in. They were ruby, the same color as the satin sheets that were now on the bed. Astrid and Faris had bought mix and match bed sets, with ruby sheets and cerulean blue pillows and accents. The new comforter was satin as well, awash with both colors and pewter. It was breathtaking and Faris loved it. For a room that was completely done for Cash only an hour before, Faris and Astrid had changed it substantially with minimal work.

The bathroom linens were now changed as well. Blue and ruby and eggplant, and Astrid had almost bought out a little out of the way candle shop of blue, red, silver and purple pillars to place around the cavernous bathroom. Faris felt at home, happy and safe. Astrid was a wonder, a true force of nature. She was happy she was Cash's sorceress and happy that they got along so well. Without the other woman's support, things would be a lot harder for her and Cassiel.

She knew her prince would be home soon. Arcady had mentioned that he was off to see Dimitri and that meant only one thing. They were probably on the Ice plains and her love was probably reacquainting himself with the lands he loved so dearly. She looked forward to his homecoming, and knew that when he arrived he would once again have the strong scent of the bitter frigid winds and the crisp taste of a first snow.

She missed that about him. She walked from the bathroom closet back into the bedroom proper and grabbed three garment bags and took them to the large closet she shared with Cash. When she turned she heard the door to the room open and she giggled. Cash had returned.

"Well there's definitely more red in here," he remarked his voice sounding lighter and more hopeful that it had years.

She ducked out from the closet and went to him. "Is it ok? You look so much better." She wrapped herself around him and inhaled his frigid scent. "You have been home."

"I have." He wrapped his arms around her. "Even got to see that dumb old cat of mine. Oscar's been feeding him... no doubt spoiling the fatty."

She grinned. "I did like that thing. Purred like an engine. So everything ok? It must be you're not inquiring about how much money I spent," she teased.

"I don't mind you spending my money, Princess. You're the only one, other than me, who has any right to."

She kissed him and smiled. "Damn right demon... I miss giving your credit cards a work out. It was always such fun to come back and see your eyes light up with all the goodies I brought home."

"And what did you buy?"

"Lots of pretty silky things and the new bedding. Do you like it?" she turned to give him a better view of the bed. "And I got you some things too. The closet looked kind of bare, and your suits, however sexy just don't go all the time."

He smiled, "Oh so you brought presents for me too?" he kissed her. "See? That's why you get to spend my money love, so generous."

She laughed and led him over to the bed. "Sit... I'll show you everything. Though I must say all the linens and candles were all Astrid. Girl doesn't even blink when she drops a grand on wax."

"She's spoiled, yet I get the feeling you could rival her on that." He sat back lounging on the bed.

"Umm she is, but she's made that bathroom more sumptuous then mine back in the fire palace. I'm going to love bathing with you in there. And I'm not spoiled... come to think of it neither is Astrid. We are loved." She winked and grabbed the large belts and baubles bag, shaking it at him.

He grinned his eyes trailing the bag. "Well loved my Princess."

"I like it when you are like this... So...." she pulled out the first outfit, an ice blue lace boy short and balconette bra. "You like?"

"Hmmmm... Very much so... you know I love you in blue."

She blushed and nodded. "Which was why I picked it." She pulled out a red little string bikini and a few pairs of boy shorts.

He groaned, "So I take it you had fun then... you know I'm going to have to ask you about Sallos sometime. It can wait but I'll need to know soon."

"Old Sally? Don't worry about him Cashy. It will be fine. Though he still really hates you. No matter." She pulled out the last set, the outfit she had asked Astrid about, and giggled, showing him.

His jaw hung loose and he stared.

"Then I take it I made a wise choice."

He nodded swallowing hard. "I think you did... though it would look much better on."

She nodded and untied the belt to her wrap dress and shrugged out of it, standing naked before him and slipped the outfit on, turning around." Well?"

He chuckled patting his lap for her to sit with him. "My mistake princess, it'll look much better off. More specifically coming off..."

She grinned and stalked over to him slipping onto his lap. "You always did like my outfits in heaps on the floor."

He wrapped his hands around her and cuddled her body to him. "I still do, though it has more to do with having you naked in my lap that it does the actual outfits."

"I love being in your lap Prince. So what's on the agenda for tonight?"

"Nothing so far. It's just me and you tonight, Princess. And the baby, of course, but I think it's a tad too young yet to be spoiling our alone time. So it's the two of us..." His hand trailed lazy patterns gently over her back cooling wherever it touched. "We're both highly intelligent demons I'm sure we can come up with something to occupy our time."

She grinned, seeing the mischief alive in his eyes. He was in a truly good mood. "Oh I'm sure we can, though I must tell you, I did have my heart set on your famous ice cream."

"I think we can arrange that... what's your flavor Princess?" he asked teasingly as he kisses her bare shoulder.

She sighed. "I'd say vanilla... but I don't like anything bland."

"I've noticed. I'll admit for a while there I thought you were going to say something overly hormonal like carrot and banana. So what do you really want love?"

"Ummm Banana sounds good... how about chocolate and banana? I'm not craving really... but it does sound good."

"Chocolate and banana it is then. I'm sure we'll have all the ingredients in the kitchen."

"Ummm but that's for later... right now..." she kissed him and relaxed fully into his embrace. "I need a little attention."

"And you have it my love. My undivided attention."

She grinned. Cash back to his former glory was exactly what she remembered. He wasn't twitchy, or broken, he was strong, and powerful again, and his mind was healing. She knew long ago he would make a great father, back when that was all that mattered to both of them. Now, he was king and would be a great father, and a wonderful lover and companion. "So maybe we need to get you out of these clothes then? I mean if I'm sitting here in this skimpy little number, you should at least not have these rough pants on, or the shirt."

"I am a little overdressed for the occasion," He admitted grinning. "And just how do you plan on remedying that?"

Faris giggled and grabbed both sides of the button up shirt he wore and wrenched, the buttons popping off the material, scattering hither and to. She quirked an eyebrow as she licked her lips. "Ummm yummy Cashy," she said. "I think that solves that problem."

"Rather effectively but you do owe me a shirt. That is unless you know how to sew a button back on?" He chuckled,

"If I don't I'm sure someone does. Feyd looks like the domestic type." Faris bit her bottom lip in thought. "Now what about these pants?"

"Let's get these off in a more traditional way."

She held up her hand and called her fire, the flames licking around her fingers. "You sure?" she winked.

"I can't say I'm not tempted."

At his words, Faris raised her other hand and willed the fire into both, the flames of the first caressing and then jumping to her left hand. She cocked her head and then let the flames die down. "Later..." she got off his lap and sucked her teeth. "Off with them... I miss your skin."

Smirking he unbuttoned his pants slowly slipping out of them. "And I miss your fire."

"Yeah, my fire missed you." She watched him kick off his pants and relax back onto the bed and she climbed back onto his lap, reveling in the steely hardness of his thighs under her softer ones. Cassiel was utter perfection of the body and the fact that he was all hers again, was liberating. She bent her head and licked a slow line of fire from his upper chest to behind his ear. It played on his skin, and then sizzled as his ice dampened it.

He hissed closing his eyes. "Mmmm you always did know just how to play me." His ice cold hands grasped her hips pulling her to him.

"Of course I do." she smiled and sucked his earlobe into her mouth, running her hot tongue along the ridge.

Growling he pulled her onto him grinding up into her through the flimsy blue silk.

Faris reared back and groaned, her body responding to his perfectly. Her nipples puckered and her fire burned hot. "God that feels good."

"Always did, always will." His lips found her nipple sucking it into his mouth his teeth scraping over the lace of the bra. He suckled and nibbled on her tender nub for a few moments fully savoring it before moving onto the other one.

She closed her eyes and gave over to the sensation he was making on her flesh and moaned softly. "Damn right... you know exactly how to play me too demon..."

"Never doubt it." He grinned wickedly kissing up his way up her chest and neck.

She wiggled on his lap and was seconds away from tearing the blue silk off her hips when there was a soft rap on the door. She looked down at him, a frown on her lips.

He growled in frustration lifting his head towards the door. "Astrid I do hope that you're not going to make a habit of this," he all but snarled at the door.

Astrid opened the door and blushed at the sight of them on the bed. "I'm sorry Cash, but... Well you have a visitor." She smiled at Faris who winked at her. "And Faris you do look divine in that frock."

"A visitor? I highly doubt that... I've spoken to everyone that I need to. I'm not expecting anyone else, at least not until Am gets curious enough and I'm giving that a few days to take hold of him. Plus he wouldn't use the front door."

"Trust me, you're going to wanna see this one. I can keep Faris company while you have your meeting if you like, Fallon is out pissing George off." She grinned and Faris giggled.

The frown that had developed on his face softened somewhat at the concept. "Fine... but it better be important."

Astrid walked in, taking the steps to the bed quickly. She crawled up and lounged next to them and Faris bent down and kissed her lover. "A king's work is never done. Go, do what you have to. I'm sure Astrid will help keep it warm for you."

"Not too warm I hope." He stood pulling his pants on and a fresh shirt buttoning it half way. "Where is this guest?"

"Kitchen," Astrid said as Faris moved to cuddle with her on the bed. She knew the two of them were a sight to Cash, the heat flashing in his eyes told her as much. Faris leaned into the witch as she wrapped her arms around her and kissed Faris' head. Astrid was wonderful, a soft wind in a horrid gale. Her presence behind Faris, wrapped around Faris, was comforting. Where Natalia was a threat, Astrid never would be, and they could be friends, and she knew probably more.

Faris smiled at Cash. "Take your time Prince."

He grinned at both of them pausing to admire the view. "Same to you, my love, I'd hate to miss the show." He winked and left slamming the door shut behind him.

Faris grinned at Astrid and then laughed. "Grumpy ice demon."

Nineteen

The scent of the Succubus gardens enveloped him as he walked into them, the cloying aroma of the roses and the Afterverse lilies rising from everywhere. This was a hay fever sufferer's worst nightmare. He smiled at one of the Succubus that was working on pruning a hedge as he walked by, intent on finding Fiona.

She hadn't been in the throne room, or the spa and the last haunt he had left at his disposal was the gardens. When they were young, Fiona loved the Labyrinth and he was sure she was probably perched just outside it, working on something.

His instincts were right as he turned the corner to see her sitting on a large silver cushion, her body in the Lotus position. He grinned. He watched as she posed, doing several Yoga positions, and then did a few he knew weren't normal yoga, but closer to the humans version of Tantra. All Camions' daughters were quite flexible and versed in the art of Qual Tai. Qual Tai was a secret, the ability to sustain unheard of positions, and the Succubus all knew levels of it.

Dimitri had seen it used countless times, even had been treated to instances at the court where he was part of the fun, but no one was as good at it as Fiona.

For that, he was a bit regretful of not having her in his bed, but it was for the best. He watched her tumble and stretch, and then cleared his throat, finally announcing his arrival to a very preoccupied princess.

She sighed holding her position keeping her eyes shut. "I'm not in the mood. If it's anything important take it to Moni."

"Forgive me princess, I'm sorry to intrude, but this is about you."

Her eyes darted open and she looked over at him. "Dimitri." She grinned. "You should have said, I thought you were one of..." She shook her head coming out of her position and standing. "Never mind. How are you?"

"Quite well, enjoying the show as a matter of fact. You have surpassed your sisters, it's fitting."

"In some ways perhaps," she growled her mood darkening at the mention of her sisters. "Of course these are the pleasure courts D, if you have enjoyed it you could have showed me just how much. You know we don't stand much on ceremony here." She smiled seductively her voice like thick honey.

He chuckled. "As much as you're tempting me here Princess, I have some business to talk to you about."

"Ah. Well by all means then on you go... Although I believe my mother's already been very clear in respect to us having no involvement in your businesses. I'm afraid that I won't be able to change that."

He grinned. "Not that kinda business. Actually I came to see you."

"Okay then."

"Can I sit?" he asked and motioned to the lounger.

"Sure make yourself at home." She sat herself down on the soft grass.

"So Cash and I were talking... and he had wanted to betroth me to you," he said quietly.

She sighed pulling at the bits of grass, "Oh... you don't seem overjoyed at the prospect."

"Not for the reason you think Fi... There's one major complication. Something you don't know." He looked at her. "I would marry you love, you're a goddess and we could have one hell of a time, but I'm not the one that adores you. Someone else is."

She sighed shaking her head. "It's always somebody else D. I'm not a complete idiot you know... I know you have your sorceress, you love her and you'll never love me." She shrugged blinking back tears.

"I have too much of my parents in me, even Moni agrees, I'm going to be alone and bitter forever. Just like them. It's the curse of the courts, so it's not your fault; you're off the hook. Just go." She sighed her lip trembling as she stood turning her back dismissively.

"Well, see I can't... Cuz I know who it is... and you won't be happy to hear it, given past events, but there're a few things you need to know," he said quickly, hating seeing her in such a state. "Because I know how he feels about you, I couldn't marry you."

"Dimitri I don't have time for this." Her shoulders slumped in defeat. "Iris, that bitch, is pregnant again. I have to organize a ball whilst putting up with the constant jeers from those harpies."

Dimitri sighed, "Very well. I'm sorry to bother you Fiona," he stood and bowed.

She turned round to him, her face streaked with tears, and sighed. "Sorry D... It's just a touchy subject at the moment."

"And it should be Princess. No one should have to be lonely. No one."

She shrugged.

"Do yourself a favor, invite Murphy over for tea," he winked.

"Murphy?" She smiled. "Strigo Murphy?"

"That's the only Murphy I know..." he smiled at her.

She sighed, "I'd love to see him again, but he was never interested in me. I might be desperately alone but the last thing I need is for him to turn me away. My heart couldn't take it... not him." She swallowed. "You and Arcady I can take but not him. It would end me D. I'm not willing to take that chance."

Dimitri chuckled. "Fi that's the thing you don't get. He never wanted Iris. His family made a deal with yours, in order to possibly create an alliance between the houses. He did what he was bade to, but he never even liked Iris. He did, however, covet you. But you were still too young at the time... and his father was hoping for a swift alliance, children. So when Iris turned him down, he just quit. Didn't want you to think you were getting your sister's leavings. He never touched her either. Why do you think he doesn't show at the balls here at the courts? He doesn't wanna see you with someone else."

She frowned wringing her hands. "Really?" she asked quietly after a while, hope in her eyes.

He nodded. "I don't lie. That's Cash's department. Murphy wants you Fi, always has. But you know him, propriety and duty drive him even more then Alexander. I don't think he wanted you to be a laughing stock if he courted you, especially to your sisters, because of his house. So he stays away."

She nodded quietly. "Ok...any chance you could get him to call me? I would but chasing after a man really would make me a laughing stock."

"Personally I think you and Murphy are a good idea. He's the exact kinda guy you need Fi, so fuck what you bitch sisters say, Iris married a fucking human, Lila married a bargained human. You are much better off I think. I'll call him."

She shrugged. "They've always ganged up on me D, I was the favorite and groomed to be queen. They'll use anything they can to get at me... I 'm just fed up being alone."

"Fuck them. Murphy is a good guy, and he's actually a demon. Neither of them can say that."

"It's not like I haven't had both their husbands. Lila's only married her because he thought she'd be queen... I can handle them both; it's not about that. I've never cared about Murphy being a Strigo. Time demons are very powerful despite the biases of the other courts."

He knew that. Strigo were probably the most powerful of all the Afterverse races, their power over time unheard of. Murphy was probably the most powerful to come out of that corner of the Afterverse in an age, and the fact that he was still unmarried and kept to himself spoke of the general distrust the other houses had for the Strigo. They looked on them as lower because, he believed, they were afraid of them. "This is true. So shall I have him call on you?"

"Please." She nodded a small smile gracing her face. "Thank you Dimitri."

"No thanks needed Fiona." He went to her and caressed her cheek. "You know I care about you a great deal. I do wanna see you happy, and I know I can't personally give you that."

"I know D." She hugged him tightly.

He kissed her sweetly on the lips. "Expect a call princess."

"I will, tell Cole I said hi. The two of you are good for each other."

He grinned. "I like to think so. Good luck darlin. We will see you soon." He blinked out and sighed; materializing back in the apartment he shared with Cole.

With that out of the way, all he had to do was get at Murphy, and the whole thing would be taken care of. He gave himself a pat on the back, it had gone much better then he hoped. Cash would be proud and he would be happy, one less thing he would have to deal with come his reentry.

Twenty

The building was beyond enormous. *Figured he would find a sorceress with the means to keep him in a grand lifestyle.* Sekhmet stood on the steps of the mansion looking it over once again. The building was old and held power, and it was right on a line. The woman Casha called his sorceress has smarts that was for damn sure. Jolie had said he had chosen well but it took seeing the opulence he lived in to make the Arcuo queen agree with Cash's mother.

Now to meet the Sorceress herself... She rang the bell and stood back waiting for the door to be answered. The woman that opened the door was short, sexy and lush and radiated power, both the warmth of her goddess and the frigid cold of the Conglacio. She was very powerful, like Cash's old sorceress Natalia, but with none of the hard and backbiting ambition. Sekhmet, or Sookie as she preferred to be called smiled at the woman in front of her.

"Good Evening, Astrid is it? I was hoping you could help me. I'm looking for Cassiel."

The woman eyed her up, no doubt feeling the power that Sookie was throwing off. "And you are?" she asked warmly, her wariness slipping.

"Sookie dear, or rather Sekhmet. I'm the Arcuo queen."

The girl bowed and smiled. "Welcome then. I have to be careful you know. Few know he's here. Please come in. He's upstairs. If you will wait in the kitchen, I'll get him." She showed her into the large chef's style kitchen and left seconds later through another door. Seeing Cassiel for the first time in almost thirteen years was going to be tough, but it had to be done. Things were now set in motion that only his help and the help of the powerful little witch he bound himself to, could bring to fruition. Telling him what she had to tell him was going to be very hard indeed, especially when he realized what it meant.

Cash padded barefoot into the kitchen his hair tousled and a scowl on his face. It lightened as soon as he saw Sookie and he flashed her a dazzling smile. "Aunt Sookie! It is you..." He moved to her kissing her cheek. "How have you been?"

She grinned. He looked amazingly well for a demon that had been exiled for the past decade and some. She returned his kiss and hugged him. "I am ever well my darling boy. How are you? Life with the witch seems to be agreeing with you."

"Indeed things have been going very well. How is Alex?"

"He's doing well, enjoying the sunshine in California, playing the hero and all. Enjoys it too much I think."

He smirked at her. "Ah well he always did know just the right side of the line to play on."

"You may be right. So tell me love, how is Faris faring? Rudolph is waiting to see you both."

"Faris is well enough. It's just a matter of finding time to get down to see Rudolph. Things need to calm down a little before it's safe enough to go... we can't have Fuerety getting his hands on her."

"I understand that. It's one of the reasons why I'm here. I could have him meet her here or at the office in the city. You guys can blink right in and out. No one will know you're there."

He grinned at her, "That would work very well, thanks Sookie... you always know just how to brighten up my day."

"I want to make things easier for the two of you. We can't have her having any stress."

"Or any more stress, she seems to be in good spirits though. I could call her if you like?"

"No, not just yet love. You're the reason I'm here actually. I have some things I need to tell you. Maybe we should sit. Do you have coffee?"

"Somewhere I'm sure." He moved around the counter rummaging through the cupboards until he found the coffee. "I rarely drink it." He smiled apologetically.

"Never mind then love. Perhaps wine?" she asked hopefully.

"Now wine I have, not to mention know where it is. Red or white?"

"Red... something dry."

"I have the perfect one," he took two glasses taking a bottle and filling them. "Now what can I help you with?" he asked passing her the glass.

"It's actually what I can help you with darling. It's about Jolie."

He paused, pain flashing over his face at the sound of his mother's name. "Oh?"

"Tell me Casha, do you miss her?"

"Of course I do, she was my mother. When she died everything stopped, but that's life, we just have to pick up the pieces and move on. It's Dimitri I feel for, he barely knew her."

"I understand. So if you could bring her back, would you?"

He frowned at her. "I would but it couldn't be done. I looked into it and it would be a cold day in the fire plains before I believe that my father had never tried."

"Your father didn't have the resources... and the knowledge." she said quietly.

"And...?"

"And you do."

"Do I?"

"Yes, now you do love. Astrid is the missing piece of the puzzle."

"Oh Astrid can bring my mother back from the dead," he said his voice laced with sarcasm.

"No, not by herself she can't. See, there are things that needed to fall into place Cash. Your mother isn't truly dead; or rather she isn't somewhere where we cannot reach her. She isn't in the Dreamverse, not really, she's more in the borderlands, what the Christians call purgatory, but not all cruel and everything. It's hard to explain."

"I'm getting that." He took the wine out of her hand setting it down on the counter. "I think maybe you should lay off alcohol Aunt Sookie. I know you took her death hard too, but she's gone."

"Cash, your mother's time in the borderlands is almost over. She has a choice to come back or to move on. Everything is in the right place for her to return, especially now that you have the crown." She hadn't told him she knew, but Jolie had told her in their communing, before she left for the mansion. It was her bargaining chip.

"Crown?"

"I should have addressed you as such when you walked in. I know Cassiel. I know what Levi did, not three days ago."

"And you know because... it's common knowledge? Or because my dead mother told you? Because Sookie, I have to tell you right now, this isn't how I expected this conversation to go."

"You actually expected to have this conversation?" she sighed.

"Honestly? No...I couldn't have predicted this."

"Look Cash, I know what the woman meant to you, to all of you. She can come home now, and she can, but she needs your help."

He sighed heavily. "Doesn't everyone these days?"

"You know Cash, never mind. I'll tell her you don't want her back. It's fine. You know, I was told to come to you, because you above all missed her the most. I'm sorry to have bothered you Highness." She stood. "Please convey my heartfelt congratulations to the princess," she sighed and turned to go.

"Look Sookie..." He sighed again. "Don't leave. You have to realize how this sounds."

"I do. Better then you do as a matter of fact. You don't want to believe it's possible. And that's okay."

"No. I don't want to let myself hope that it's a possibility only to have the whole thing shot down. I lost her once and if it wasn't for Dimitri it would have ended me."

"It's not easy Cash... but it can be done." She shook her head. "Look, you want proof right?"

"I do..." He answered carefully.

"Well there's only one way I know."

"And that is?"

"It's called dead speak. It's when the voices of those who are waiting speak through electrical equipment. Something like that white noise phenomenon."

"Didn't that film go horribly wrong? I think I remember everyone dying at the end..." he said with a half smile.

"I have no idea. All I know is the humans have figured out dead speak to a fault, but I know very well how to use it. I could show you."

"Uh huh..." He nodded frowning. "Sookie, exactly how long have you been able to communicate with the dead?"

She frowned. "Cash my name isn't Sekhmet for kicks you know. Times change, and so does the communication."

"Oh... well that makes sense. Have you ever talked to Faris's mother? Is she still hanging in there?"

"Lillith isn't on the same plane. She was worshipped, and allowed continual worship in her non-corporeal state. I cannot reach her," she smirked. "Though Jolie could."

"Really?" He smiled, "Well that is something I'll have to talk with her about... how exactly is it that I would go about doing that?"

She smiled. "Do you have an external microphone here? And headphones to attach to a computer?"

"I might, but it's not going to be here in the kitchen."

"Obviously. There's an IP address," she said writing down the address. "It's set up by someone who apparently knows what it is. There's a button, like a play button in the center of the page. Click it. You'll hear static. Then speak into the Mic. She will answer."

He nodded. "Ok... though I know I may be the recently crowned king of the Conglacio demons but this conversation has to have been one of the most disturbing ones I've ever had and I've seen someone throw a live werewolf into a furnace. I have shivers. I don't think I'll ever look at you as my fun Aunt Sookie ever again."

She smiled and walked to him embracing him. "I'm still fun aunt Sookie love, I always will be. This is important though. She should be able to explain it better than I can. Contact her. And when you're ready, contact me. I'll be waiting to help with the preparations, should you decide to do what she asks." She kissed him on the cheek. "I love you Cassiel, like you were my own blood. Trust me okay?"

"I do." He smiled weakly at her. "But you've been hiding my mom from me... From Dimitri."

"No, not really. There're reasons why I have only come to you now, but it is better to let her explain them herself darling. Look Levi doesn't know that I know of. She wanted first contact to be with you." She smiled and a tear ran down her face. "She's so proud of you."

"She should be," He grinned at her wiping the tear away with his thumb. "I turned out great. I was always the good one you know."

She smirked. "Sure you were love. I must go. You decide what you will do okay? Speak to your mother. Time is running out and you need her more then ever now." She turned from him and blew him a kiss, then blinked from the house back to her palace in the Afterverse.

He wasn't convinced, but if Cash was anything, he was curious. He would do as she said, and he would speak to his mother for the first time in over three hundred years.

Sookie smiled to herself and turned from her throne room to the hallway that led to her office and war room. She had a lot to do if she was to help with what was to come.

Twenty-one

Cash was scared. The possibilities of Sookie's words terrified him. In his youth he would have done anything to get his mother back. Now things were different. Things were complicated. He had more in his life than just Dimitri. He had the child and Faris. He couldn't afford to do anything that would put them or his kingship in danger.

Then there was the possibility that she, like him, blamed him for her death. Levi had played a strong part in it as well but deep down Cash had always known that if he had treated the bastard as he treated Dimitri then Jeanette would never have had cause to call the duel.

Cash had always despised duels and his father for allowing his concubines to have one. That day was the one Cash had repressed more than anything. He envied Dimitri for being so young because no matter how hard he tried; the day would never leave him. The day he really grew up, the day he'd had to.

He'd sworn as his mother lay dying that he'd flat out destroy anyone that had taken part in the duel, even those that had supported the whore that had ended his life.

Destroy them as they had him. So as she died in Levi's arms and as Dimitri cried silently in his he began to plot.

He supposed he really should have thanked Jeanette for making him the cold, calculating, heartless fuck that he was. Before Jolie's death he'd been considering living topside with a family of humans he'd grown acquainted with. He'd been spoiled and soft, more concerned with childish rebellion and human rights than any real demonic activity. Oh how he'd changed.

With his mother dead, revenge consumed him. He channeled it well plotting silently as he looked after Dimitri and his father's court. There was no sense in rushing things. That never boded well, only to take the time and learn his enemies. To start with, his list was short, numbering only Jeanette herself and his half brother Gabriel. That was until he dug deeper. Jeanette had been pushed into challenging his mother, pushed by Gabriel, who in turn was puppeted by the Overlord himself, Feurety.

This left him with something of a new challenge, something that was worthy of his skills. There had always been friction between the ice court and that of the fire. Feurety was well known in his extreme distaste of the Conglacio. The king had hoped to destroy them passively. Eliminating his mother quite effectively destroyed his father. If Cash hadn't been the man he was it would have been simple for Feurety to gain control of their court through Gabriel. Thankfully Cash stepped up to run the court with the much needed help of Oscar.

He hadn't quite been ready to take the Afterverse by force though. He still wasn't sure if he was. Yet at that time he had a promise to fulfill so he learned all he could. Made alliances and pushed buttons from the inside. Feurety welcomed him into his court and confidence with open arms. Just as Cash had suspected, the old demon sought to use him to influence the Conglacio court and Cash was never one to let that illusion fail. Until Faris.

Faris complicated things. It was a habit that she'd picked up along the way. He loved her dearly but he could have had his revenge by now. He had it set up and he was taking his time waiting for the perfect moment. He wanted Feurety in pieces.

Lilith had been easy to turn against him, her vanity making her the perfect target to set herself up for worship by humans. It only took a nudge and surely nothing that he'd ever take any real credit for, especially around Faris. She'd had to grow up without truly knowing her mother much like Dimitri had. It was sad but necessary from a tactical point of view. Fuerety, due to his own laws, had to publicly execute his own wife. It was almost poetic, but not nearly enough for Cash. He'd made Fuerety feel pain and he'd liked it.

Faris had, rightly so, blamed her father for killing her mother. It turned her from him as Cash had turned from Levi. It gave them something else in common. He wanted it made perfectly clear if only to himself that Faris had never been a part of his revenge. Though he knew it killed the fire king that they fell for each other. He'd toyed briefly with the idea of seducing her but had quickly dismissed it as distasteful. He'd decided that he'd show mercy and leave her out of everything reasoning that he could always deal with her later if she took offense to her father's obliteration. Imagine his surprise when she seduced him.

So he waited, as always, biding his time and making friends, being everyone's friend. They all loved him and he was good at manipulating them. Doing favors and gaining them in return. It was hard work. All up until that fateful day when an eight year old Dutch girl summoned him...

Summoned him! The audacity of it all. Summoning a demon is a complex ritual one which even the highly trained witched could rarely do. First you needed a name and a spell and for that you needed a very special book. Centuries ago witch families would ally themselves with demons. The outcome was always highly profitable for both demons and witches. Demons got souls and the witches gathered power. Some great families would gather up the summoning spells of hundreds of demons over the years.

The Romanov family happened to be one such a family. Their collection of spells and powers were well known throughout all the verses. Legend had it that they had allied themselves with more than just demons. That was all hearsay though so he didn't put much stock in that. The family books were kept strictly in the family bound by magic to follow the closest family member with the gift. Of course everyone knows of the Romanov's fate at the hands of the mysterious Grigori Rasputin.

So imagine his surprise when he was summoned into the disgustingly pink bedroom by a little Dutch girl with the ancient book in her hand. The book that had a summoning spell for Fuerety, the book that, if he'd played his cards right, would have spelled out the end of Fuerety's reign in the Afterverse. Unfortunately Faris fell pregnant and Fuerety couldn't allow that. The child died and Cash was forced to play his hand ahead of schedule.

The rest was history, an unpleasant history. Yet he'd survived, both he and Faris had and Cash was almost certain that they were stronger for it. Even Cole had learned her lesson though she'd never gotten the spell book back. Cash had assumed that Fuerety had kept it, though not knowing much witch magic he'd barely be able to use it.

Rushing into things wasn't Cash's style, it never ended well. So as he sat in his locked office in front of his computer he began to get cold feet. As bad as it sounded, his whole life had started when he'd lost his mother. What would it mean if he suddenly had her back? Would she blame him? Sookie had said she was proud of him, but proud how? He wasn't the son she'd left. He wasn't exactly ashamed of how he'd turned out. It wasn't like he was bad at what he did, he just wasn't the perfect son. Or the man he'd hoped to be. Dimitri was, though and he deserved to know his mother, in the end it all boiled down to that...and possibly Cash's own curiosity.

He sighed powering up the computer and plugging in the headset. He double checked the door knowing for a fact that if Nightly got wind of what he was doing he'd never hear the end of it. He typed in the address that Sookie had given him waiting to click the sign on the center of the screen.

It came up and he took a deep breath. He took off the headset, stood and moved across the room. *Fuck if I'm doing this sober.* Pouring himself a scotch he downed it in one, pouring another to take back to the computer. He took the bottle with him. He sat again gingerly putting the head set back on. He clicked the screen. "Hello?"

Static crackled through the headphones for a moment, as if he were speaking through a walkie talkie. It was as it died that he heard the faint lyrical voice. "I was wondering when you would get up the nerve to do this," it said and sighed, "Hello my darling."

He jerked back from the computer. "Mom?" his voice cracked, his throat suddenly going very dry. It was her voice; he hadn't heard it in so long.

"Yes... It's good to hear your voice darling," she said quietly.

"It is you..." He took a gulp of scotch. "My god...Dimitri's going to think I've gone insane...have I?" he asked the screen.

"No, not that I know of. And Dimitri won't think anything of the sort," she chuckled. "How are you? I have been watching, and congratulations are in order. A child, and king, and a powerful sorceress, you're doing well for yourself Cassiel."

"I try my best." He breathed a sigh of relief, unsure of the emotions flooding through him. "How are you? I've missed you... we all have." His chest tightened, he'd missed her so much. He was actually talking to her, his mother. A single tear slid down his cheek and he quickly wiped it away.

"I'm existing. And I miss you all so much. I watch you all, that's usually all that's open to me to do. I'm sorry about what happened thirteen years ago Cassiel. I saw it all, and my heart went out to you, and to Faris. You did what you thought was right though, and I'm proud of you," she sniffed. "I have always been proud of you."

"I'm not the boy you left, mom." He sighed.

"No, you're not. You're a man, and a better one I didn't think there could ever be my love."

He smiled feeling better, his mom always knew just what to say. "There's Dimitri too, he grew up just fine."

"Dimitri... "She chuckled. "My brave Dimitri. I know. You raised him well love, and I'm proud of him as well. I'm proud of all my children. But you, you're my first, and therefore always my favorite. Tell me about you and Faris, and this sorceress."

"Thanks mom." He knew he was grinning stupidly but he couldn't help it. He was talking to his mother; her voice just filled him with so much excitement. It was like being a kid again. "What do you want to know? You said you've been watching."

"I don't watch you all the time love. I do give you all your privacy. Tell me about the sorceress first..."

"Astrid? She's a great asset. Powerful, loyal and with her comes Fallon. Fallon's a little bit whiny but, given current events, I think he's going to be a worthwhile investment. Plus Faris loves Asty which is always one less thing to worry about."

"Very true. I never liked Natalia. Girl wasn't right for you. Astrid is, and it's a bonus she and Faris get on. She's a sad thing though... I have watched her since you have been at the mansion, and she seems so sad."

Cash growled softly at the mention of his old sorceress's name. Natalia had served her purpose and, despite Faris' and apparently now his mother's extreme dislike of her, she wasn't necessarily a bad person. Cash and she had been good together, they'd connected. He wouldn't have been able to bind her otherwise. The fact that he'd been sworn to protect her then tricked into letting her die was something that still wounded him deeply. He sighed looking up at the roof; he really didn't want to discuss Natalia right now. Or ever. It took him a second before he could respond to his mother's comment. "Astrid is sad mom. She's had a shitty run of things."

"How so? She's beautiful, sexy, wealthy, she has you and her lover... and that smelly monster that roams the house..."

"She's an orphan, her parents died in a boating accident, unhelpful people that they were. She rejected her god and turned to worshiping Lillith... I think you can guess how that ended."

Jolie gasped. "It couldn't have ended well, poor child. What did Lillith do to her?"

"Forced her to kill two children, unbeknownst to her that they were her cousin's. Poor Spinner has never quite recovered but loves her cousin enough to never tell. Astrid served Lillith for a while before breaking off from her. Lillith, unpleased, cursed her... she'll never have children," he said quietly. "She'd be a very good mother."

"She had no right to do that... none. She was always a spoiled cow, but this is horrible," she said softly. "Something needs to be done about that."

"Can it? I know, for personal, I'd like to make sure that Lillith stays gone permanently. However if Astrid's curse can be undone I'd stand to make a whole lot more from the deal, especially if my hunch about Fallon is correct."

"Hunch? Well it is possible..." she said quietly.

"Possible how?"

"It's complicated, but it is doable. Did Sookie mention anything to you about..." she trailed off, sighing. "It can be done... but it would need to be part of the proactive work to bring me home."

"Ah..." He smiled glad that she'd dropped her original question about Fallon. "And how exactly do we go about bringing you back? Because I do want that, you back here...with us. My kid needs at least one grandparent."

"Your child will have your father regardless, but yes, it's complicated," she chuckled. "Dying is so easy. It's bringing the dead back that's the bitch. Your witch will have to be involved, and you, your father and Dimitri... and..." she trailed off dropping her train of thought. "And that traitorous bitch too."

"We'll get her, Levi didn't kill her. Course her whereabouts are a little iffy, last I heard he'd had her imprisoned out on the fire plains. We'll get her though." He took a deep breath. "I don't expect it to be easy, or else people would do it more often. Astrid would help whether the curse was removed or not but she'd do anything to have it removed. I'd rather my child's grandparent be you... Levi's not exactly with it recently, despite him finally making a brilliant decision."

"Your father will be fine once I'm home. Though I don't know what he shall do with the sweet girl he's kept... She's a joy that one," she chuckled. "And I can take care of Lillith, but it has to be part of the bargain. Nothing in the cosmos is for free Cassiel."

"Mother that's practically my ethos, I think I'm perfectly capable of working a suitable bargain. Telling me how is like teaching my gran to suck eggs..." He frowned. "Did my gran suck eggs? Does anyone's?" He shook his head forcefully. "Never mind it's a horrid saying and I promise never to use it again. The point is that I can make a bargain and I'll deal with Thisbe when the time comes. So don't worry about either one."

She laughed, a light tinkling sound. "Cassiel you misunderstood me my darling. I like Thisbe, she's kept your father from skirting over the edge for a while now and she's kept him somewhat sane. I have a lot to thank her for. Your father is the love of my life Cassiel. My little icicle, there's going to be a lot of surprises with this, and it's going to take a lot of power..."

He raised an eyebrow, "Icicle? You have to stop that right there; you can't come back and starts calling me baby names. It's not proper now I'm king. I'm not going to kill Thisbe I'm just going to keep her happy and out of the way. Or out of the way until I can think of someone to keep her happy with. As for power... I have my fair share."

"Yes love, I know you're a big bad demon. But what I mean, is Astrid in good standing with a Goddess, and if so what's her power set? This is important Cassiel... And I'm your mother; I can call you anything I want. You used to like being called my little icicle."

"I used to want to be a farmer and be married to a plump little French wife. I used to care when a human died. I used to beg for their lives. I used to be a lot of things mom but no longer. Thankfully I grew out of all that and I'd appreciate it if you didn't call me embarrassing pet names." He growled "At least in front of anyone who'll make me suffer for it."

"Deal on the last part," she giggled. "So? About the witch?"

"She's in very good standing with her goddess, who is Ishtar."

"Really? How is it you swindled her as your sorceress?"

"I'm just that good," he smirked at the screen.

"I'll just bet. So if she is with Ishtar, the goddess isn't upset about the power drains from her when she attends you? She doesn't mind that she is partly yours? You got a good deal love."

"Astrid's never mentioned it, if anything, she's said that Ishtar likes me... or maybe that was Fallon. Either way the goddess must know that I'm good for her."

Jolie chuckled again. "So what's her power set, I mean how does she gain the favor of her goddess?"

"It's physical. She needs to..." he trailed off not particularly comfortable discussing sex with his mother. "She gains and replenishes power through sex."

"Leave it to you. Well then it was as I figured. Before the ritual, you will need to pull another binding on her, and she will have to be with her lover as well. She will need the power."

"I don't see much of a problem with that, it's prying her off of Fallon that's normally the problem."

"It would work best if both sessions were close to each other. Say by hours... or if it was done together would be ideal, but I don't really want to know the details of your sordid sex life. After that, the ritual must be done soon after, again hours count. We only have one shot at this, and it's in three weeks time."

"That can all be arranged... not the with Fallon part. I can barely be in the same room with him let alone the same..." He cleared his throat. "So hours apart is good. Does it have to be three weeks? Sookie mentioned that you had your reasons for waiting this long to come forward... what exactly would that be?""

"The veil between the worlds thins considerably in three weeks, enough for soul transference, so yes, we must wait in order for it to be effective, and for the body to be transformed. I had to wait because all dimensions have rules. I was killed, and it was before my due time. The fates don't take kindly to that, so they put me here. I had a penance to work off my soul, to prove the love for your father and my children was real, and that I wouldn't make the same mistake twice. It's almost done, my penance, and if I can bridge the gap to that plane, well I can go home. If not, then I must move on."

"Penance?" he asked not liking the sound of it.

"Yes. Penance."

"Which was?"

"Why do you have a hunch about Fallon?" she asked slyly. "A secret for a secret."

"I'd love to mother, but it's a theory unconfirmed. A working theory if you will. It's loosely based about what I've pieced together about Snow and what I have on him. It seems to fit but I'll need Ammit to confirm my suspicions. When I have them you'll be the first to know."

"Okay love."

"And your penance?"

"A night's infidelity."

He felt his eyes widen, "Really? With who? Before you died? Was I born? Does Levi know?"

She sighed. "Questions answered in order are yes, a noble, yes, I can't very well have congress like this with the living, yes you were born and yes, you think your father would have gone to Jeanette if we didn't want a play night?"

"Huh..." He sat back stunned at what she'd just told him, shocked even. The seconds ticked by as he poured himself another drink deep in thought. "Gabriel. That was the night he was conceived. The bastard."

"Yes... One night, and a lot of regrets, at least on your father's end. If he hadn't of been born..."

"No wonder he went mad... and all for a night of fun. Nothing in any of the verses is for free... you left while she was pregnant, couldn't stand the sight of him looking after her."

"No... I left for other reasons..." she coughed. "This might not be the best time."

"Reasons? He sent you away?"

"No, Your father would never send me away, for any reason. I was pregnant too." She sighed.

Cash chocked violently on scotch he'd been sipping sputtering it everywhere. "You what?"

"Look it doesn't matter love..."

"What? Why not? Why don't I know about this?"

"Because it doesn't matter Cassiel." She sighed once again.

"Cassiel? What happened to icicle? Look mom I have to know...is there some other bastard running around? Another Gabriel? God it's not Bethany is it?"

"No, and it wouldn't be that lunatic either. I had enough sense to stay far away from the Celo even before I was gifted to your father."

"So what happened?" Suddenly it all made sense and his heart fell. Her hesitation and why he'd never heard about this before. "Did you lose the baby? Oh mom I'm sorry... I... I know you were upset when you came back, I just put it down to Gabriel."

"Don't worry about it love... Okay? And please don't tell Dimitri. Or your father that I told you."

He nodded solemnly feeling bad to have forced the tale from her. "Of course, they won't here anything from me."

"That's my boy. So you have some work ahead of you... and I have to enter the dream realm to see your father."

"I really don't want the details of that mom."

"And I won't be giving them to you. If you see your father tomorrow you'll know why love."

He blinked groaning. "I don't actually have to see him tomorrow, do I?"

"Cassiel, Your father and you might have your issues, but I will not come back to a family divided."

"Divided? Who said anything about division, I love old Levi," he said with as much enthusiasm as he could manage, which wasn't much.

"Cassiel..." she warned. "I might be incorporeal but I know the score."

"Then you should know that he started it. The man's a waste of time and space. He was never there for us and even before you died he was never all that good...you could do better. You know I'm king now, there's nothing to say that you have to go back to him, he has his bit of fluff. Tell me what do you think of Amos? He should be a wonderful lover and he's a good man." He frowned, thinking better of it. "Well maybe not so much and Cam's always a bitch... how about that nobleman...what was his name?" He fished gently; Cash was nothing if not opportunistic.

"Your father is the only one I have ever wanted Cassiel. He gave me you, and Dimitri... and I love him. I want to go back to him... I need him."

"I don't like him... not that it matters if he makes you happy, you won't hear me complain...much."

"I better not. He's my husband and your father and Cassiel... I will have order in my family."

"Yes mom," he answered out of old habit, suitably chastised.

"I do miss hearing you call me that. So love? Three weeks? Can you arrange it?"

"I can, I trust that once I make a bargain I'll be able to introduce Astrid and Sookie and let them work out the mechanics?"

"Yes. Sookie has the spell book, stole it a long time ago from the library in Alexandria. Alexander and his boys didn't need the knowledge of life and death. Astrid should be able to procure everything and your father, well he will get Jeanette, I'll make sure of it."

"And so everything will fall into place."

"Indeed my darling. You go and speak to your princess, and your sorceress. If you wish to reach me again..." she snickered. "You know how. Just not till tomorrow ok?"

"I have no intensions of interrupting anything mother. My mind has been through enough these past few years."

"Darling. It will be good to hold you again, and to see you face to face. You relax, Okay? Rest up... We will be together soon my little icicle."

"Not that name again," he groaned then paused hesitating on his last words. Loathe as he was to end the conversation he was drained both physically and mentally. He didn't want to lose her again. "Speaking face to face will be worth waiting for. I love you mother."

"I love you Cassiel. My dashing and wonderful first born. You need me; you know how to reach me. Sleep well darling, and hug that princess of yours for me will you?

"I will indeed. Good night mom." He signed off removing the headset. Tonight had certainly been one of interest. He had a lot to think about. Shutting his eyes he sat back in his chair. Bringing back the dead... He sighed deeply draining his scotch. It was quite a task that he had set upon him, one of many and nothing that he couldn't handle. He would have to talk to Faris about this and Dimitri would think he was crazy. Perhaps he was. He felt sleep tug at him and had to force his eyes open. Falling asleep in his office would only serve to piss Faris off. He'd have a good night's sleep and in the morning everything would make more sense. He laughed shaking his head as he left the room heading up to bed, like things were ever going to be simple ever again.

Twenty-two

Faris lifted her head from the pillow as she heard the door open. Opening her eyes, she saw Cash and gave him a sleepy smile. She was alone in the bed, only recently vacated by Cash's sweet sorceress. They had cuddled and talked about the child, and Faris saw the envy in Astrid's eyes. When she had asked Astrid why she couldn't have them, and Astrid told her the story, she was dumbfounded. To think her mother's exile had twisted her into such a bitter and evil soul...

She knew what her mother had become, and why her father had banished her, but she had never known the extent of it all. Now that she did, saw how badly it affected someone that she was growing quite fond of, she wanted no part of her mother.

There was a time when she had missed her mother, had wished desperately to have her back in her life, but not anymore. No, the twisted evil bitch could rot in whatever nether world she was in for being such a petty bitch.

She smiled as Cash craned his neck to see over her lounging frame and shook her head.

"You just missed her. Fallon showed up and Linus led him here to her. She left in a flurry of kisses and growls, and they weren't coming from Fallon. That dog is insane."

Grinning she sat up, still in her pale blue frock and looked at him as he turned on the light. He looked a little pale and it worried her. "So what did Sookie say?" when he gave her a quizzical look she smiled. "I pried it outta Asty when you left. Everything ok?" she asked and patted the bed next to her. "I'm lonely and you look like shit."

"I feel like shit." He sighed collapsing into bed next to her.

Well, that isn't good. What happened?" she cuddled to him and ran her fingers down his far arm, letting the heat seep slowly into his skin.

"I really don't know..." He relaxed into her touch letting his head fall on her pillow. "I think I just need to sleep on it, let things work themselves out."

"See now that bothers me. You're never one to just..." she shrugged.

"Just what?" he sighed. "Faris, it's been a long day... for both of us but that last conversation really stretched the limits of what I consider normal. I'd rather not talk about it. How was Astrid?"

"Poor girl. She's envious I think... It hurts her she can't give life, but more so that she can't give Fallon a proper family. She will be ok though, I think."

"I think so too, I may have found a way around it."

"Oh? How would you manage that love? I mean I know you're powerful, but breaking a curse of a goddess on another plane... hard to say the least."

"You don't think I'm just that good?"

"I think you, like all of us, have limits... and no amount of souls you have is going to change that you don't have a godhead."

"Very true but I do have my fingers in a lot of pies so to speak." He sighed deeply running his hand along her side. "Truthfully this one blindsided me."

"So tell me love," she snuggled closer to him and nuzzled his neck breathing in his clean and crisp scent that was uniquely Casha. She loved that he smelled like the crispest snowy day, and while as a Cento the scent should repel her, she found it a most intoxicating aphrodisiac.

"Promise that you won't think I'm crazy?"

"Casha when have I ever thought you were crazy? When you brought little Cole home? When you tried for the throne? Never."

"I hid Cole from you and I didn't exactly talk much to you after I tried for the throne. What I'm about to tell you is insane. If you told me the same thing I'd... well I'd think you were pretty far gone."

"Casha, you have survived on this plane for thirteen years with a minimal amount of souls... and you're still you. So tell me love."

He frowned at her taking a deep steadying breath. "I was just talking to my mother."

She gaped at him. "Your mum? Like Jolie? Really? How the hell did you manage that?"

He winced shutting his eyes as if not wanting to see her reaction. "Through the internet."

"Well shit. That's..." she shrugged. "Who told you how to do this?" she asked carefully.

"Sookie... she made me really."

"Well leave it to Sookie to get all mystical with technology. So what happened?"

"We talked." He lay back on the bed his eyes still shut. "She wants to come back. Reckons that she can..."

"Really? Is that really possible?" she held him, aware of the fact that he needed comfort, and her acceptance. If he said he spoke to Jolie, he did. She wouldn't nay say him. Stranger things had happened.

"Apparently so, I need to talk with Astrid in the morning. She'll be the one doing the spell and in return she'll get the gift of life and in return I'll get the family line and our baby will have a very powerful line of witches... or more."

"Well that works out doesn't it? What do you mean by more love?" she asked and rubbed his shoulder idly.

"I have a theory about Fallon and Snow, and no, I can't tell you. Not until I've spoken with Ammit. And if we have a little girl and they have a little boy I'm sure we could manage to demon him up a little for her. It would be a good match; if anything Fallon and Snow are ruthless. They make good advising counsel, no reason to expect their children to be any less."

"That's true. And Astrid is very powerful, so either way it should work out for the better. I trust you Cash, so you don't need to tell me everything."

"When I know love you'll be the first to know. Unless of course my dead mother's hovering over me watching... which is a whole new level of unsettling."

She laughed. "Ah but she won't be dead then will she? You think Astrid could really do it?"

"I think if anyone can it'll be her. I didn't choose her for her cooking abilities, though they are excellent."

"Indeed. Though Feyd surpasses her in the baking department."

"He's an enigma as well. At least life's never dull with the friends we make." His hand moved to her belly gently cupping it, the cool from his hand seeping though into her.

She purred, enjoying the feel of his ice permeating her skin. "Umm that feels good. You know when the babe is agitated this is going to help a lot..."

"It likes the cold. Can't blame it really. Sookie said that she'd arrange for Rudolf to visit us."

"Oh wonderful. I was meaning to get around to it. And of course it likes the cold. I might be a cento, but its still part of you." She sighed, "But you're right in the friends department. You have some strong and interesting friends and allies. You chose well with this lot Cashy."

"I always choose my friends carefully, Princess."

"I do agree. So a meeting with Rudolph... What do you think it will be?"

"It doesn't matter to me. A son would be great, but I'd adore a little princess. I'll just take what we get."

"I agree. As long as it's healthy." She smiled at him. "Thank you."

"Why thank me?" he grinned at her. "I haven't done anything that I'm aware of"

"You brought me here, took me back. You didn't have to Cash." And she meant it. If he didn't want her and didn't come for her when she let slip that she was pregnant again, she would have hidden on her own. But as it was, he did want her and they were going to be the family they wanted thirteen years before. It was fitting, somehow, that they were both stronger then they had ever been now, and that they had a chance to make things right.

"I won't ever say it much but... I love you Faris. I couldn't have done anything else. These past few years apart only served to prove just how much I need you. When I thought that you hadn't fought... hadn't once tried to come and see me.... It put me in a bad way," he admitted. "It drove me deeper thinking that there you were in the Afterverse not caring, not needing me. It killed, unnecessary paranoia brought on by no souls and a vampire for company. You have no idea how I felt when you said that you still wanted me, that you needed me. You had every right to turn away from me Faris. I wasn't exactly very good to you. One could take the view that I brought all of this on myself."

His admission was a bombshell. She was stunned, but more so, the love she felt amplified. Casha had never told her he loved her, not really even though she knew he did. It wasn't him, and she never pried it out of him, never pushed. Hearing it though, it made it all better, and everything they both suffered. "Casha, we all make choices we have to live with. You chose what you thought was best for us, and I never once really hated you for the games. Hell I played them too. You chose me," she fingered the ring on her finger. "And I never stopped wanting you or us. I love you too Cassiel, always have and I always will, no matter what happens."

"I know that now." He pulled her tighter against him cuddling her.

She sighed. "Come on, you have always known."

"I know, but having you back with me carrying our baby does firm up my suspicions somewhat. Nobody would have blamed you for walking away, especially when this is only going to end when either I or your father dies."

"Cassiel, my father isn't a good man. He's a selfish and despicable person, bent on making everyone as miserable as him. You are not going anywhere. And daddy's time has passed."

"I couldn't agree with you more. So when shall we set up our meeting with Rudolph?"

"Soon I think. I'd like to know what kind of baby clothes to buy and Astrid said she would love to do a nursery," she beamed. "You really did pick well with her Cash."

"I did indeed although she does have her bad qualities. Thankfully they don't outweigh the good. How about tomorrow?"

"Tomorrow night then? " she purred and slipped her hand under his shirt and caressed the tight planes of his stomach. "And what're her bad qualities? The woman is generous, beautiful, sexy, doesn't mind sharing, involved and thoughtful. She didn't have to spend an hour with me making out on the bed, but she did," she said nonchalantly.

"Very true, Princess. Something I would have loved to have witnessed."

She giggled. "And I'm sure you will... she's quite... well..." she blushed. "It's been a long time since I enjoyed something like that."

"Since Chastity. You two were always a sight to behold."

She blushed harder remembering her friend. "Yeah you did seem to enjoy watching more often then not. I wonder whatever happened to her? She was the only real human friend I ever had."

"I'm sure she'll turn up though she'd be quite an age by now. Maybe she's living happily ever after with Amaro."

The thought struck her as wrong. "No, no if she was I would have seen her. I hope she had a brilliant life though. She was wild and amazing."

"She was," he agreed.

She yawned, thoughts of herself and Chastity and Cash playing in her head. "Ummm I'll have to look her up," she said and closed her eyes. "Cashy I'm sleepy," she muttered and yawned again.

"I can tell that by the yawning and the eye shutting." He settled down next to her gathering her into his arms. "Sleep then, Princess," he whispered gently into her ear. "Tomorrow we'll talk to Rudolph and find out if we're having a little boy or girl. Goodnight love."

Twenty-three

Fallon and Linus had found Astrid snuggling with Faris and Fallon, after Linus had cuddled with her and Faris, had twirled the new pewter colored g-string she bought around his finger. She had then taken her leave of the princess, and Fallon had carried her to their room, murmuring about the bag of lingerie he had found on the bed when he returned back, and his favorite pieces, and what he wanted her to model as soon as they got back up to their third floor suite. A balconette bra still clothing her ample breasts was the remnants of the little fashion show, Fallon grabbing her when she finally put on the pewter g-string and bra, ripping the bottoms off and guiding her to ride him as he asked about her evening.

"Fallon, nothing happened with me and Faris... though no doubt Cash will be asking her the same questions. She needed some cuddling, and we talked. She's a dear."

She rode him slowly, arching as she did so and shut her eyes, reveling in the feeling of his hands sliding up her thighs, then one stopped and played on her clit, the other traveled north, to cup her material covered breast.

"If you want though, I'm sure it could," she teased.

Astrid giggled and bent down to nip Fallon's chest. Still astride his hips, his body nestled inside hers she reached back and squeezed his thighs. She was getting even more limber these days, what with both Cash and Fallon keeping her well satisfied. He groaned as she softly worried his flesh with her teeth and then reared up, her silk covered breasts skimming his chest. "I missed you cookie..." she murmured and then sobbed, arching as she came under the ministrations of his hands and body.

He chuckled kissing over her chest and thrusting deeper into her. "And you know I missed you vixen."

"So how's it going? I mean Georgie got any clue you guys are planning his demise?" she purred and closed her eyes.

"Not exactly what I want to talk about right now vixen," he growled rolling them over to grind her into the bed. "Tell me more about your cuddling with Faris."

She groaned. "Ummm I figured it would go back to that. Does it turn you on that we were all comfy in the bed, that she had her hands all over me?"

His body trembled over hers. "You could say that, where exactly did her soft warm hands go vixen... How did it feel?"

She kissed him, nibbled his bottom lip and squeezed his hips with her thighs, and dug her nails into his flanks. "Umm first just on my hip, we were spooning, but then she turned..." she moaned as he swiveled his hips.

He sped into her gripping her tighter as she spoke. "Turned vixen?"

"Umm she turned to face me.... and we talked... and kissed... she's a very good kisser Cookie." She arched and gasped. "And then her hands were on my sides and moved slowly and cupped my breast, and her thumbs teased me. Umm it was really good."

"Very good," he panted roughly in her ear as his hand moved to thumb her clit twisting it deliciously.

She cried out, enjoying the attention he was lavishing on her. "Faris is very sexy..." she whispered.

"Not as sexy as you vixen... the two of you are quite a sight to behold, though I wish that I'd gotten to behold more."

"I told you, I'm sure it can be arranged... after the baby of course..."

"Of course."

She wrapped her legs around his waist and shuddered. "Fuck... umm baby I'm close.... " she moaned and closed her eyes, letting her body go, feeling the fantastic fuzzy sensation she always got when Fallon brought her to the edge.

"Jesus Astrid!" he shouted grinding himself into her as he came spilling himself into her.

She followed him over the brink, and panted, her body and his slicked with sweat. "Christ Fallon..."

He rolled them, still panting, draping her on top of him. "Always a pleasure vixen."

"It better be Cookie... You're stuck with me till the end of time." She sighed and licked a bead of sweat off his chest. "She's really happy about being pregnant," she said quietly.

"It's a happy thing, from what I can gather."

"I would think so," she sighed again.

"And how exactly does it make you feel Vixen?" He asked her carefully. "Are you okay with this?"

"With Cash having his heir? I'm ecstatic for him and Faris. He should have been a daddy thirteen years ago. I'm saying it's well over due."

"I know, but with having a baby in the house... are you ok with that? I know you Astrid," he said using her real name instead of Vixen. "I know this has to hurt you. If it's too much then... we can have them leave, there are other places for them to go."

"I'd never make them leave Fal. Cash is my demon, and he's in trouble. So is Faris, and I love them both. They are part of the family Fal, the only family we have however dysfunctional. And you're right, it does hurt, but it's not the fact of knowing a child is in the house."

"I know..." he sighed.

"Fallon, seeing them both so happy because of it... and knowing it's something I can't give you... that's what hurts."

"Children aren't important to me Vixen. I don't even think I'd know what to do with one." He sighed again this time deeper. "It's not something we can change, I have you and that's all that matters."

"I know, and I have you, but I would like to give you a proper family. Neither of us really ever had that. And I have always said you would make a great daddy. It's my stupidity that put me in this position, and I accept it, but I really don't have to like it."

"I hate to see you in pain. Maybe there's a way around it, if it's a curse surely there's a way to end it? You know I'm not big with the witch-crap but there must be some kind of cure."

She gave a small, bitter laugh. "None that I have found, and believe me I have looked. I'm sorry to spoil the afterglow Cookie..."

"Not spoiled, this has been on your mind since you found out she was pregnant. Maybe Cash knows something or a way."

He cuddled her closer to him stroking her back reassuringly.

"Vixen you're all that matters to me, you know that, I had a family and it's not an experience I'd like to repeat. Alice... Snow even is the sanest out of all of us and she's pretty far gone. I like the family we have here."

She thought about their extended family, of Ashlyn, and Feyd, Casha, Faris, Arcady and Snow, even Spinner and Dimitri and Cole... It was if they had all found a place to belong, together. "I love our family too, but it would have been nice to have a little boy or girl, with your skin color and my eyes... Still, we do have Linus."

He chuckled. "We do and he loves us. I'm not saying kids wouldn't be nice and you're the only one I'd ever want them with but if it's not a possibility... Don't beat yourself up about it Vix. It was a mistake; we've all made them. Hell I'm banned from Thailand and I'm to be executed on sight in Budapest for stupid mistakes and who knows if I'm capable of it. I've been hit in the nuts enough times to be sterile," he joked lightly still cradling her.

"I highly doubt you're sterile cookie, not with your sex drive. And please, between you and Feyd and Arcady I think the states are the only free zone left to you guys," she giggled. "You always make me feel so much better."

"That's what I'm here for love."

"Too true. So you liked all the knickers I got?"

"They were very sexy... you know I love it when you dress up."

"And I love to dress up for you. Speaking of under things, unhook the bra... its comfy, but I'd much rather feel your skin against mine."

Grinning he obliged her unhooking the bra and helping her out of it. "I prefer this too." He smiled throwing the garment across the room.

"You just like undressing me," she giggled and looked up to him. "So tell me about Georgie. Feyd drive him to drink yet?"

"Not that I know of but we did get him into Pinky's looking for Ashlyn. Took him half an hour before he caught on. He's getting restless though and I'm sure Falwell's getting some interesting phone calls from him. Plus little Snow has her eye on him, which is disturbing. He's mine, if anyone kills him it's going to be me."

"I wouldn't expect anything less. You know, I think Arcady said something about the Incubus Court having access to a warehouse. When you decide to do it up you might wanna remember that. I don't think I can get bloodstains out of the basement grouting."

"Good thought, I'll talk to him, when the time comes."

"See? I'm always thinking. But we really need to figure that shit out. I would hate to spell fire him for coming snooping around."

"It would mess up the carpet."

"True, but carpet is easy to replace. I'm perfectly capable of defending myself but with Faris in such a delicate condition..." she trailed off.

"I know Vix, Georgie's being taken care of as is Falwell and I'm sure Faris is more than capable of taking care of herself as well."

"I know, but you know hormones and such. I'm happy Cash is here more often then not when you guys are out fucking George's day up."

"He'll keep you safe, Morrison and Snow as well. Plus Dimitri's pretty much just around the corner now. Things are about as safe as they can get here. I know I'd hate to have to break into the place." He stroked his thumb over her cheek. "It's going to be ok, and you shouldn't be like this Vixen, you're the brave one."

"I am. I do worry though."

"There's such a thing as worrying too much. Don't obsess on it love, your wards could stop a herd of stampeding elephants dead in their tracks."

She beamed with pride. "I know, I know. And you're right. So what's on your agenda tomorrow? Think you have time for breakfast?"

"Sure are you planning on cooking or should we get up just after Feyd does?"

"I was going to make Crepes... I miss Paris so I figured something French."

"French I can do," he chuckled kissing her, "As you very well know."

"Ummm you do French just about every night," she giggled and sighed, rubbing her nose against his. Their relationship was truly perfect, physically and emotionally. She relaxed fully against him and then bit the skin just about his nipple. "You wore me out cookie. You always do."

"Then we should get some sleep, you've got crepes to make tomorrow. They don't just make themselves you know."

"No they don't. If they did I wouldn't eat them," she grinned and kissed him sweetly. "Everything is going to work itself out, and I love you Fallon."

He kissed her back his heat seeping through into her. "I love you too Vixen. Always will."

Emotionally content and physically exhausted she squeezed him and shut her eyes. Fallon had a way of making things all better for her, and lying in their bed, with his scent surrounding them both made it abundantly clear that she really was where she needed to be. If the fates wanted something else for her, they would provide it. Snuggling, she closed her eyes, listening to Fallon's breathing become even as he drifted off. She smiled to herself and set off to join him.

Twenty-four

Sallos sighed wearily as he descended the stairs into the throne room. He was not looking forward to this conversation. The overlord of the Afterverse was well known for his ability to sniff out a lie. Sallos had always strived to be truthful with him. Lying to the king wasn't something an intelligent person did. All made worse by the fact that he was helping the Conglacio. The child would be Cento regardless of its father. He just had to keep reminding himself that.

The king was in his study immersed in a dusty old archaic text of some sort, a small brandy glass next to him. He'd always hated coming into this study ever since the first time when he was seventeen. He'd been covered in blood then, not all of it his. Tamsyn, his baby sister, had been hanging on him crying with their cousin Jocelyn standing just in front of him, her bright green eyes glaring defiantly. Towering over them stood Fuerety's hound a hulk of a Cento with the name of Blaze.

Sallos had no idea why the king had had his parents and uncle hunted down and killed but it had never really mattered. He was always grateful to him for sparing his and the girls' lives. Sallos had pledged allegiance to Fuerety that day, swore to become his hound and protector until death. It was a pledge he'd never broken. Not even when he saw the things Jocelyn had had to do to keep her end of that allegiance. In doing his part he kept Tamsyn safe from the madness hoping that she at least could lead a normal dignified life. Of course that all went to hell when she got herself pregnant by a human and died in childbirth.

Sallos knelt on the faded red carpet his eyes submissively on the floor.

"My lord," he announced himself trying to keep his thoughts to himself.

"Good news General?" Fuerety asked looking up at him.

Sallos kept his position on the ground not daring to look up. "No my lord, I'm afraid not." He paused taking a breath. "I haven't located her as of yet."

The king cursed and, in what was an unusual display of emotion threw the brandy glass across the room. "I'll have that Caligo's head on a plate for this."

Sallos felt a spark of hope. "Yes my lord, shall I see to that right away?"

"No." The king answered with finality. "You will not rest until you've found my daughter. Remember that you have more than your life to lose Sallos."

Sallos slipped looking up at his king. He was threatening Tammy.

Fuerety smiled at him. "Do not forget that it's my word alone that allows her to survive here. It would be unfortunate if something were to happen to her."

"I understand." And he did.

"It's unhealthy for you to keep your loyalties divided so."

"Of course sire." He agreed almost automatically telling the king what he wanted to hear.

"I don't expect it to become a problem Sallos."

"It will not sire," Sallos monotoned.

"Good. I expect you to find my daughter before she does some irreversibly stupid thing, as children are want to do."

"I'll find her sire. I'm just having difficulties finding any leads. No one has heard anything from her."

"And what about Cassiel? Have you located him?"

Sallos cringed inwardly, if he told the king he had not he'd presume they were together. "I have."

"And?"

"Faris is not with him, as far as he's concerned she betrayed him. They've had no contact. I believe he's had relations with Bethany."

"Bethany?" Fuerety cursed. "That's certainly something to watch out for. There are rumors that she'd been spending time with the Conglacio, but I'd believed them to be just hearsay."

"Faris must know this. She'd never go near Cassiel if she believed he'd been with her. She loathes her above all else. I believe she's sulking somewhere, you know how the princess can be."

"I am aware of her moods. I'll have Aldinach watched in case the old fool tries to petition the exile back."

"Wise, my lord."

"You find my daughter Sallos. I'm holding you personally accountable for her disappearance. Now get out of my sight," Fuerety dismissed.

Sallos stood thanking whomever it was that watched out for him and made that possible. He was starting to form a plan; he'd have to talk to Cassiel though.

Twenty-five

Jolie looked out towards the barren wasteland that was her dwelling place and sighed. Talking to her first born had been thrilling, and went much better then she had hoped. He was not insane, but rational, and still the calculating overachiever she always knew he would be. Cassiel was going to make a fine king once he got home, and an even better Overlord, one that would rule justly and not hurt those that depend on him.

Now that she had spoken to Cassiel, who she knew would talk to Dimitri, it was time to pay her beloved husband a visit.

She left her bedroom and went to the viewing room, a small chamber with windows almost all the way around it, and a large scrying pool in the center. This was where she watched her family, all of them, in their day-to-day mundanity.

She sat at the edge of the pool and closed her eyes clearing her mind of everything but the task at hand. When she opened them she saw Levi, thankfully alone. She didn't have a problem with his concubine, but for this, she needed her lover alone and open to all possibilities.

She watched through the water as he strode from the bathroom to his bed, one he always slept in alone. The girl, Thisbe, her apartment was for play, but his place was his alone. She came over and spent time there, but never spent the night. She respected his privacy, and his rules and Jolie liked that.

Levi dropped the towel onto a chair and Jolie smirked. Her hubby had indeed been keeping himself in prime condition and she longed to run her hands down his chest and over the tight plains of his stomach. She would, and soon.

He settled naked on the bed and lounged back, turning on the television and closed his eyes. She could feel him slipping into the land of dreams, where she could interact with him. It would be moments she knew, until she could walk into the dream room and hold her husband for the first time in over two hundred years. She smiled as she felt the last dregs of consciousness slip from him, and the door to the dream room clicked and swung open slowly.

She stood and walked into the room. The mists were thick in this room, as they were the entrance to the Dreamverse. They caressed her as she walked in, acknowledging another of their kin, a resident of the ether. She closed her eyes and willed herself to him, and walked only stopping as her feet hit cold stone.

She opened her eyes and smiled. She was in their bedroom in the Conglacio palace, or a version of it that the Dreamverse picked up on. She looked down and saw that her outfit had changed as well, to a gauzy one shoulder sheer gown, fastened at the right with a large ice diamond. *Well hell, I look pretty damn good.* She thought and then realized that it wasn't her wishes that made her look so good, it was his, and he was there.

"Long time no see *Coban*..." she said using the old language's word for beloved. The languages of the Afterverse were never used, and well forgotten, except by those versed in them. Few of the old guard still existed, but all the royalty of ages passed knew it, and used it sparingly. The old words had more power over a demon then anything and to use them spoke of reverence and dedication to the person you were speaking to, especially a love name.

Levi stood in front of the bed staring at her in a pair of midnight blue silk lounge pants, and nothing else. The look on his face was priceless, as if he never expected to see her there, even though it was what he was wishing most in his subconscious mind.

He took a step towards her before reality, a deep incurable pain, spread across his features. "A dream," he whispered softly to himself shaking his head.

"Yes and no. I'm here, really here husband, but yes, it is a dream." She moved closer and smiled. "I am quite real though."

He looked up into her eyes the extent of his suffering showing through to his soul. "How?" he asked unwilling to let himself hope.

"Wishes? Will? What does it matter? I'm here, and so are you."

"Can I trust it? It wouldn't be the first time my mind has lead me astray."

She walked closer and reached out to him, not closing the gap between them, leaving it to him. "You can my love. I'm real, here, and I need you to hold me," she smiled. "So this is how you see me? I don't think I ever wore anything like this in life. You're still a kinky thing Levi."

He smiled suddenly at her, his blue eyes lightening up. The simple gesture took years off him and it broke her heart that she'd never truly seen him smile since she'd died.

"It is you my love," he practically cried out stepping towards her and gathering her in his arms. "Forgive me," he begged slipping to his knees.

"For what?" she looked down at him.

"Everything," he whispered.

"There's nothing to forgive my love. Things happen." She went to her knees in front of him and kissed him sweetly.

"You never should have fought. It's all my fault... I've missed you so much."

"I did what I had to do to be your unrivaled love. And I still am. You did right by me Leviathan, never doubt that. I have missed you too, every minute of every day of every year."

He nodded holding her close. "I love you, so much."

She closed her eyes and drank in the emotions he was throwing off. It felt so right to be held by him again, felt good to know that his love for her hadn't diminished. "I know, and I love you too. Else wise I wouldn't be here."

"He looked up at her unshed tears in his eyes. "Why are you here? Now? It's been so long."

"Because I'm finally allowed to be. Love, it killed me these years not being with you, knowing you dreamt of me, and looked for me and I couldn't come."

"But now you can... that's all that matters."

"For now yes. We have tonight."

"Only tonight? Its not enough time."

"For now. And you're right it's not enough time. Luckily your time here lasts as long as you can sleep and you sleep like the dead," she grinned. "Tell me of your life," she said carefully, hoping to draw some conversation out of him even though her body was screaming for her to climb into his lap.

"It's been..." he shrugged and shook his head. "It's been hell without you. True hell."

"You haven't been stuck in an ethereal realm with no one to talk to, though I see your point. You have been keeping busy?"

"I abandoned our sons, my kingdom. My guilt and pain consumed me... I see that now. I allowed Cassiel to be exiled."

"But you did right by him recently," she said quietly.

"I can never make things right between us. Dimitri is more forgiving."

"Dimitri is more me then you. Cassiel... he was ever your son... and ever will be. You will stand by him when he goes home and kills that lunatic right?"

"I will, he won't need my help but it's a gesture I'd be a fool not to give." He paused looking at her. "There has been another my love. Thisbe. She's a sweet girl, helps dull the pain. I don't love her as I do you but I do care for her."

Jolie touched his face. "I know about Thisbe, and I'm grateful to her for keeping you sane when I could not. I don't bear her any ill will, maybe a little jealousy for being in you arms when I wished to be, I wouldn't be a demon in love if I didn't. She's been good for you, and to you, and if you didn't care for her well I wouldn't be happy with you."

He smiled at her brushing a stray hair from her face. "My love... always so understanding."

"I am that. Tell me, what would you do if I was able to come back to you?"

He looked at her speechless. "Anything."

Jolie moved in and placed a soft kiss on his lips, his whiskers tickling her face. "Anything my love?"

He nodded jerkily. "Yes... why? Is it a possibility? Can you?"

"It is. I have come to the end of my time here, and with the right situation, I can. I want to, and Cassiel is going to make sure it will happen."

"You've spoken to him?"

"I have. Only moments before you." She grinned and ran her fingers down his chest, making them cold, and licked her lips in what she hoped was an inviting gesture.

"And he said he could make this a reality? Bring you here?"

She nodded. "He and his sorceress... and Sookie of course."

"When?"

"Soon. A few weeks. We have to wait for the veil to thin enough for a soul transference." Her fingers traced the band of his pants.

"So until then we have tonight."

"We have tonight," she giggled and cocked her head. "I hope that little girl hasn't mellowed you..."

He shook his head pulling her down onto his lap growling. "No, there are things that I do that are purely yours my love. No one else's." He kissed her with a searing passion.

Jolie's head spun at his dominance. It was as if the years apart never happened, he loved her with the same ferocity, and the same blind abandon he always did. She moaned and melted into his body her hands working the muscles in his arms and shoulders. He was still in perfect physical condition and she thanked the fates for it. No man in her life had ever turned her on like her king.

"I've missed this so much, having you here in my arms."

"As have I love. Show me how much *Coban*... We have time..."

Gathering her in his arms he lifted her carrying her to the bed and gently laid her down. "I've dreamed of this for so long," he smiled wryly, "I guess I still am."

"Not really. Its real... and depending on how vigorous you are you'll feel it when you rouse. But I don't want to talk anymore Love, I need you. It's been over two hundred years for me." She grinned and palmed him through his flimsy pants.

Kissing her he brushed the straps of her gown off her shoulders. He closed his eyes willing the rest of it away leaving her naked in front of him. He showered her with kisses starting at her jaw line working down her collarbone to finally take a pert nipple into his mouth.

Everything felt more erotic here in this realm, or it could have been that she was overly sexually frustrated. Two hundred years was a long time to be horny, that was for sure. She arched and gasped as he nibbled on her tender flesh, and even after all the time apart he still remembered what her body liked, and how it liked it. Just enough teeth, this side of pain, and her whole body thrummed.

The temperature in the room dropped as his power began to rise. The heat from his body seared into her as he pressed himself to her gently laying her back on the pillows. "You're the most beautiful woman I have ever laid eyes on, my love," he spoke gazing up at her his irises now a solid blue.

She smiled, seeing the love and adoration he always showed her in his eyes. Her king missed her, needed her and she was more than sure now that she was doing the right thing. "Beautiful eyes my king. I have waited so long to see you look at me like that again."

"I didn't believe I'd get the chance." He willed away the rest of their clothes and smiled triumphantly. "My dream, my rules. I much prefer this." His eyes moved over her as if committing everything he saw to memory.

She grinned and stretched, making a real show of it, like she knew he liked. "I love your rules."

"As do I." He lets his fingers stroke over her, caressing over her soft skin.

Jolie arched and purred, smiling. "You're still a tease Levi... though a woman could get used to this attention all over again."

"If that woman is yourself then you're going to have to. Never mind though, we'll ease you gently into it." Grinning he leaned forward licking a frosty cold line over her belly.

"Oh..." she gasped and shivered. It was the one thing she truly missed about being alive that had nothing to do with her family, the feel of Conglacio ice. Under her King's tutelage, she had mastered hers in her old life, and she was getting reminded now of just how amazingly creative he was with his. "I missed your ice."

"It's been hard living without yours... I don't often call ice anymore."

"Well you should do it more often in the future," she mused and pulled him up and kissed him, wrapping her legs around his waist.

"I will." He kissed her hard one hand moving along her thigh drawing a spider web of ice.

She purred again and smiled. "Levi, I have waited over two hundred years for you... the teasing can wait... please..." she begged softly.

At her words he shifted his hips sliding himself deep within her. He let out a pleasurable hiss in her ear as filled her. "Mmmm my love."

She closed her eyes and sent a silent prayer out to those who watched that she would feel the splendor of her husband once more in the flesh. "Levi...Sweet hell!" she moaned and tightened her legs around him.

He began slow and steady thrusts taking his time to enjoy her fully. "Sweet my love. Very sweet," his soft lips kissed down her throat and back up again to find her lips.

They made sweet and perfect love, both murmuring words and sentiments of love, and promises of devotion. The vows they had never spoken bubbled to the surface, leaving them wrapped in emotion. "I love you Levi, I always have..." she whispered in his ear. "Nothing ever compared to you. I was made to be yours."

"I know, you're the queen of my heart. My queen. The only woman who will ever be queen in my eyes," he sighed breathlessly into her.

"I never cared about that. I only wanted you my love... Only you since I met you," she arched under him. "All I wanted was you."

"And you have me... you always did."

"And I will again... another chance.... Oh gods harder..." she crooned and panted, the orgasm cresting. Normally she would ice up during this part as he liked, but even in dreams certain things were off limits. Her powers would only return to her once she was flesh again. The sex was good but it needed that extra to be stellar.

His hands gripped her hips, as his body obliged her wishes pumping harder into her. Sensing the problem his power rushed over her covering her exposed body with an intricate pattern of ice.

Tears stung Jolie's eyes and she looked at her husband. He remembered, and he did it for her. A lone tear fell as she arched and came for him. The feeling was overwhelming. He was committed to them still, and nothing was going to change that.

A groan escaped his lips as his body followed her over the brink coming with her. He immediately kissed away her tear, as they both lay panting with exertion. "No tears my love. You're coming back to me."

"I am... Sweet darkness I will. I missed you. Missed you making love to me," she sighed. "Do you remember our first time?" she asked wistfully and kissed his shoulder.

"I do. I could never forget the way you looked. My heart was in my throat all night, I felt like a nervous school boy on his first date."

Jolie chuckled. "Well it was our first date. I knew the stakes even then. Knew that if I were to have you and be in your bed I would have to show you. Too many others wanted that spot and not because they wanted you," she said as she remembered the four other noble daughters that were also vying for the spot she held still to this day, the Queen of the Conglacio, and ruler of the king's heart. The only one to destroy that peace was Jeanette, and she would pay dearly with her life, and the life of her son.

"You had me, you always had my eye. I was determined to have you but I didn't want to scare you or make it look like I was using my position to bed you."

"Your position never was an issue Levi. You could have been a scribe... it didn't matter to me. I loved you, loved how you danced with me, and how you asked for me by name when you were presented with the option of a concubine."

"You enchanted me... you still do. It was hardly a hard decision and it was the right one. We had two wonderful, if headstrong, sons. My only regret was not marrying you until it was too late. I could have prevented everything had I stuck to my gut instead of tradition."

"I never blamed you love. Never. If you didn't stick with tradition, we wouldn't have had the chance to have Cassiel."

"I know. The verses wouldn't quite be the same without him."

"No, that's for sure. He is the best chance we have to make things right. I'm glad you did away with the old mating laws though. I do like Faris, and she's perfect for him."

"She's strong enough to give him a taste of his own medicine. She's doing a good job of whipping him into shape."

"She always has. They are good together, like you and I. He listens to her." She snuggled into him and sighed. "And Dimitri, so happy finally with Colette."

"True. It's not a match that I would have picked for him, but he does love her. His eyes always light up at even the mention of her. I've always indulged the boy more than Cassiel. The reason being that he's always made it easier," he chuckled. "Dimitri has more smarts than Cassiel when it comes to manipulating us both. He has his Colette now and I'm sure it's much healthier for him."

"And for her. That girl is destined for great things my love. She's the right choice for him. Our boys chose for love, no matter how much Cassiel likes to think it isn't about that. They turned out wonderful. Strong, healthy, and powerful," she sighed, knowing they would have to talk about two other additions in their lives, one a point of happiness, another, well the reason for despair.

"Our children," he whispered. "How can we not love them?" He sighed deeply. "I told Cassiel he could kill Gabriel. The boy's too twisted to ever become anything useful."

"I don't think it mattered that you gave your blessing Levi. Cassiel knew Gabe was the reason why I'm here. He's been living on borrowed time since Cassiel was exiled. I wouldn't expect anything less from our first born." The smugness in her voice was hard to miss. She detested her husband's bastard more than his mother because unlike Jeanette, he was much easier to manipulate for reasons of power. She knew Jeanette thought she loved Leviathan, but really she loved the idea of him. None but Jolie loved him for real and she was ready to prove it to the world.

He nodded silently. "He's still my son, despite all he's done, it wasn't easy."

"It isn't supposed to be. Sacrifices have to be made. You think I wanted her to grow up without a mother? I didn't and I don't, but that's a sacrifice I made to be with you. She's grown now, doesn't even know me Levi, and the boys don't even know they have a sister."

"I promised you I wouldn't tell them. Milo has kept her quite hidden from the others along with Sookie. I hear she spends a lot of time at the Arcuo court. The prince has taken a liking to her although I'm not sure if she shares his feelings."

Jolie grinned. "She has other suitors, ones we would both approve of. I'm proud of her Levi, and I want her there when I come back. My entire family," she sighed. "And Milo. He's a good man for keeping her safe all this time."

"He's done well. The boys should know. I've always been of that opinion. Keeping secrets, especially from Cassiel, is tiresome and difficult. She could benefit from her brothers' protection, or should I say over-protection. Knowing Cassiel he'll try and lock her in a cupboard somewhere to keep her safe, which isn't too far off from where she's been."

Jolie chuckled and sighed, happy that the love of her life was remaining true to his normal attitude about Milo and wasn't being a jealous sod. She kissed him and then smiled. "True, though I think he's going to have his hands full there. She's more me than Milo." Jolie bit her lover's lip and then cocked her head. "We only have a little time left love. Then I won't be able to contact you till I arrive. Those are the rules. Shall we cut out the chit chat and get back down to business?"

He nodded. "Very much so, do you want me to tell them?"

"No... Cassiel is already on to it. We'll let it sit for a while. Give him a mystery to play with." She grinned. "But I suggest you see Milo before hand. Let him know."

"I'll see to it." He kissed her once more.

"Good. Then see to me before the magic fades my love I wish to be aching from overuse by the time you leave me."

Twenty-six

Astrid stood over the stove with spatula in hand, ready to flip the most recent crepe she was making. She grabbed the handle, and slid the spatula under the thin pastry and in one swift motion, flipped the crepe, and then went back to the griddle side of the overlarge range, to tend the bacon, sausages and hash. Everyone in the house had a different taste, and Astrid liked seeing them happy. She hummed as she cooked, a nonsensical little ditty designed to keep her mind occupied as she worked.

Fallon had already eaten, along with Ashlyn and Feyd. The boys had a morning meeting with Georgie, and Ashlyn had a pedicure appointment with Faris, who had come down just in time to have a glass of juice, and nibble a few pieces of bacon. They had left in a flurry of concerns coming from Feyd about Ashlyn's welfare. Fallon had just winked and promised to be home for tea.

She knew Cash was on his way down. Her body could feel him getting closer, and she knew that was the bond they were sharing. She was still craving him physically, but it was lessening each day.

She knew though that once she was in his full presence the need would be overwhelming, but that really didn't matter. She had her green light and planned on using it.

Cash walked into the kitchen and made a yummy sound and she giggled. "Was that for me standing here half naked, or cuz you're hungry demon?" She turned and smiled at him. "Coffee is made, so is the tea."

"I'd say because I'm hungry but my reflexes are always slow in the morning." He kissed her cheek moving past her to grab a mug and filling it with coffee.

She grinned and shook her head. "Fair enough. So how was last night with Sookie?"

"Interesting. Informative. It's been a long time since I spoke to her." He took a drink out of the mug leaning against the counter.

"Could you be more vague?" she asked with a half smirk.

"I could, but that's not why I'm here. We need to talk."

"I figured as much. You waited till everyone left so I knew something was up. So dish Casha... I'm intrigued."

"I have a proposal for you. Something that I think will interest you."

"Casha," she said and turned smiling. "Everything you say interests me."

"Oh course it does but this has the potential to grant you something that you've always wanted." He set the mug down taking her hands in his. His eyes met her. "I want you to work with Sookie, she needs your help with something very important to me."

"Of course Casha. You're my demon, if it's important to you, it's important to me." Her words rang true to her as she heard her voice relay them to him. He had never hurt her, and she had bargained to be at his beck and call. Whatever it was, it didn't really matter to her. She would do it.

"In return I've found a way to destroy Lillith and her curse on you," he paused taking a breath, "But to that there is a condition."

She blinked. As usual, Casha had given her a way for all her dreams to come true. She would be stupid to say no. "Okay... I should be asking you what it is, but I don't really care, unless it's harming Fallon, or losing him or any of our friends."

"Noting so horrid..." he grinned wickedly, "Although could we maim Fallon?"

She frowned and punched him in the arm. "No."

"Ow," He frowned rubbing the spot. "I want the line bargained to me... I'll be good to them; they can even be demons, full demons. Full Conglacio powers."

"Our children? Full Conglacio? Casha it's possible, but if I have children, you know I will have a witch as well, if only one. That's my family's bargain with Ishtar. So we will have to modify it. I'll agree, if the fate of the children is left up to nature. If they are to be witch, they must be allowed to choose to be a sorceress or not." She smiled. "That way I keep the protection of my goddess as well."

""Of course I've accounted for that. If you have children that, for whatever reason, aren't demon then I won't lay claim to them. You know I want to keep on the right side of your goddess."

"Fair enough. Fallon would want the kids protected, and full Conglacio powers can do that. They would be a noble family correct?" she asked and gave him a plate of crepes and bacon.

"Of course, just like Snow, although they wouldn't be princesses and princes in their own right like she is... but noble enough."

"Noble is fine, I never asked for royalty." She grinned and nodded. "We have a deal. What is it I have to do?"

"With Sookie?"

"Yeah with Sookie. We can close the bargain later. The fates have heard me agree. I can't go back on it now."

"She needs your help in..." he frowned to himself. "I don't know what's the term? Reanimating? No that's a little zombie-ish..." he shuddered. "She thinks she can bring Jolie back to life. Now I don't think there will be zombies involved. You'll really have to talk it over with her."

"Soul transference?" she asked, eyes wide. "Casha that's very hard. There're a lot of factors involved."

"You didn't think I'd give you something that big for free did you?"

She laughed. "No I suppose not. So your mother huh? It's doable, but it's going to take a lot of power, and a deeper bond between us. Also, we need a body, someone that is expendable."

"It's being arranged for. My father..." he cleared his throat. "Levi has had someone sitting around just waiting for the task."

"Well that clears that up. So how do you know all about this? Sookie told you?"

He took a deep breath. "Yeah, more of less."

She frowned. "You are lying."

"And badly which means I'm uncomfortable." He checked his watch. "Oh look at the time, I better go. I have to talk to Dimitri before Cole steals away his attention."

"Casha. Tell me. Please? Have I ever doubted you?"

"Your doubt has nothing to do with this. You know what you have to and Sookie can fill you in on the rest later on. I have to go. I'll talk to you later." He kissed her cheek blinking out of the kitchen.

She frowned and looked at his partially eaten meal. Cash didn't hide things from her, he promised he wouldn't, and now that he was she wasn't sure why but there was that gnawing feeling that she needed to trust him. She sighed and picked up her cell, hitting Fallon on speed dial and set to leaving him a message about what she had just done.

Twenty-seven

Dimitri walked into his living room, his hair still damp hair curling around the tops of his ears. Cole had just left for her afternoon shift with Thisbe, his father's concubine. He smirked, recalling Cole's devout willingness in the shower not twenty minutes before, and the soft little cries she made, as he loved her in the pulsing water.

Things were working out well. Cole was in his bed at last, his brother was finally king, and his father wasn't being a shit anymore to Cassiel. Healing had begun, and Dimitri took it as a good sign.

The call he got though, the one from Cassiel minutes before, threatened to stifle that healing. His elder brother had been speaking wildly, babbling about something he couldn't quite place. All he knew was that Cash was on his way to the apartment, and that whatever it was; he was very excited about it.

He padded barefoot into the kitchen, and opened the fridge, grabbing a jug of juice and drank right out of it, then looked around for something to eat. *Fuck it, Cash is coming over I'm ordering in.*

He grabbed the phone and called Jade Empire, the Japanese take out restaurant, and ordered several choice items, as well as soup, salad and a bottle of plum wine. Knowing Casha, he couldn't a sit down talk, so eating would be part of it. He hung up after giving them the address, and left the kitchen, walking back towards the bedroom when the doorbell rang. *At least he's using the bell and not porting in,* he thought as he went to answer the door. Casha stood on the other side of the door with a smile on and right away Dimitri was wary. "So what? Find out what you and Faris are having?" he asked as his brother pushed past him to the living room.

"Not yet, Sookie said she'd send Rudolph over tonight."

"Ok so what's got you all hopped up?" he grinned. "You didn't catch Astrid and Faris in bed together did you? Did you get it on tape?"

"No but that's in the works, Faris and my sorceress get on very well, which is good for a change."

"I'll say. Astrid is a gem Cash, a true gem. So why all the fanfare? You rig fire pant's crapper with explosives?"

Cash frowned at his brother. "Exactly how old are you? Or has having only Snow for company rotted your brain?"

He shrugged. "I'm in a good mood, as you are too. So tell me what's up, and quit with the cloak and dagger."

"Ok... but hear me out before you have me committed... or laugh. If you laugh at me I'll not be best pleased..."

"Ok I'll bite. No laughing. What's up?"

"I spoke to mom last night. Sookie made me do it."

"Really?" he grinned. "How?"

He sighed. "You're laughing... and it was through the computer."

"I'm not laughing, I'm smiling. Through the computer? Mom has the internet?"

"No. She's dead; I don't think the dead have the internet. She's in the Ether now... apparently she can affect certain things. It's like white noise, and before you start I know those films ended badly. Sookie assured me that this was safe. I spoke to her D... it was mom."

He smiled. "Well shit. I think that's good news. What did she say? Is she ok?"

"You don't think I'm crazy? She's... as well as can be expected, I guess."

"Why would I think you're crazy? Hell stranger things have happened. What's she been up to?"

"I don't know... floating around, watching? Stuff like that. She's coming home... I think. Astrid and Sookie are going to work on it, apparently it can be done."

"You're kidding. Really? Fuck that's fantastic. How though, and does dad know?"

"I guess... she said she'd tell him. I guessed that there was going to be some sort of sex involved so I didn't ask too many questions."

Dimitri shuddered. "Agreed there. Thank the gods I wasn't old enough to remember them doing that shit."

"I tended to be out and about at those times. She did love the old prick... you know she told me to stop fighting with him?"

"Um Cash, she's mom... What else would she tell you? You're a bit past the whole 'eat your greens' stage."

"He starts it. Anyway so we're bringing mom back... we had a weird conversation though. She had an affair around the same time as Gabe was born. I think she miscarried."

Dimitri blinked. "Whoa, what?"

"It was a weird conversation. When you're dead you just think about all the things that you should have said."

"I'll take your word on that, seeing as I haven't been dead, or talked to the dead myself. So mom had a thing? It's not unheard of, but a kid? Miscarriage? That's some heavy shit."

"Tell me about it... it would have been before you, around the time of Gabe. She went away for a while, I assumed it was because of Gabe and that bitch lording it over the castle."

"Yeah I bet that sucked. So then what? Me?"

"It's not like the stork just abandoned you at the door one day Dimitri. Yeah, you were next."

"Hey he might have... The ice stork." he snickered.

Cash sighed heavily, "Perhaps, it's better than the alternative thought. How are things with Fiona?"

"I think it worked out... We'll know soon I'm thinking. So about mom... She's coming back... what about Thisbe? I mean she's a sweet girl, having her heart crushed like that isn't going to be easy on her."

"That's his fault... he'll have to deal with his mess. You know Cole is rather fond of her, I guess you could take her on..."

Dimitri laughed and shook his head. "No I don't think so. If I didn't want the queen of the succubus I'm not taking on a concubine."

"Suit yourself. I'll have her dealt with..."

"Well don't kill her. She may be useful."

"I know. She undoubtedly has skills unparallel by any back street whore and you'd know."

"Considering she's a royal concubine and is the highest paid dancer at Pinky's, yeah I would think so." He sighed. "Mom coming back, Thisbe getting the shaft... shit I'm surprised Dad hasn't run in like a lunatic spouting about her." He turned his head as the soft tones of the bell sounded. "And that should be lunch."

"What did we get?"

"Japanese. And a fine bottle of plum wine." He walked to the door and opened it to see his father holding a plastic sack and bottle of wine. "And since when are you moonlighting as a delivery man?"

Leviathan walked in and grinned, then saw Cash and his smile grew wider. "Kill two birds with one stone." He pushed past Dimitri, and went to the table setting the food down. "I take it you told him?" he asked Cash as Dimitri closed the door and walked towards them.

Cash waited till his father had moved away from the table before approaching it rummaging through the bag. "I did. You could have gotten here first though, would have saved an explanation from me." Coming out of the bag empty handed he moved away. "Your tastes in food never cease to amaze me Dimitri."

"There's Negamiayki in there for you, and crab Rangoon so quit your whining, Highness," Dimitri said and opened the bottle.

Leviathan grinned at them. "I would have been here earlier, but I had things to do. I need to ask though, is it really possible Cassiel? She said it was riding on your sorceress."

"If it's possible then Astrid can do it... she has a lot riding on this, and Sookie seems to think it can be done."

"Sekhmet would know. She was always the mystic of the bunch. Your mother didn't go into details. What do you need from me?"

"I don't know yet, but I'll let you know when I do."

The old king nodded. "Do you need her?" he asked quietly.

"I will... when the time comes. Let her rot for now."

"Won't here me complain. And Gabbe?"

"It's not his time yet... But it will be. If I kill him before I take my place it'll arouse suspicions. I have Oscar keeping an eye on him."

"Good thinking. Oscar is a good one. Much like his father was."

"If only it had rubbed off on Drake." Cash sighed turning to Dimitri, "Any word on him yet?"

"Aside from Sallos mentioning him, no. Sandor mentioned she spoke with him."

"Good, hopefully he's there, staying out of the way."

"Well Old Sally didn't mention being in Marrakech, either way." Dimitri shrugged.

"Either way he's out of my way."

Levi nodded. "Loose cannon that one."

"Really?" Cash bit out sarcastically, "I'd hardly noticed."

"He needs someone to truly knock him on his ass," Leviathan said around a forkful of noodles. Dimitri watched his father and brother bicker, amused that in almost fifteen hundred years, his father had never learned to use chopsticks.

"Yeah if only there was a king that could have been holding his people accountable for their actions, imagine how great that would have been? And now he's all my problem... although, Dimitri, he is technically your bodyguard."

"True, and my little experiment with Snow didn't work out, and she's the craziest and most brutal female I know aside from your Faris."

"Very true."

"So until we find someone to knock some sense into him we are SOL."

"So it would seem. Just as long as he stays out of my way, and you refrain from telling Snow she was an experiment, things will go along nicely."

"Like I would do that. I'm not stupid, unlike you... Did you tell Faris about Bethany?" he smirked. "Did mom mention her? Slap your ass for being naughty?"

"No but she did mention what an annoying brat you were."

"See now that isn't something that mum would say."

"Funny because that's exactly what she said," Cash grinned.

Dimitri frowned. "Mom wouldn't ever call me a brat."

"An annoying brat."

"See that just doesn't sound like mom. Though I could see her calling you that, and spoiled," he grinned.

Leviathan shook his head. "Would you both stop? You do know she's probably watching right now."

Cash started to look over his shoulder then stopped himself. "Fine, I have better things to do than fight with my bratty brother anyway." He chuckled muttering something under his breath.

"Just wait till mom comes back..." he grinned. "So you are going to see Rudolph then?"

"No I'm not, thankfully, you know how I am around him. He's coming to us, it's safer."

"Yeah. You'll let us know though right?"

"Of course, if just to gloat more than anything. Any designs on your own yet?"

"Kids? Cash, Cole and I have been together what three days? We have time for children."

"But you're having sex right?"

Dimitri grinned. "Have you seen Cole? I would be an idiot to not be."

"Then be careful... you're old enough to skip the dangers of unprotected sex right?"

Dimitri laughed, all traces of hostility between the three of them gone. His mother had done the impossible from her misty world, brought them together for a semblance of normalcy, a glimpse of the family they could have been had she lived. It seemed they were all getting a second chance at making the mistakes in their lives right, and he hoped that whatever was ahead of them would be worth the pain and the road to redemption they all had to travel.

Twenty-eight

Murphy looked in the mirror once more and frowned. Usually not one for vanity, he was worrying now that he wasn't in any way presentable. Seeing Princess Fiona for the first time in probably a decade and he was like a schoolboy again. The woman was perfection, always had been but he had kept his distance after the failed betrothal to Iris. He was grateful for that. He was a Crown Prince yes, but he loathed the idea of marrying for duty. Marrying Iris would have been for duty. All he had wanted though was Fiona. His father didn't see it as profitable, especially because she was younger than he and wasn't in any position to take the side of a King. Murphy on the other hand thought differently. Fiona was everything he wanted in a girlfriend and in a princess. From the time she was a teenager, Murphy watched her from afar, her flirtatious ways, her talents for singing, her wonderfully limber body, her unsurpassed beauty...

And here she was agreeing to see him for tea. He knew she had yet to marry, and didn't have suitors, and secretly, he was glad for it. It meant that he still had a chance at happiness with her.

He never approached her after the situation with Iris, not even during the balls when everyone was fair game. He was sure she would think he was just settling, when it really had been the other way around.

He didn't deserve Fiona. Not in the least. He was one of the only Princes, aside from Alexander, that didn't have any prospects for a princess and political marriage in his future and while he was fine with that, his father was not.

So this wasn't for anyone else but himself. He was to see her today, and hopefully get her to accept his invitation to the ball coming up at the Cento court. If not... Well it was back to square one, but he would have had at least one date with her.

He smiled again and sighed. He looked presentable, his black suit and Strigo green shirt immaculate, his hair and goatee trimmed and presentable. He looked down at the small package he had. He had chosen the gift special for her, and he hoped she would accept it, let alone enjoy it.

Realizing he had taken more time than usual at the mirror, he blinked to the Succubus Lands and walked into the Palace, to the reception room. He saw Althea, one of the younger succubi and she bowed at him and left, he assumed on her way to fetch Fiona.

Seconds later a dark haired man sauntered through the door that he had expected to see Fiona come through. He walked with the lithe sensual grace that the entire race of incubus seemed to posses. Moni smiled brightly when he saw him.

"Murphy," he greeted warmly. "The man of the hour. She's changing her dress... for the fifth time. The first wasn't enough, the second was too much," He frowned counting them off on his hand, "The third Iris said made her look "hippy" and to be quite honest I'm not sure what was wrong with the last one." He sighed.

"Women have far too many clothes, especially in this place, she shouldn't be long though. How are things?"

Murphy chuckled and shook his head. It was nice to know he wasn't the only one with nerves. "Things are quite well Moni. And with you?" he asked and bowed to the other man. Murphy might be a prince, but Moni was as good as king. Moni shared Queen Camions with the king, and his council was kept by the queen. He had more power than most.

"Can't complain." He shrugged flopping down on the couch in a lazy cat-like move. "So where are the two of you headed?"

"New York. I have reservations for the crystal room at Tavern on the Green. I hope it will be appropriate."

"I'm sure it will. It's a beautiful setting. Of course it's been a while since I've been there... I like that you're taking her somewhere nice. Few men go out of their way when a Succubus is involved."

Murphy smiled. "Fiona deserves the best," he said in a low tone. "And I'm not the kinda asshole who thinks just because she lives off sex that she's an easy lay. Not that this is what this is about."

"I never thought that you would be, I remember you Murphy, and that kind of guy doesn't get near Fiona. Sex isn't everything. Just because we live off sex doesn't mean that sometimes we're not capable of holding hands and cuddling with the one we love..." He broke, an emotion passing briefly over his face, pain maybe but it was gone before Murphy had a chance to catch it.

He was saved from having to react as Fiona walked in wearing a dark ruby dress, which clung to her body perfectly and fanned out from her hips allowing it to move freely around her. Her dark hair was worn in curls cascading around her shoulders.

"Moni you're not depressing him are you?" She smiled nervously at Murphy.

"Of course not, Princess," Moni shook his head standing.

"Good. Then thanks for keeping him company. You better go as I saw Iris headed your way. She wants to discuss baby names again and I don't wish that fate on anybody. I think Cali's in the garden carving, Iris wouldn't go near her so you're reasonably safe there." Moni paled visibly clearly the idea of spending time with Iris not settling well with him. He bowed to them both saying his goodbyes and left quickly.

Murphy smiled. "Nothing changes I see." He bowed at her. "You are stunning Princess. I'm quite pleased there are constants in the Succubus courts that have nothing to do with immature and bitchy women." He grinned.

She smiled wryly at him. "I wouldn't be so sure Murphy. I'm afraid bitchy has been a running theme down here lately." She looked at the door Moni retreated through. "He didn't say anything crazy did he? He's been a little antsy since my mother left. Not that I blame him, it's been open season on the poor guy recently."

Murphy shook his head. "Not at all. He seems sad though." He offered her his hand. "We can chat more about Moni at lunch, if you would like to go that is. I have reservations at Tavern on the Green for fifteen minutes from now."

"He's very sad, emasculated even, my mother destroyed him. She does that." Fiona shrugged taking his hand. "Lunch sounds perfect though I'm sure we can think of something better to talk about than pool old Mo."

He chuckled. "I think so. Come." He took her hand and blinked them to a copse of trees in Central Park just at the small parking area near the restaurant. "I hope this is ok. It's a beautiful day and blinking to my apartment here just to get the car seemed contradictive."

She nodded, "It does, plus you can never get anywhere fast by car."

"Not in this city that's for damn sure." He let go of her and offered his arm. She took it and they were quiet as they walked up and saw the Matre'd. He smiled at them and showed them to their table in an out of the way corner of the room. The crystal twinkled and spilled rainbows hither and to, blanketing the table in color. Murphy waited for Fiona to sit, the Matre'd helping her and then sat himself. "Ruby is a good color for you Fiona."

"Thank you." She smiled at him. "I was toying with wearing Strigo green. It would have been nice to match."

He gave her a sly smile. "And you would look breathtaking in it I'm sure. But matching like that would have to be for a ball or something." He blushed. "Now before I sputter compliments all over you, shall we order?"

"Let's." She grinned at him her eyes sparkling with amusement.

Murphy motioned the waiter over, ordering a merlot. He looked at Fiona and smiled. "I don't know what your tastes are, so I'm sorry to say I can't choose something you would find thrilling."

"Oh I'm sure you could." She grinned looking at the menu. "My tastes are pretty normal... no tuna fish and banana pizza or anything."

"So then you would trust me to order for us?"

"Might be fun," she nodded, "But if it's putting too much pressure on you I can do it myself."

He blushed. "No, I... well..." he looked at the waiter. "The lady and I shall have the truffle salad, with the raspberry vinaigrette. Also, the poached salmon with the cherry crème sauce and the basil and rosemary cauliflower. Oh and as an appetizer we will have the spicy prawns with the lemon and ginger butter." The waiter nodded and left and he looked at Fiona. "Is that ok? I have a love of rich foods. Sandor says it's my main weakness."

"It all sounds yummy. Food's a good weakness to have, one of the better ones I think." She smiled leaning forward. "How is Sandor?"

"Good I think. I haven't seen her for awhile, just talked on the phone or over email. Dad still doesn't approve of her position as the Madame in Marrakech, but what can he do. She still pining for Drake I think, though she hasn't mentioned him lately."

"No? Well maybe things will start to look up then. Drake's an unhealthy obsession."

"I think you may be right, but she loves him. Always has. I feel for her because of it. I know he cares for her, but not like that."

"It's not a good situation, then, so few are these days. With the state of the Afterverse there seems to be very little hope for any of us."

"Indeed. Though I like to think there're still flashes of it. Take right now for example. I never thought I would be sitting anywhere alone with you princess."

"Really?"

He nodded and blushed. "I didn't think you would be agreeable to a date, after, well past events."

"Past events? You mean Iris..."

He nodded. "I didn't want you to think I was working my way down the line."

"I don't think you ever worked her, did you?"

He chuckled. "Gods no."

"Good." She smiled looking relieved. "Besides I think I'm higher up the line than she is."

"Actually you're the top." He winked at her as the waiter came and set the salads in front of them. "And Iris isn't my type."

"She's not many peoples' type."

He laughed and picked up his salad fork. "All too true."

She lifted her fork, eating carefully. They sat in silence for several minutes. "How is the court doing? I haven't heard much from the Strigo recently."

"We exist... nothing out of the ordinary. The three rigs we have right now are working splendidly, and our holdings on this plane are increasing. So it's all business as usual," he said and forked a bit of the salad into his mouth. It was delicious, the vinaigrette the perfect flavor to enhance the truffle mushrooms hidden throughout.

"That's always good to hear."

"I guess so. And you? How have things been for you? What are you doing with yourself these days, aside from running the court?"

"Nothing but, I'm afraid. Running the place takes up most of my time. There's a lot more to do than I thought, thankfully I've had Mo around to help me out. Though I've now ended up running interference between him and my father, which is always a little delicate. So between that and my sisters I haven't had much time to myself. I kinda miss the days when it was all harp practice and salsa lessons."

That perked him up. "Salsa lessons? You dance?"

"'Fraid so and in most styles. Except for disco... not that I couldn't it's just against my morals. Back in the days when mom and dad could bare to be in the same room with each other they used to love to dance. They insisted that we all learn."

This was good news. Murphy's other guilty pleasure was dancing, and it was a gift from the fates that the woman he was so enamored of was into it as well. "Really? You just said the magic words. My mother did the same with Sandor as I. You know, there's a great club here in New York. Swing dancing on Tuesday's and Salsa and Cha-Cha Thursdays, I'd love to take you," he said hoping she wouldn't shoot him down.

She beamed at him, "Truly? It's been so long... I can never really find a partner at the same level as me...well other than my father, but it's not the same."

"I know what you mean. It would be fun I think... though I think we would have to trade out for this." He grinned.

"Oh yeah?"

"Uh huh." He sipped his wine and nodded to the waiter who brought their appetizer.

"I'm sure that can be arranged."

"You're not even going to ask what it is I'm wheeling towards?" he asked and grabbed his knife and fork cutting the prawn. "Have you had these before?"

"Nope but they look tasty." She smiled, "So what are you wheeling towards?

He cut a piece off and dunked it in the sauce then placed it in his mouth and chewed. "The Cento Ball."

"I'm listening." Smiling she followed suit eating a prawn.

"Well I had hoped that you would let me accompany you to it."

"I wasn't going to go... for a few reasons but mostly because I'm avoiding Fire pants." She sighed. "He's wanted to talk with me since my mother's disappearance. I guess we could though, I mean it couldn't be that bad with you with me."

"Your mother tends to go walk about a lot. He needs to talk to your father, not you. So don't worry. I'm sure I can keep you dancing all evening so as to make sure he won't have the chance to corner you."

"Perfect." She beamed. "Then it's a date."

A date. The words coming out of her mouth directed towards him. "It would be quite a wonderful night." *And I plan to make it just that.* They ate in silence, and when the main dish came, they both were very impressed with it. "Now this is decadence... don't you agree?"

"Indeed, I love Salmon, a commendable choice."

"And the cherry crème is a perfect compliment. I'm glad to see you enjoy this. Gives me hope."

"For?" she asked grinning as she ate a piece of the fish.

He grinned. "Future dates, that is if you're willing. If not then..." he trailed off and blushed deeply.

"I'd like that. It's definitely something that I'm interested in... I'm glad you called."

"I'm glad I did too. You're every bit as enchanting and adventurous as I thought you would be."

"Do you do much thinking?"

"When it comes to you? Hell yeah. You just might be my favorite subject."

She giggled blushing hard. "I just bet I am."

He winked. "You are."

"Really?" she asked her eyes twinkling. "And just what do you think about?"

"Several things," he grinned and reached across the table and ran the pad of his index finger over the top of her hand. "You wouldn't believe it but you're in my thoughts more often then not."

"I'd like to believe it." She smiled heatedly at him.

He smiled. "That's a good thing, cuz it's true. So do you want dessert? I'm loathe to let this date end."

"Dessert sounds good. I'm enjoying myself way too much to let the night end. We could maybe go for a walk after...?" she asked hopefully.

"I was hoping you would say that. So the big question is dessert here or ice cream at Rumplemeyers?"

She grinned. "Ice cream I think."

He nodded and squeezed her hand and then motioned to the waiter, who promptly brought their bill. They were out in the late afternoon air moments later walking through the park towards sixty-eighth street and the exclusive ice cream parlor. He grabbed her hand as they walked, Moni's words in his mind about the little intimacies and her race. He wanted her to feel comfortable, and didn't need her to think that she was only good for one thing. Instinct was also driving him to kiss her, but he wouldn't even presume to think she wanted that from him. She might enjoy his company, but that didn't mean she wanted to get physical.

She squeezed his hand pulling him a little closer to him so that their shoulders brushed. "This is very nice. It's been a long while since I've had a nice meal with a perfectly normal man. Well there was Don but I think it's safe to say that my virtue is pretty safe with him."

Murphy almost choked. "Quite. Poor Don. I blame his mother for his... issues. If she wasn't such a used up slut and a bitch he wouldn't be batting for the other team."

She chuckled. "She almost makes me glad I had Camions for a mother."

"Cam isn't so bad. She's the queen of sex, she's gotta keep up the reputation."

"I guess. She just doesn't have to try so hard...still though I'd rather have her over Ammit any day of the week."

"I agree to that. Still, you grew up to be one hell of a woman Fiona."

"Thanks Murph, you're not so bad yourself you know? Charming, sexy, kind... there's a pretty long list you know."

He grinned and sighed. He wanted to kiss her so badly, especially now that she was accepting the guy he was. True, there were a lot of things she didn't know but he wasn't hiding anything half as bizarre as Drake did from the world. He squeezed her hand gently again. "You think?"

"Of course. You're a catch Murph..." She grinned. "I'm surprised you haven't been snapped up already."

"Well my situation in the Afterverse isn't one where I have the princesses lining up to bed me, let alone marry me so its not that far fetched."

"No? I find that a little hard to believe..." She grinned eyeing him up and down. "And you're perfectly beddable, if you don't mind me saying."

That got yet another blush from him. "Damn Fiona... don't even play games."

"Who said anything about playing?"

He stopped walking and turned her to him. "You just keep getting better and better."

"I do?"

He growled. "Do you have any idea how fantastic you are? No other demon has ever flirted with me."

"That's very lucky for me, but they've been missing out." She smirked at him.

"I'm glad you think so. And I'll tell you a secret."

"Please do..."

"It's lucky for me that the only one I ever wanted to flirt with was you."

She practically glowed, "Now who's playing?"

"Not me, that's for damn sure." he grinned. "You're everything I thought you would be. And I severely want to kiss you." There, he said it. "But I'm not going to."

Her eyes widened in surprise, "What? Why?"

"Because I'm not officially courting you Fiona, and I don't take liberties, no matter how much I want to."

"Oh," she sighed her shoulders sagging a little. "I suppose that would be the proper thing."

He sighed. "I don't want there to be talk... And I don't.... ah fuck it." He pulled her closer and kissed her fiercely. Everything stopped. His power flared of its own accord, and a haze drew around them. Time stopped for him, as if it knew it had to make the perfect moment last. She felt amazing, her lips soft and fantastic.

She groaned softly into his mouth. Their bodies fit perfectly together as she slid her hands around to the small of his back pulling him closer.

Good fates but she was perfect! Everything felt right. He broke the kiss, his magic still flaring around them. He looked at her and groaned. "I have no willpower," he said almost apologetically.

She licked her lips her face flushed. "I'm glad you don't. If you did then I wouldn't have just had the best kiss of my life. I hope you don't suddenly find some... I'm going to expect another kiss soon."

His heart leapt. She enjoyed it. "I would be happy to oblige you in that Fiona. But first I think Ice cream."

Twenty-nine

"I need Amaro," Sallos said blinking into Cash's office.

"And I need a special amulet that automatically makes me the undisputed ruler of the universe but it's not likely to just fall into my lap with a wish, if such a thing were to exist."

"Don't play games with me Cassiel, I've just had my nuts roasted by Fuerety. Not to mention he's threatened my entire family."

"Not my problem," Cash dismissed looking back down at his papers. "Faris is dealing with the Cento side of this. I don't have the time right now."

"Oh but it is your problem Cassiel, you'll just have to make the time. It would be an awful shame if Faris found out that you've been frolicking around with Bethany in your top side time."

Cash looked up at him the fear stark in his eyes. "You wouldn't, it would kill her. It would kill us both Sallos and it's not like there was any frolicking going on. It was once; she took advantage of me when I was at my lowest. Trust me I'm doing everything in my power to cover up that momentary lack of judgment on my behalf."

"I don't care what it was, it's an easy way to get what I want. Which is Faris back home and my life not being dragged through your affairs."

"He'll kill the child."

"Not if she claimed it as Jacob's."

The demon in front of him paused considering. "True. It would still destroy her... you'd have to live with her. Eventually I'd take the Verse and once I hold the throne then..." he shook his head. "I don't have time for threats. Why do you need Amaro?"

"Because Fuerety needs something, he's very close to sending Blaze after her and once he's unleashed..." He shook his head. "I don't have the stomach for that anymore. They'd be nothing left."

"A tad melodramatic but I get the point. Nobody wants to come face to face with Blaze or Pyre for that matter"

Sallos shook his head. "He won't send her, its just Blaze we have to worry about."

"I'm sorry to say that I don't know where Amaro is," the demon answered, his tone glacial. "I wish I did, I've been expecting him. Although when I see him I have my own plans for him, ones that don't involve having him laid out like a sacrificial lamb. You're going to have to come up with something else." He stood grabbing his papers. "Now if you'll excuse me I really have to go."

Sallos grabbed him as he walked by him, his flames barely held in check. "There is no other way Cash."

Cash's ice-cold eyes met his. "I appreciate what you're doing Sallos. Trust me I do. It's a little late but it's appreciated. I'm not cento so I can't comment on how you do things, but I don't barter my friends."

"Oh no? You forget that I've seen Natalia, recently. I've seen what happens to the women that believe you love them."

The ice demon's eyes narrowed viciously, the fury in them plain to see. "I didn't kill 'Talia. Nor did I wish her dead."

"Still failed to protect her didn't you?"

"It's rather hard to protect one from Faris, she can be rather tenacious when she wants to be." He swallowed hard stepping forcefully out of Sallos's grip. "I doubt that I'll have that problem again, Faris quite approves of my new sorceress. Now," he cleared his throat. "Blaze is a problem, he can't be sent after us. But that's your end of things; I can't be concerned with that. I have too many balls in the air as it is. I'm not hosting the parties up here; I'm trying to hold things together. If you need somewhere safe to leave the kid I can arrange that for you. As for everything else you signed up to be on our team, Faris' team, you're more experienced dealing with the fire king than any of us. Find a way."

"It's not just about Tam! It's my life, my honor..." Sallos growled seeing no way out of this situation, the Conglacio was never going to cooperate even for the sake of Faris and the child. "Fine," he answered in a forced calm. "I'll find another way, but don't believe for one second that I'm sacrificing everything for you."

Sallos turned and stepped into the Ley-line before he could here the Conglacio's come back. He had things to do and Cassiel had put him in a bad enough mood.

The first thing he had to do was find Kris and Tammy. Once he knew they were safe then he could make arrangements for her. There was no way he could leave her with Kris any longer than necessary. Kris was a friend but he was still loyal to the throne and that, for the time being, meant Fuerety. He'd never ask him to go against their king. It wouldn't be fair.

The vineyard in Mexico was rather small in comparison to some of the properties that he owned but it as the one place in the Ververse that he truly felt at home. It was the perfect place to keep his niece and a giant fire demon out of trouble, although it was hard to tell just who would be getting into the most trouble. He walked up the sun bleached stairs into the wide arched doorway. The main living room was spacious and bright the normally pristine interior was now cluttered with empty junk food cartons and sweet wrappers. He winced knowing she'd be hyper, it didn't matter how many times he repeated himself they just wouldn't listen. He bent to tidy a little, hearing her giggles coming from the other side of the house. Lifting some rubbish he threw it in the bin on the way past.

She was on the bed bouncing to try and touch the roof. Kris was collapsed on a chair in the far corner of the room. He looked like Sallos felt, exhausted. It didn't take much to figure out that Tam was being a handful. He leaned against the doorframe watching them both. Tammy looked just like her mother had when she was younger.

Her head snapped up and her grin widened. "Sally!" she screamed jumping off the bed and gripping him in a viselike grip that threatened to squeeze all the oxygen from his body.

"Hey kid." He grinned back relieved to finally be seeing her again.

She pulled back punching his gut, "Now where the hell have you been?"

"Don't cuss," he winced, staring back up. "I've been running some errands, but I'm here now so there's no need to keep Kris up much longer." He turned to his friend. "Thanks for the help."

The huge demon rose concern worrying at his face. "Are things ok?"

"Fine," Sallos nodded dismissively. "Tammy why don't you go and get your things ready?" She looked up at him ready to complain but one look at his face and she moved off muttering under her breath.

Kris waited until she was out of ear shot before asking, "What the hell happened?"

"Nothing, Fuerety wanted me to do some things for him."

"And?"

Sallos shrugged, "And I did. Will you be going back now? Just because you've been looking after Tam, doesn't excuse you from your duties." He smiled changing the subject.

Kris's dark eyebrows turned into a scowl. "I was only helping."

"Thanks Kris, I don't know what I would have done."

Kris nodded, "I'll see you two back home then." He said as he blinked out on the nearest line.

Tammy came though a few seconds later her bag in hand and a frown on her face. "Something wrong isn't it?"

Sallos sighed looking at her, he never could lie to his sister and now it seems Tammy. "Yes."

"Is it something I've done?" she asked her lip quivering minutely.

His heart almost broke at the sight of her, "Don't be silly, I've just managed to get us in a bit of a bother. It's nothing to worry about, I'll just work better knowing that you'll be safe elsewhere."

Instead of complaining like he'd expected her to do she nodded. "So where is this safer place?"

He grinned at her. "I'm taking you to see an old friend of mine. You haven't seen her since you were young."

"Her?" Tammy asked with perfect child tact.

"Yes, her. Now come on."

Taking her shoulder in his hand he blinked them down into the incubus courts. Alabaster's rooms hadn't changed much in over fifty years. He was beginning to think that this was a bad idea. The incubus courts were no place to keep an eight-year-old girl hidden. He groaned thinking of someone else that could look after her. He couldn't hand her over to Cassiel to look after, then the demon would just have something else to hang over him. Alabaster was the only person he trusted to keep Tammy safe.

"Plush," Tammy remarked looking around curiously.

"It's not bad. Come on Tam," he took her hand loosing his nerve. "This was a mistake."

"Sallos?"

The soft voice came from the other side of the room as the body it was attached to walked through the alcove. She was tall, long chestnut hair to the small of her back. Her eyes flashed in the perfect lighting of the room, amber then gold. She was a vision, pretty and lithe, her long silver dress sweeping the floor as she stood there. "Is that actually you?" her hands went to her mouth, dropping the leather bound book she carried. "Is that Tamara? Dear fates it's been a long time."

"Wow." Tammy said from behind him mirroring his thoughts.

His mouth dried up at the sight of her, she looked even more beautiful than she did in his memory. "It has," he offered, smiling weakly.

"I... Sal you look like shit, what's going on?" she walked forward her hips swaying naturally, accenting the seductress she was. It wasn't something she did consciously, but it was something that never failed to get his blood pumping.

She stopped shy of them and looked down at Tamara. "Hi," she said softly.

Tam grinned, "Hi. I told him he looked like shit too."

Alabaster grinned. "I'm glad we agree. I haven't seen you since you were a year old." She looked up at Sallos and sighed. "What is it?"

He frowned at Tam, "Try not to swear in front of her, she's impressionable." He smiled apologetically, "Is there somewhere we can talk?"

Alabaster smiled and nodded and then looked down at Tammy again. "Do you like books? I'm sorry to say I'm not privy to the workings of the mind of an eight year old, so I'm not sure what to offer you to do while Sallos has his clandestine conversation with me."

"Do you have any juice? I'm kinda thirsty," Tammy asked reminding Sallos that all she'd eaten in the past day was most likely junk.

"And would it be possible to get her something to eat? I think Kris has been letting her eat anything she wants."

"Yes of course. Let's get you a sandwich and some pasta salad and some Kool-Aid. King Amos is rather fond of the stuff..." she smiled. "So why don't we take you to the kitchen, and you can eat while we talk?"

"I guess."

Sallos smiled at Alabaster. "You're an angel and that would be perfect."

Alabaster took them to the kitchen where she quickly fixed a sandwich of turkey and cheese and mayonnaise for the child and one for Sallos. She placed it in his hand and then turned to Tamara to serve her some macaroni salad.

"Anything else you want Hun, please don't hesitate to root through the kitchen. Grady is the only incubus about today and he's a cookie hound so if you find them and he's about, he's going to make you share. We will be in the room next door okay?"

She looked about unsure about being left alone. "If you need anything just shout and I'll be right through," Sallos reassured her.

"Ok," she said sitting down. "Thank you Alabaster."

"You're most welcome Tamara, and I have to tell you, you look just like your mother." She smiled.

"Uncle Sally says that all the time," she answered sadly.

She went to her knees and touched the child's hand "Don't be sad Tamara. Your mother was exactly like you, pretty and smart, and dazzling. You should be proud, you're her legacy."

Sallos winced, waiting for Tammy's usual violent reaction to her mother's name but instead he was surprised to see her smile. "I guess I am."

"Eat little one, we will be back in mere minutes. Oh and there's some pudding in the fridge..." she turned to Sallos and motioned for him to follow her. Once they were safe behind closed doors she watched him carefully. "So it's been... ten years. Why now?"

"You're good with her." He smiled looking at the closed doors unable to look at her.

"I had a lot of practice with my nieces. Answer the question Sallos. It's not that I'm not happy to see you, I just want to know why now after all this time?"

He sighed; she was always to the point. "I need your help, with Tamara. Things are getting too dangerous for her with me. I take it you're aware of the situation?"

She nodded. "Luckily Amos and Cam have chosen the right side this time. What do you need from me Sal?"

"I need someone to look after her, take her away from it all."

"So you thought of me. Brilliant Sal, no one would ever think I would have her since you have been so careful to avoid me all the time."

He watched her for a moment trying to detect sarcasm in her voice. "You'd have to take her topside."

"I spend most of my time there as it is Sal, there's nothing wrong with that. You need my help, you have it, have I ever turned you down?"

"No you haven't, but ten years is a long time."

"Nothings changed Sallos, nothing." She looked down and sighed. "And here I was thinking you actually missed me."

He smiled his body aching to touch her. "I did. I do. Maybe the shift in power won't be such a bad thing."

The look in her eyes as she stared at him was filled with hope. "I'll do this for you Sal, but only on one condition."

"Anything."

"Kiss me, kiss me like you're saying you're not leaving again."

He crossed the distance between them in one step. He lifted her against him pressing himself to her. "I never wanted to leave." He kissed her letting all of his passion and frustration out on her.

Alabaster gasped and moaned into his mouth, grasping at his shoulders then wrapping her arms around him as her body melted into his.

He kissed her for all he was worth, not knowing when the next time he'd see her again. The past ten years without her had been unbearable.

Alabaster broke the kiss and gave him a satisfied smile. "You do take payment seriously Sallos."

"I do... but that was more me, than payment." He kissed her again lightly.

"I do want to believe that. So where would you like me to take her?"

"Anywhere, it's best I don't know."

She nodded and smiled. "Very well, but I'll leave word with Fiona where I can be reached, so that you can find me if you need to. You think she's going to be ok with me? She doesn't even know me."

"Like you said you have experience. She'll not like it but it's time off school so it's not all that bad for her. Just take her shopping."

"I can do shopping... and let her decorate her room." Stroking his cheek, Alabaster gave him a lazy look. "I'm going to miss you all over again. It's not fair."

"True but maybe this time there's hope in our situation. If the king dies... I'm no longer indebted to him. I'll be free of him."

"And if he doesn't? I have faith in Cassiel, all the pleasure courts do, but I'm not hanging my happiness on his winning. Ten years alone is hard to bear."

"He has to, if he doesn't I'll be killed with him."

"I won't let that happen Sal."

"I know angel, but it won't come to that. I'll make sure Cassiel succeeds."

"Then I will be waiting for you, like I always am." They kissed again and she moaned into it, her body taught once again, as if unable to let him go.

"It won't be long now Cassiel will want to move soon after the baby's born."

"Baby?"

"The child," he said carefully. "Faris is pregnant."

"Truly?" She smiled a sad smile and sighed. "That is good news. Cassiel has a lot to lose now. I hope she's safe."

"She will be. Faris always could take care of herself."

"There's the truth of it."

"I trust her decisions, as the future monarch I must."

"She was always more level headed then either of her parents, but I suppose that is due to you having a hand in her upbringing."

"I've tried my best, though there were some things I could never talk her out of."

She nodded. "The heart wants what the heart wants Sal, that's true of us all."

"Us especially." He laid another kiss on her lips.

"I won't lose you in my life again Sallos. Not when it's all I have left."

He wanted to argue but he knew how she felt. Parting from Alabaster always killed him. "You won't."

"So what is the plan then? Do I even get an evening with you? We could take Tamara to my apartment, I'll have to pack a few things anyway," she offered.

"I don't know, I should have given my report already." He looked at the door to where Tammy sat. He didn't want her to get the wrong idea, not that he was entirely sure what the right idea was.

She nodded. "I see. So how's this? I'll take her topside to my apartment, and get my stuff together. Won't leave till the late morning, I have some travel plans to arrange, so the option is open if you want to spend some time with her."

"I'll try. Unfortunately as soon as go to the king the chances are that I won't be coming back for awhile. Sugar-coat it as I may but I've failed to find the princess, I don't fail, he'll want to know why."

Alabaster frowned. "All the more reason to come for a little while. But I won't press you. You will do what your damn honor dictates as always," she bitterly offered.

Her words stung him more than if she'd slapped him. "I guess I will," he sighed stepping away from her.

"Don't get sullen Sallos. I have a right to be bitter. Ten years without you, Ten years of hurting and being utterly alone, and you come to me, ask me for help which I gladly give, and tell me that there's a possibility you're going to be punished and that you would rather go and do that over spending some time with your niece and myself, whom you claimed to love once upon a time.

"This is all for your damn honor Sal, and I'm sorry but that fuck doesn't deserve it and never did. Not when he stopped you from having a life and being with the one person that truly loves you!" Tears swam in her eyes and she shook her head. "It doesn't matter, it really doesn't."

"What do you want me to do? Leave with you? Run away? I can't do that Bas and you know it... it has nothing to do with my honor. I don't want to go and get punished, nothing could be further than the truth." He took her hands in his. "I want to run and hide, I do, but it's not going solve anything. All I want to do is curl up with you in front of a fire, or to be back on the beach." He sighed heavily. "The longer I'm away the more he'll suspect I'm up to something."

"You're right Sal. I... it's not fair. Not fair at all."

"Our situation never was." He pulled her to him holding her close. "I don't suppose a few more hours would do much harm."

"Don't patronize me Sal. You already made it plain where you need to be. Go say goodbye to your niece. I suspect it will be some months till you see her again."

"I'm not patronizing you." He slumped suddenly very tired.

She held him then. Cuddled him to her and sighed. "None of this is fair, ever. I'm forced to endure here alone, you're forced to work for a lunatic that's out of his tree and never the twain shall meet." Sighing, Alabaster kissed his forehead. "Maybe things will get better."

"They can't get much worse. I've failed you... there's nothing I can do to make up for that."

"Failed me? No, not in the least. We are both victims of circumstance. I was destined to be the property of a man that doesn't want me, and love another man that I can't have. It has nothing to do with you failing me."

"It feels like it."

"That's because you're always so hard on yourself. That's gotta change if we are ever going to move forward."

"I'm sure it's something we can manage."

She smiled, the hope she was projecting making her features come alive once more. "One day at a time love. So are you going to go say goodbye?"

"More of a 'see you later' than a good bye." He bent taking her lips into his once more, enjoying the feel of her against him.

Alabaster's whimper was one of desperation as his lips parted from hers seconds later. "Keep that up and you won't ever leave this pantry."

"Works well with the desire to run and hide, doesn't it?" He flashed her a quick grin. "But hiding in a cupboard, no matter how well stocked won't solve my problems. Plus Tam wouldn't stay out there forever."

"True. She is going to ask you know, about it. She's smarter then she lets on I think, picks stuff up."

"You don't know the half of it. I'll tell her what I can, that she's in danger. If she asks you, be honest just leave out the parts where I'm going to be in pain for the next little while. She may be inquisitive but she's still only eight."

"And about us?"

He smiled up at her. "Tell her that I love you very much and once this is all over we're finally going to be together. Tell her that I'm going to ask you to marry me and hopefully you'll say yes. Tell her that we're fed up being pawns in other peoples' games and that it's about time we started living our own lives."

She laughed and shook her head. "I just figured she would ask if we were involved, but if you really mean what you say..."She giggled and gave a brilliant smile. "I do love you Sal."

"I know," He kissed her again. "I love you too and I mean every word."

"I know Sal, I know. As reluctant as I am to leave here, we should get back to Tamara. I don't want her to think she's been abandoned, and I think you need some time with her as well. We will have our time together soon."

"We will. That's a promise." He kissed her again letting his hands move over her hair. "We better go back through before Tam finds Grady and starts quizzing him on exactly what an incubus is."

She laughed and nodded. "That would fluster the hell outta Grady cuz he couldn't very well give his requisite 'I could show you if you want' to an 8 year old. And we have been in here long enough to rouse suspicion. Come my love, let's not dally."

Sallos laughed with her, "If he tried I'd kill him, come on." He opened the door letting the light floor around him.

Tamara sat at the table with an imp sitting in front of her, both munching on a cookie. Alabaster went closer and grinned. "I see you have met Oswald. He didn't try to steal your sweater did he? He likes yellow."

"Nope he's been very good. He even found me some cookies."

Alabaster pet the little hairy imp, who looked like a fuzzy ball with a goblin face and very shrewd and calculating eyes, with a long purple tail and smiled.

Asmodeus, the Incubus king, had had Oswald a long time, and while he was constantly a thorn in the monarch's side, the little terror made the courts more lively and that was why he was allowed to remain. "Oswald, take another cookie and say goodbye to Tamara. She and I have to go soon."

Oswald the imp took another cookie from the plate on the table and then looked at Tamara and bowed his little head. "You come see Ossy again yes? Good we eat cookies together. Safe... Tammy safe ok?"

Tammy grinned at him patting his head. "I will, you be safe too Ossy," she answered then frowned then looked at Sallos. "Wait where am I going with her? What are you doing?"

Sighing, Sallos took a seat next to her. "I need you to go with Bas for a little while, things aren't too safe here right now, love."

Alabaster went to her knees next to her. "We are going to go topside Hun, and take a vacation. No school, lots of shopping, horseback riding, and anything else you could wanna do."

She looked suspiciously at her. "What's the catch?"

Alabaster looked at Sallos. "You won't be able to see your uncle for a while."

Her eyes shot to Sallos, "Why? What are you doing?"

"Things are just getting a little dangerous for you to stay down here. I'm sorting it out but its best you have someone to look after you properly."

He watched her think it over. "And no school?"

"No school Hun, though if anyone asks you're being home schooled, which in a way is true, you're going to be learning about the almighty dollar and how to ride," she smiled. "And I would love to have you around Tamara. It's been a long time since I could just be a girl and hangout."

"I don't want to." She blurted out running to him. "Sallos I'll be good, don't make me go, you need me." She grabbed him hugging him. "Who'll look after you?"

"Tam? He doesn't want you to go, but you have to come with me so he can be safe, and so can you."

"Tammy, it's not going to be forever. It's only for a little while till I sort something out. I'll make your birthday in two months I promise." He held her tightly.

Alabaster looked down to them and caught his eye and nodded. Tamara would be ok, and his woman, the woman that still waited for him, would see to it.

"Promise?" She asked looking up at him. "Can I have a party?"

That was his Tammy always bargaining. "Yes, you can and all the ice cream you can eat."

Thirty

Sallos steeled himself as he once again walked empty handed into Fuerety's throne room. He knew this wasn't going to go well though the time spent with Alabaster and his niece had lifted his spirits. At least he now knew they were both safe, no harm would come to them. He could take his chances with Fuerety knowing that. He strode into the room taking every effort to keep his body language confident and neutral. His king could sense weakness like a shark could sense blood.

The king was sitting in his study as expected. Normally he'd be there reading a dusty leather bound book or staring out the window surveying his kingdom. This time, much to Sallos' horror, he was sitting opposite another. His blood ran cold. Blaze sat surrounded by shadows. He'd never met a Cento who had such an affinity with the darkness as Blaze did. Between them sat an old backgammon set and it looked as if they were half way through a game. He'd seen that set a thousand times but he'd never seen it in use.

He bowed low to the floor trying as hard as he could to ignore the feel of Blaze's eyes boring into his head. "My lord."

Fuerety inclined his head his full attention on Sallos. "Where is my daughter General?"

"I don't know sire."

"That's..." he paused dramatically as he pretended to search for a word. "Disappointing."

"I agree, I've done everything that I could and there's still no sign of her." Sallos answered keeping his head low to avoid seeing the look of fury on his king's face.

He'd already steeled himself for what was coming so the kick to his ribs was expected. The second however took him off balance knocking him onto his side. He stayed where he was praying that the king would lose interest.

"No," Fuerety spoke calmly moving around him. "I've put too much work into you Sallos. Too much of my time and effort has gone into making you what you are."

What that really meant, he thought bitterly, was that the king had spent his time ruining him. He felt the bite of another kick dangerously close to his ribs. Demons could heal damage quickly but Fuerety could dish it out faster than he could heal. It wouldn't be long, he knew, before he'd be begging for the simple kicks.

It didn't take long to start as Fuerety lifted a crude metal sword. He began beating him viciously with the flat of the blade. The sword roared with fire singing into his clothes. Sallos was almost sick as his ribs crunched, his own blood bursting into his mouth. Breathing became impossible and all he could do was spit blood and pray that the darkness would take him soon.

The beating stopped as soon as it had started. "Kneel!" Fuerety commanded.

It took him awhile, blood pouring from his nose and mouth. His ribs crunched sickeningly as he levered himself to his knees. The pain in his left leg was excruciating, his knee swollen beyond recognition.

"You're lucky Sallos. I'm growing tired of torture today." The king's simple words dripped with malice that made him look up despite the pain.

He didn't want to know, he knew he didn't but it didn't stop him from asking. "Tired sire?" He croaked hoarsely.

"Yes tired. Blaze was helping me earlier as we were waiting for your return."

Sallos looked at Blaze for the first time taking in more than his shadowy shape. His hands were stained a deep red from blood. "What have you done?" he asked though the answer terrified him.

Blaze shrugged calmly shutting his eyes as Fuerety answered for him. "I've done what is my right to do, in the search for my daughter. I asked Blaze to check in on your niece, she seems to be absent."

His heart stopped. Had they gotten to her and Alabaster? No there hadn't been enough time he'd just left them. Which meant they'd gotten to somebody else. Who could it be?

Gathering himself as best he could he met the kings eyes. "I sent her to her paternal grandparents. I felt you were right, the Afterverse is no place for a half human."

"Indeed." He spat out sarcastically. "Her whereabouts are no longer required. I have what I need now."

He heard a noise behind him and turned to see the smiling face of the bastard Conglacio prince. He slammed a metal chair down pushing it into Sallos' broken form. "Please General," he leered, "By all means take a seat."

Rage boiled through him. He was familiar with the chair it was one they often used for interrogation and one that was already blue with ice. That the king was using Gabriel the bastard was a bad sign indeed. His lie about Bethany and Cassiel may yet come back to haunt him instead of the Conglacio. One look to the king and he knew that he'd have to sit on the frozen seat. Nothing burned more than ice.

Gabriel wasn't as accomplished as his half brothers but ice was ice. It didn't take much to hurt. The Conglacio still had his hands on the back of the seat. In his last act of defiance he levered himself up into the seat ignoring the ice searing into him. He used the pain in his aching body to fuel his fire as he sent it through the chair and up to the unsuspecting Conglacio's hands. Gabriel yelped throwing himself back cursing.

Fuerety smiled, amused at the smug bastard's pain. "Enough," he commanded, "Blaze, the cuffs."

Blaze stood silently towering over Sallos. He placed one hand on his chest pushing him back into the seat with no regard whatsoever for his slowly healing splintered ribs. Sallos coughed at the pressure, his lung capacity severely limited. The other Demon strapped his neck to the high back of the chair tightening it securely before moving onto his hands and legs. The chair wasn't often called for but it was almost as lethal as the blows you could be dealt whilst in it. No matter what happened he had to remain loyal to the princess.

In the past when the chair had been used there was normally a tray of tools. Sallos hoped their absence was a good sign although looking at Blaze's bloody hands he wasn't convinced. He could feel his blood pumping through the pulse at his neck, the sound loud in his ears. Blaze finished the last strap pulling it tightly drawing a scream from him as his ruined leg twisted with a pop.

The Conglacio behind him snickered. "Well shit, if that's all it takes I can go home now."

"You're not done here just yet dear prince." Fuerety told him. "This is a lesson on failure and applies to you as well. I don't tolerate it, either in myself or of my people."

"I have no intention of failing you." The Conglacio answered cockily.

"As I'm sure neither did my general, although that is what we're here to find out. I'm not sure which I'd prefer, your incompetence or your betrayal. Let us find out, shall we?" He looked at Sallos expecting an answer.

"I don't think he's much up for conversation old boy." Gabriel's voice laughed. "Let's see if I can help."

Icy fingers stabbed through his shoulders adding a fresh wave of pain to him. Through a haze of red Sallos saw Fuerety's frown at the Conglacio and he instantly knew one thing. Fuerety's pet Conglacio Gabriel may be, but he was living on borrowed time. That was what happened when the king befriended you. At least Cassiel could play that game, Gabriel was a fool. A dead fool. Maybe, a delirious part of Sallos' thought gleefully, once they'd settled all this betrayal nonsense the king would send him to kill the bastard.

He glanced up at the king who smiled at him as if reading his mind. "Now, now General," he cautioned. "This is all for your own benefit. I need answers and I feel that you're hiding something from me. Of course if I had the child we could have had a calm discussion instead of all the dramatics, that you've hidden her away reeks of guilt. You've expected this. And I'm afraid with no other close family..."

"Pyre." He interrupted gaining himself a twist in those icy fingers.

His shoulders were now achingly numb, the cold seeping through him stealing away his heat. The pain was excruciating, his knee ached and he barely had the use of his lungs. The cold stopped his body from healing itself letting his original injuries hurt so much worse. None of it, however, compared to how much he didn't want to carry on listening to Fuerety.

"Pyre is valuable Sallos, as you should be. I look after those I have value in." He smiled tapping his bloody sword off his leg. "Try not to interrupt. I considered all my options carefully before coming to this somber conclusion." He struck the sword off the floor causing the sound to vibrate through the room and Sallos' head.

The door opened at his signal revealing another chair similar to the one he was currently sitting in. It was the figure tied to the chair that Sallos' mind refused to accept. Slowly the bleeding and beaten shape began to take form. First he saw the huge shoulders and heavy build that made up Kris. Sallos felt himself go cold as he tried to make out the damage that had been done to his friend.

One eye had been completely removed from the socket, the blood left to pour down Kris's face and front. His chest had been mutilated with what looked like shards of ice poking through his skin. This wasn't the methodical look of someone who'd been tortured for information it looked like a free for all had been called out on the demon's skin. Chunks of him were missing and bleeding profusely. Very specific parts were missing too; Sallos shuddered to think where they were.

He felt the bile rise to the back of his throat. Kris's feet were smashed to a pulp and he was missing most of his fingers. Sallos swore praying that this wasn't what was in store for him and then instantly feeling the shame at his thought. This was all his fault.

If it hadn't have been for him Kris would still be whole, in every sense of the way. There was no going back for Kris, his friend couldn't heal from most of these wounds. The pain he was in suddenly lessened in comparison.

"Apparently he really didn't know where you and the child were," Fuerety told him matter-of-factly.

Sallos glared at the bastard hating him. He'd always known that the king was sick but this was on a whole new level. He was a monster, they all were. How could they stay so calm in front of this mess? Kris hadn't deserved this, no one deserved this.

Sallos knew the horror showed in his eyes but he just didn't care anymore. There was no more illusion. No pretending. "He doesn't know where her grandparents live," he answered the king numbly.

Fuerety cracked a smile rolling his eyes. "Now you tell us. Your incompetence knows no bounds General. You could have saved your little friend here had you let us know what you planned."

Sallos shook his head, his vision hazing over. He prayed that he'd pass out, he didn't want to be here, to see this madness. He'd had enough. Closing his eyes he prayed for oblivion. It was only the sound of Kris's terrified pained mewling that forced them back open. Gabriel was towering over him pliers in hand as he made a bid for Kris's mouth.

"Of course. Once we realized that he had nothing to tell us we had no further need for his tongue." The Conglacio grinned gleefully prying Kris's mouth open causing blood to pour from his mouth.

True to his word his friends tongue was gone along with most of his teeth. The bastard placed the pliers around one of the few teeth left causing a more panicked moan from Kris.

"So tell me general. Do you know where my daughter is?" The kind questioned coldly.

Horrified Sallos shook his head as the terrified eye of his friend met his own. "No... I don't."

"Wrong answer." Gabriel grinned grinding the pliers as he extracted the tooth as painfully as he could.

Kris's eye squeezed shut, his noises animal like in its pitch and desperation as he fought uselessly against the bonds.

"Then this is the price of your failure," Fuerety said gravely.

They repeated the process, asking him questions he couldn't answer then mutilating Kris further. That was the price of his failure, the king repeated over and over. Taking his ears and bursting his eardrums, then telling him it was the failure. Fifteen minutes later Kris was nothing but breathing, sobbing meat.

Sallos looked at the ruin of a man that had so recently held his niece, comforting her. Kris had protected Tam, looked out for her. Written her note for her, taught her swear words, lovingly cooked for her. This was the price of failure. Fuerety was right, Sallos had failed his friend.

"So General, now that we're clear on that point. Why don't you finish the job?" Fuerety said as Blaze released his bonds. "If you're with us, General, then finish him off. Prove your loyalty."

Blaze pressed a blade into his palm as he pulled him to stand; the demon's grip on his shoulder the only thing holding him back from lunging at the king and his pet Conglacio. The rage soon passed, fear taking its place. He didn't want to end up like Kris, a shapeless ball sobbing in pain. It didn't matter how brave you were, that punishment would break anyone. Pushing Blaze's support aside he stumbled over to Kris with a crack from his leg falling into the ruined demon.

The screech from Kris sounded loudly in his ears as Sallos sought out anything to stop it. He brought the blade up in his hand quickly finding his throat and slicing it, silencing his friend permanently. Whether he did it to end his torture or Kris's he didn't know. Once it was over he felt ice-cold hands pushing him back off from the body throwing him onto the floor.

"See?" Gabriel grinned down at him. "Now that wasn't so hard. In fact it was rather fun. I've almost got myself enough Cento teeth to make a chain out of," Gabriel sneered laying into him with his feet.

Sallos welcomed the cold beating, letting it seep into him, anything to take away the scene that he'd bared witness too. He wished that they'd take his eyes as well as he was sure that Kris's body would be forever burned into his retinas. The beating lasted for what seemed like hours, nothing but the sound of the impacts and the crunching of his bone, before stopping suddenly. After a few heartbeats unmolested he dared open his eyes.

Fuerety looked down on him, disgust written all over his face. "That will be all General," he dismissed as Kris's blood, mingled by his own, soaked through Sallos' clothes, "And clean yourself up, you're a mess."

Sallos rolled over painfully smearing blood all over the floor. His dignity was gone, as was his best friend. Nothing mattered at the moment not the princess and her damn rebellion, the cold within him refusing to warm, his broken and bloodied body, Cassiel and his coupe or the people watching him try to stand. If Fuerety had pushed him over right at this moment and questioned him again he would have spilled it all. None of it was worth his friend's life, but it wouldn't bring him back. Nothing would. He sobbed rolling uselessly over onto his back.

"Blaze I expect him to be gone by the time I get back from talking to my dear Conglacio friend." With that he strolled out of the room with the bastard in tow.

Sallos took a deep breath struggling to even lie flat on his back. Closing his eyes he mustered all his strength turning to rest on his good hand and knee. His vision hazed red again and for a second he thought he'd pass out. Guilt wracked through him, it was his fault, and he deserved to be where Kris was. Strong arms lifted him up in one move.

"It's not easy watching a friend die, let alone ending it yourself." Blaze's voice sounded in his ear. "Trust me I know."

"Leave me alone." Sallos croaked trying to twist out of the other demon's nightmarish grasp.

"You're freezing," Blaze stated ignoring his protests.

Heat flooded into him, through the demon's hands and despite himself, Sallos moaned trying to draw in as much of it as he could.

"I'll take you home."

Sallos felt the familiar feeling of being pulled through the lines. His house was exactly as it had been when he'd last seen it. Kris's note was still on the fridge complete with Tammy's smiley face. Blaze, the demon from his childhood nightmares, almost tenderly carried him up to his room and sat him down on the bed. He took the tatters that had been left of Sallos' clothes and threw them onto the fire, which had sprung to life in the hearth. The heat felt good on his bare skin, healing almost. He never wanted to leave it. Blaze started to inspect his wounds first gently moving his knee then getting him to lift his arms so he could look at his ribs.

After inspecting his arms and face Blaze rocked back on his heels and sighed.

"That knee will have to be seen to now or you'll never regain full use of it. I can take you to a healer or I can do what I can for you from here. I can't guarantee that you won't have a limp. It's dislocated but the whole joint looks shattered."

"Whatever," Sallos answered, numbly staring at the carpet. "I'm not going anywhere."

Blaze nodded. "Then I'll do what I can. Bandages?"

"Bathroom."

The other Cento left the room silently coming back sometime later with a bag of bandages and a glass of water. "Drink," he said pushing the glass into Sallos' hand. Sallos did as he was told tipping the cool water into his mouth and shakily sitting the glass aside.

"Good, you'll need to keep drinking. Sit up straight and I'll tape your ribs before I set your knee."

Blaze got him to take a few deep breaths deciding where the most affected areas were before firmly taping him up. He took a warm damp cloth from somewhere wiping most of the blood off him.

"You're being awfully nice, would of betted against you ever giving me a sponge bath," Sallos said humorlessly.

"I'm not being nice. It just doesn't stand to reason that I should leave you coughing blood on your doorstep."

"Very gallant of you for a mad man. Didn't know you had a grasp of first aid." Sallos grunted as Blaze pressed down on a rib he was taping.

"I've been patching myself up since before the king was born. As for mad, it happens. Once you lose everything your very identity comes into question."

That information perked at him, something he could almost bring himself to care about. "You're older than Fuerety?" If it was true then Blaze was indeed ancient.

"I advised his father. It was an age ago."

"Before you lost your identity?"

Blaze smiled, a terrifying action on its own. "So it would seem. A time when the dragons still worked with us, trusted us." Something close to pain or disgust flitted over his face.

"I thought dragons were a myth."

"No they existed, the king had them all destroyed for fear of rebellion."

"And your friend? Was he a dragon?" Sallos asked bitterly, unable to believe that this monster had once had friends.

"No, he led their rebellion. He believed he could save them and fell right into Fuerety's plan."

"Save?"

"This'll hurt," he said as he grabbed Sallos' leg twisting it into its proper shape drawing no more than a grunt from Sallos' pain ridden body. "When I said that they worked with us I really should have said that they were slaves. Not all of them, earth dragons lived peacefully with the pleasure courts and the Strigo enhancing their power. The water dragons were trusted and valuable assets of the Conglacio. Fire dragons were slaves and warriors and the air dragons were the play things of the illusion and shadow courts." He spoke calmly as he bandaged the knee in place.

"Your friend tried to set them free?"

"Montrose committed suicide by warring with Fuerety. For all his might, charm and seemingly endless powers his spirit was crushed by those he'd set out to save long before I marched him up the steps to his demise."

"You killed him."

"In a way, I fetched him for execution. As I said his choices and the dragons' killed him. I'd like you to remember that, he was willing to die for them but when it came down to it, it was mostly dragons cheering on his death. Don't put your life on the line for anyone who wouldn't return the favor."

"And Fuerety? Would he?"

"Fuerety is our king and we are his dogs. His motives are quite simple, he'll keep us as long as we're still useful to him."

"I don't want to be useful to him."

Blaze tisked, "I'll put that down to post beating talk. Going against him is futile just as dying for a cause is pointless. You have to win Sallos; it's the winners that write the history. Poor Montrose is barely remembered by the people who were alive during his time let alone the scores of demons that came after him. Even Dragons are legend."

Sallos shook his head. "So there's no point in fighting if you can't win and don't fight for people that wouldn't die for you. Is that really thousands of years of wisdom condensed?"

Blaze grinned, "Of course not but it's relevant to you. You have a good thing going here, don't screw it up. If the king has called for me then something is brewing. There will come a time where you have to choose sides and you want to be on the side that doesn't get crushed horridly. Fuerety will win, and it's not because he particularly deserves to or that everyone loves him. It's because that's what he does. He wiped out the whole of the dragon race and most of Montrose's Conglacio. I doubt very much that if it comes to war he couldn't handle his protesting daughter and whomever she's conned into protecting her. Don't be one of her patsies."

"I don't know where the princess is."

"I hope not because you know the consequences of lying, it's much worse than failure. It won't bring me pleasure to kill you in that way. You have faith in the king's ways don't let what happened here tonight change that."

Sallos took a sip of water. "I won't." Faking loyalty shouldn't be a problem considering up until a few days ago he'd been that guy but the horror of tonight had changed all that. Fuerety was a monster, and that was the only word Sallos could think of to describe him. Him and Gabriel, they both had to die. "You know this has to be the longest conversation we've had."

"True but then I've never had anything to say to you before. I see a lot of you in myself."

"I'm not you Blaze."

"We'll see about that." He gave Sallos a chilling smile before porting out.

Thirty-one

Faris paced the room for the sixth time in the past hour, wringing her hands. Casha was late, Rudolph was late, and she was getting antsy. She had skipped dinner because of her nerves, and she was starting to think that might not have been a good thing overall.

Knowing what the sex of the child was made it all the more real. Back when she lost the other child, she never knew the sex of it and that, in a way, helped her cope. Without that knowledge, she didn't over obsess over what could have been, or thought up names. It was unfortunate, and it hurt but not as bad as it could have. All that knowledge could have killed her, and then where would she be? Certainly not here right now with a second chance at her heart's desire.

And now she was here waiting to hear that her fondest dreams were coming true. A baby was what they needed to mend the rift between them; an heir was what they needed to guarantee the safety of their family and those they loved. She wasn't sure what she was hoping for, but she had a feeling Casha wanted a boy. What man wouldn't? Once they knew, everything would fall into place though, and then the names would be decided, and the plans would be set into motion.

She paced once more, her back to the door when she heard it open, and then shut quietly. The cool presence in the room could only be her prince and she relaxed considerably, knowing that things were going to be ok, just as long as he was with her.

"I thought you weren't going to show up. Rudolph is late. I hope something hasn't happened to him."

"I'm sure he'll be here soon..." he smiled reassuringly kissing her lightly.

"I know... It's just... It's exciting right? I mean this is a happy time and... " She searched for the right words and found nothing. They were doing it right, but she was still scared and nervous about it all. "Knowing the sex of the child makes it that much more real."

"I know it does, but it won't change anything. It's real already." He patted her arm and moved to pour himself a glass of water. "It is exciting."

"You know we never even thought of names, not even back..." she looked at him and then down at her minute bump and sighed. "I just don't want history to repeat itself."

"It won't." His voice came firmly. "I won't let it. I'm king now and we have a lot more support. He'll never get to you again, I promise." Sitting the water down, he took her into his arms. "Last time I overestimated his sanity. I didn't believe for one second that he'd do that to you. To us."

"I know Cashy, I just... this is just surreal." She snuggled close to him and nuzzled his neck.

"It is a little." He admitted kissing the top of her head. "But in a good way."

"Yes, a very good way. So you have any ideas for names my love?" she asked and giggled, starting to feel a bit playful.

Cash always had a way to make her emotions exactly what they should be at the time, and now, she knew she needed to be positive for both their sakes.

"Names? Not really... nobody is getting named after my father though," he paused in consideration for a second. "Or yours. What about you though? Any one that you've been thinking of?

She had been thinking, but it wasn't something she wanted to decide on her own. "A few, though I wouldn't want to make any of the children after past rulers, its not, well safe."

"Or original," he pointed out. "So tell me what you've come up with."

"Well for girls, I like Andrea, Chloe, Aubrey and Aramantha," she said and kissed his nose.

"All good options and for boys?"

"Well, I like Brandt, and Sebastian, and Gage."

He made a face. "Hmmm, well I like Gage and Sebastian's okay."

She grinned. Gage was her favorite. It was apt, the one name that she kept coming back to was the very one Cash liked. "Well then that settles it." She kissed him. "A boy named Gage then."

"If we have a boy."

"Well you have a fifty percent possibility of that." The words spoken were cultured and soft, and Faris turned and stood, looking at Rudolph, who bowed from the waist.

A tall and dark figure, Rudolph was the epitome of the Arco court noble. His shoulder length hair was a deep chestnut brown with darker plum highlights, his eyes a bright and starry turquoise, same shade as the other full males in the royal family.

As the queen's brother, he was the surgeon to all the royal families, and has been the attending physician for all the Afterverse children for the past five hundred years. He was also the only person Faris trusted to help bring their child into the world.

"My apologies for being late. Lady Hestia is with child as well but a bit further along. There have been complications, and I didn't want to raise suspicions by not attending her quickly. The two of you don't need the extra attention from the Afterverse." He turned his gaze to Cash and bowed. "Highness, congratulations on your new position."

"Thank you." Cash smiled at him, "News travels fast, I see, and I appreciate your discreetness. No further attention from the Afterverse is required, I'm afraid we have a little too much."

"Word has not traveled, but my sister is always abreast of every situation. You both are fine, and you know you hold the support of the Arcuo, as well as many of the other houses. So shall we see what the new heir is? I do admit I'm happy to see you back together at last. Highness, if I may?"

Cash let her go, stepping to her side but keeping within touching distance.

The doctor went to her and knelt in front of her placing his hands lightly on her belly. She felt the quiet power of the Arcuo flow through her, a delicious fuzzy pressure permeating her womb. She breathed slowly, allowing the other demon to do his job.

Minutes later Rudolph took his hands away and then stood smiling at them both.

Cash waited for a few heartbeats before asking, "Well?"

Rudolph grinned wider and looked to the two of them each in turn. "It seems history is partially repeating itself."

"In what way?" he all but growled.

"It's a boy, as was before the unpleasantness. You have your second chance Highnesses, and he will be very powerful."

"A boy?" he asked in disbelief before turning to Faris grinning. "Our boy?"

Faris blinked her surprise. The news of the first child had reached her long after the incident, when she had begged Sallos to tell her in a fit of melancholy, and now it seemed they were truly getting the second chance at it. "How far along am I?"

Rudolph smiled. "Almost a month Princess."

She looked at Cash and then smirked. "My betrothal night."

"That was a possibility." Cash chuckled.

Rudolph smiled and bowed again. "You're progressing well, and because of the power level of the child, you might go into labor before the normal time. It's common with Royals and powerful children. Both of you were early births."

"Then there's no doubt our son will be as well... and powerful."

"Very powerful. I always knew it would be so if the two of you ever had children. My congratulations on this as well. My sister will be glad to hear of it. And I'm sure you have family and friends you wish to tell. Princess Faris, I will need to see you in two weeks since your progression is going to be quicker then most." She nodded. "King Cassiel, I will need you to keep her from exerting herself for the next month or so, and no wild copulating."

Cash flashed him a grin, "I can only try my best."

Faris blushed and then punched Cash in the arm. "We will be on our best behavior Rudolph. Thank you."

The other demon grinned. "Then I should take my leave of you both. I'll see you in two weeks then Faris, here at the mansion."

"We'll see you then." Cash answer pulling her close.

The space where the doctor was standing was suddenly empty, as he made use of the large ley-line vein that ran under Crypt. Faris giggled and looked at Cash, going to him and wrapping her arms around him. "A boy, a little boy. This is it Lover, no going back now."

"There was never any going back Fari. So little Gage then?"

"Yes, a little boy named Gage... Ooh!" she squealed and hugged him close. "Now Astrid and I can do the nursery, and go shopping for baby stuff... I'm happy Cashy, really happy."

Laughing, he squeezed her tightly being careful of her belly. "And I should hope so too. A baby boy and the prospect of shopping, you've got your card full for the next while love. I do want you to take it easy though."

"I will, you'll be here to take it easy with me won't you? We will get a chance to really reconnect."

"I will. Nothing sounds better to me than a little reconnecting." He grinned.

"Yeah? How so?" she giggled and grabbed his ass.

"Judging by that I think you know. So shall we tell everyone or shall we do some reconnecting first?" he grinned wolfishly kissing her.

"That's up to you, though I'm a very happy demon right now..."

"That makes two of us. It's probably wise to tell then before Astrid has a fit... plus I wouldn't mind telling Dimitri."

"Then let's tell the family." She loved saying the world and meaning it.

They were all family now, no matter how ragtag a union it was, and now they were making that family larger with the edition of the first child of the new children of the Afterverse. It was a heady notion. "Who do we tell first?"

Thirty-two

Dawn broke over the Cascades, the sunshine glinting off the snow covered caps. Alabaster stood on the balcony of the log home she owned just outside of Dalton, a sleepy ski town that had recently seen some economic action. The house was a refuge from the courts, the cities and her king, and few knew exactly where it was located.

Tamara was asleep in her bedroom, her arms wrapped around the teddy Sallos had given her before leaving her for the fire palace. The poor girl was exhausted, but she was safe, and that's all that mattered. Well, not all.

Sallos had been gone from them for hours, and she wasn't sure what had happened. It was killing her, not knowing where her lover was, and what kind of shape he was in, but she had promised to not go looking for him. It was a promise she didn't plan to keep. If he was hurt, needed someone, she wasn't going to leave him alone.

Something must have gone wrong or he would have come to her, found them already. She had the nagging feeling that he was in need of help, and she felt this strongly, she went with her gut.

She walked inside and went to the landline, calling Fiona.

"Its dawn, who is this?" her niece's sleepy voice sounded in her ear.

"No word?" She asked cautiously.

"What? Oh no sorry, nothing." She yawned again.

"Look, I need to know, can you come here? Watch her for a little while? You know I don't trust anyone but you."

"Of course. Far be it from me to ever stop a woman from tending to her true love."

Alabaster thanked the stars that her niece understood her passion. "Thank you," she said and hung the phone up, just as Fiona blinked into the living room, wrapped in a fuzzy blanket, wearing a pair of white and grey flannel pajamas. She looked at Alabaster and shook her head. "You look terrible."

"No worse then I have in the past six months, which is why I have been avoiding everyone. I'll be back soon, I... I just need to know. Try not to wake her ok?"

"You got it Bast." Fiona went to the couch and plunked down snuggling into the cushions and Alabaster grabbed a ponytail holder and pulled her hair up, blinking to the Arcuo court, and the only surgeon in the Afterverse, Rudolph.

She raced down the halls towards his office, knowing without a doubt he would be there. The doctor rarely slept, he just morphed his appearance to give the visage a little time off.

This was one of those times. She opened his office door, forsaking any propriety and preamble, and was greeted to a completely different face then the one she knew and trusted well.

Usually a tall lean man with dark hair and bright blue eyes, Rudolph was blonde, had bright green eyes and a full beard, though his frame remained the same. He looked up, accustomed to people barging in unannounced, and frown.

"Princess Alabaster? Is the king well?"

She nodded, a bit out of breath. "I'm sure Asmodeus is fine, though I haven't seen him for some time. I need your services, and, sadly, they must be given with the utmost discretion."

Rudolph rose and nodded. "What's the problem?"

"I'm not sure." She quickly ran through the problem at hand, with Sallos asking her to take Tamara, the reason why and the plans they had set into motion. Rudolph listened intently and nodded, grabbing his Jacket.

"So you don't know where he is? Have you checked his residence?"

She blushed. "No, I haven't, but honestly I didn't want to get there and be at a loss if something did happen."

"Perfectly understandable Princess. Let us check his Residence and go from there."

They blinked to his place to find blood streaking the floor, as if he were dragged through the hallway, kitchen and into the bedroom. Alabaster sobbed and followed the blood, Rudolph hot on her heels. The sight that greeted her tore at her heart.

The man she loved was laid up, alone, and apparently in a large amount of pain. She looked at the bandages, all neatly battlefield dressed and she knew one of his comrades helped him here. She sent a silent prayer to those who watched over her that Tamara wasn't there to see this. She went to the bed as he opened the eye that wasn't swelled shut and grabbed his hand squeezing gently.

"Sal! Sweet Darkness, what happened!?"

Rudolph came closer and waited, as if he knew Sallos was not in a trusting mood.

Sallos jumped at her voice wincing silently. "Things got bad."

She bit her bottom lip, trying desperately to hold back tears. "I would say so! Goodness.." she murmured and squeezed his hand. "I brought Rudolph, and I'm glad I did. Please... Sal..."

"I got it easy," he told her his voice hoarse. "I'll live, I'm sure the doctor has other things to tend to. How's Tam?"

She closed her eyes and nodded. "She's fine, sleeping at the place in Dalton, Fi is with her."

Rudolph moved closer. "General, I think the princess, as well as myself would feel better if I examined you quickly. You need attention, as well as some tonics."

Alabaster shifted on the bed as Rudolph set to work on Sallos, and she concentrated on the positive. He might be a mess, but he was still alive. "Baby, tell me what happened."

"I killed Kris," he murmured, his voice reflecting the obvious pain he was feeling.

"What? How the hell did you manage that? Why would you do that?"

"I had no choice." He shook his head gravely closing his eyes. "He wouldn't have made it."

Alabaster's eyes grew wide at what he suggested. If Sallos was this hurt, she could imagine what happened to Kris. She liked the other demon, he was one of the only ones that knew about her and Sallos and approved of it, just like he cared for Tamara like a father would. Kris wouldn't be coming back now, and Sallos had killed his friend out of mercy. She shook her head and leaned in to kiss the small patch of unmarred skin on his forehead, careful not to touch any of the blooming bruises. Seeing him like this, her proud and virile warrior, brought low and left for dead, her choices were clear, and she knew what they had to do. "Fuerety did this to you both? Just him?"

Rudolph stood and then looked at Sallos. "The knee is going to have to be reset, and those ribs, three cracked two broken. You need serious medical attention Sallos. If you'll permit me, I shall return with my nurse, and the appropriate medicines and tonics."

"Please Rudolph, and be quick about it. I don't need to tell you..."

"Yes, yes, utmost discretion."

The surgeon nodded and blinked out of the room, leaving Alabaster with her lover. "Tell me everything." She said quietly.

"Can't..." he shook his head. "Not just yet. Look you have to tell Cash that Blaze is out and Gabriel..." he winced at the sound of the Conglacio's name. "He's working with Fuerety."

So the fire king and the bastard of the Conglacio? This wasn't very good at all. She nodded. "I'll make sure he gets the information Sal, but, I can't leave you here, not alone. We need to get you out of here." She looked at his dressed wounds and then frowned. "Who cleaned you up? Pyre?"

"No, Blaze did. Fuerety is keeping Pyre away from me, which isn't surprising, I doubt she'd approve. Though she wouldn't dare speak against him."

"Blaze? I thought he was insane." She shook her head knowing full well that Fuerety's strategy of keeping Pyre away from Sallos wasn't anything more then keeping the only family Sal had away from him, twisting Pyre away from where she should be, standing with her cousin.

Rudolph blinked in with Sereeta, his nurse just then. The woman bowed to Alabaster and then set to work on his leg with Rudolph, while the princess held his hand. "Once you're stable, we gotta get you out of here. I don't trust that son of a bitch to not come and finish you off because he had the thought on a whim. You're too important to me, and to Tamara."

"I'm not going anywhere, someone needs to keep an eye on things."

"This isn't negotiable Sallos. I'll not lose you when I just got you back. Let someone else do it. Right now you need to worry about Tamara, myself, and healing, but not in that order. If things are as bad as you're hinting at..."

Rudolph looked at them both. "I can make sure that Cassiel knows everything, Sookie has been back and forth to his topside retreat several times, and I needen't tell you she has no love for the Cento court. General, it is imperative you allow yourself to heal once we are done here. You cannot do that here with a possibility of an attempt on your life."

"No attempt will be made, he doesn't want me dead. He wants me operational and on his side. I've paid for my incompetence in his eyes. Bas love, I want nothing more than to go back with you but I can't. There's nobody else that has the king's trust. If I run now then he'll hunt us down if I stay I can destroy him from the inside. Especially now he has Blaze out. Blaze is insane but I can deal with him... Maybe even turn him to our cause. I owe it to Faris and I owe it to Kris."

"You have a point, but you can't heal correctly here, alone, and he knows that. You will be useless, worse off then Pyre and Blaze."

"She's right General. These injuries could make you lame, and this was probably his intent. He no doubt counted on you not getting the right kind of medical attention, and that you are is going to have him look towards your way with his unkind eye. He might have been punishing you, but this was meant to be one that you wouldn't fully recover from."

"Then don't fix it." he growled swatting at the physician. "I need to be here."

"So you can walk with a limp for the rest of your life? I'm sorry honey I love you but you're no pimp! Why would you deliberately lame yourself! No, no I can't let you, we need to figure something else out."

"Then let me know when you think of something Bas, because where I'm sitting there is no other way. Fuerety will expect me to get help eventually. He hasn't ordered me not to. He's just thinking that I'll have a few days of agonizing pain before I manage to leaver myself out of bed to seek it. I doubt he wants a lame general... He'd have been better off killing me if that were the case and he didn't kill me. He doesn't want to replace me at this stage."

She closed her eyes. "I can't leave you alone Sal, it's not an option. You don't need to be the hero Sallos."

"I don't want to be a hero love," he told her softly. "They tend to die horrifically and I've seen enough of that for one lifetime. I don't plan on being the hero... I'm just going to do my job, with a little of my own interpretation of exactly what that means. I'll give him no reason to kill me love, I promise. I want to live. Once this is finished we can be together, the three of us. I think a little pain and fighting is worth that. We won't be apart much longer."

She closed her eyes and shook her head. "Then what do you want me to do? Tam is going to start asking questions, and she's not stupid. If you're not home, she's going to want to know why."

"Tell her what you have to, I've always tried to be honest with her. Tell her that I've had to stay here to work and that I'll visit when I can. I'll still make her birthday... Though Kris won't. Don't tell her about him. Leave that for me."

"I wouldn't, something like that..." her train of thought derailed as she sighed. "I'm going to be here nightly till you're better Sal."

He smiled, "I can live with that."

"And probably after as well." She looked at Rudolph and Sereeta and nodded. "Patch him up as best you can, please."

She watched as the surgeon and the nurse tended to the love of her life silently, now holding a wet washcloth to his head to clean up some of the dried and oozing blood. He was still under there, the man she gave her heart to so long ago, and she wouldn't lose him now, not when they were so close to being happy.

This incident was a hurdle but nothing more. She wouldn't let Fuerety even think about doing this to anyone again, and she knew that Sallos was already plotting his own revenge against his ruler for what was done to Kris. Gabriel, well he would pay either way, though once Faris found out his involvement in this she will call for blood, which she knew Cassiel would gladly grant in one way or another. The bastard of the Conglacio was really living on borrowed time now, and nothing would change that. The only question was when it was going down, and Alabaster knew, without a doubt in her soul, that it would be soon.

Epilogue

Cash sighed heavily sitting the phone back in the cradle. It was bad news indeed; Gabriel was working with Fuerety, though it wasn't terribly surprising. Cash had long known that there was a connection between the two that ran back as far as Gabriel's mother. He'd always been willing to bet that the Cento king had used the bastard to give Jeanette that twist that she needed to call out his mother. Cash had just never had proof of it before only hearsay and instinct.

What upset him the most was the sheer ferocity of Sallos' wounds. Rudolph had accounted everything the Cento had told him and of the demon's condition. Sallos would live but he was going to be very sore while he healed. Fuerety had Blaze at his side now, a thought on its own that sent shivers down Cash's spine, he wouldn't need Sallos' fighting skills. Yet it didn't sound like the King at all to create such a powerful enemy amongst his own ranks. Cash hoped it was a sign that the old king was slipping and not that it was something else that he just couldn't account for.

Cash was dreading telling Faris, no doubt she wouldn't take the news very well. As far as Cash knew, she was good friends with the Cento Kris as well.

His death was no doubt aimed at her as well as Sallos. The news would hit her hard especially in her condition. The last thing he wanted to do was cause her discomfort, but she would have to know. It wasn't something that Cash could keep from her and even if he could he wouldn't. Cash wasn't stupid enough to start causing mistrust in his own camp not now that they were getting closer.

His half brother would have to be dealt with but he would be a good distraction for Fuerety. Cash knew only too well how much of a distraction the bastard could be, and if he could wish that on anyone it would be Fuerety. With some luck the Cento king would take him out for Cash, saving him the bother. Oscar had said that Bethany and Gabriel were an item, that was something they had to keep an eye on. The two of them having a child together would be very bad indeed. In Cash's opinion Bethany or Gabriel doing anything other than dying painfully was very bad indeed. If the two of them were in league with Fuerety things would go south very soon. For a start Sallos' misplaced lie about Cash and Bethany would be discovered instantly.

Cash poured himself some water from an iced decanter on his desk. Taking a drink of the cool liquid he set his mind away from the if's and buts of his half brother and firmly onto things he was capable of controlling from his position here.

Spinner would be meeting with Donavan very soon and the Effusio prince should hopefully be able to put him in touch with Amaro. That's if the prince would be willing to help the cause. Cash often got the feeling that Donavan would be perfectly happy living the human life.

The price of having Ammit as a mother, he was rather damaged by her.

The queen herself had been ignoring all of Cash's attempts at a summons but with his kingship intact he could now go to her when he decided the time was right. He still had Fallon's soul to barter for and a few other things he wished to discuss, the man's lineage for a start. Fallon was starting to intrigue him. There were a lot of things about him and Snow that pricked at his curiosity. Things that, if he was right, and he was sure he was, would prove very good for him when Astrid had her children with their line neatly bargained off to him. Their children would be very powerful indeed and would serve his son well.

His son. Cash had to smile at that thought. He was going to have a son, their second chance. Gage would want for nothing, he would make sure of it. A little princess would have been wonderful too but a prince was Cash's ideal. It was a shame that he wasn't going to be Conglacio but Cash didn't care what race the child was. He wasn't Fuerety and he never would be, blood meant more than ice and fire. He was going to teach his son everything he knew even though it would take them both quite a while to learn. Cash only hoped that he would be a better father than his own, he didn't know what he would do if Gage grew up resenting him as much as he did his own father.

Leviathan had come through for him in the end but with that came a whole new set of problems. Thisbe would have to be dealt with once his mother returned. The girl was going to be difficult; she'd been with his father for a long time.

Cash had little doubt that that would have taken its toll on her. She'd been dependant on his father's whims for so long that she wouldn't know much else.

Leviathan had sheltered her and it would be very hard for her to adjust to normal life. Cash just hoped that she'd make it; the girl had grown on him.

There was so much to do and so little time in which to do it. Sighing, he rubbed at his eyes and finished his glass of water. He couldn't put off talking to Faris for much longer. Hopefully she'd be out of her bath by now and he could comfort her in bed soothing her as he told her the bad news. Silently he made his way up to the bedroom from the study. The house was quiet, all its inhabitants safely tucked into bed although not necessarily sleeping.

He pushed their door open to find Faris sleeping, well and truly passed out on the bed. The sight of her and her bump warmed his heart. The woman may always complicate things for him but he wouldn't have it any other way. Not wanting to wake her, especially for bad news, he pulled the blanket over her tucking her gently in. Bad news could always wait until the morning.

He left her sleeping peacefully and crept downstairs in search of the kitchen. No doubt the dog would keep him company for the price of some leftover carrot cake and a bowl of hot cocoa. He grinned; thinking of the look Astrid would give him when she realized he'd been feeding the dog sugar and the colorful abuse Feyd would send his way when he found out that it was the last of his cake. Not to mention what Ashlyn, Faris and Snow would say when they discovered that all of the cake was gone. None of that really mattered though. Cash was king now and if he wanted to stay up late eating all the junk food with the dog then he could. *Yeah right.*

He laughed shaking his head as he made his way down the stairs. Things were certainly interesting. He'd always believed that once he became king everything would just fall into place, become easier. In real life though, it was just the opposite. He had more things to juggle than ever before. Just as he caught one thing three more came flying in his direction. He just hoped he was a better juggler than Fuerety.

Linus met him at the entrance of the kitchen and he smiled lifting the pup his mood lightening. "Come on then pup, let's see what they've left us in the fridge to eat."

About the Authors

Stella and Audra Price are multi-published, award winning authors of the Eververse books, including many not yet in print. They have opened the minds and hearts of readers and reviewers alike with their tales of Were-snakes, Satyrs, Djinn, Unicorns, Fallen Angels and Demons, and live daily in the Eververse.

Sisters, they are bi-continental, and spend the bulk of their time bringing their books to life. They are currently working on the next few books in the Eververse series simultaneously.

They love to hear from fans and readers alike, and you can reach them at their website, www.stellaandaudra.com, their message board: www.shadowheights.com/forum, or at their respective email accounts:

Stella@stellaandaudra.com or Audra@stellaandaudra.com.